Desert Fire, Mountain Rain

Also Available by Amy Schisler

Novels
A Place to Call Home
Picture Me
Whispering Vines
Summer's Squall
The Devil's Fortune

Chincoteague Island Trilogy
Island of Miracles
Island of Promise
Island of Hope

Children's Books
Crabbing With Granddad
The Greatest Gift

Spiritual Books
Stations of the Cross Meditations for Moms (with Anne Kennedy, Susan Anthony, Chandi Owen, and Wendy Clark)
A Devotional Alphabet

Desert Fire, Mountain Rain

A Buffalo Springs Story, Book 1
By Amy Schisler

Published by:
Chesapeake Sunrise Publishing
Amy Schisler
Bozman, MD
2020

To the many women who make sacrifices every day to protect our country. May God keep you safe.

In memory of Helen Sprance (1924-2020), reader, friend, and inspiration to many.

One

"We've been hit. We're going down, I repeat, Seal Team Three is going down." Jeremy's words filled the small command center in the Middle East like a thick smoke, blinding and choking Andi. It took only a split second for her to reach for the mic and respond.

Andi pushed down the button and fought to find her voice. Her throat was tight as she struggled to answer the distress call. "This is command. Blue One, Repeat."

"Blue One to Command. Repeat, we've been hit. We're going—"

The radio went silent.

Andi bolted upright and gasped for breath, her throat dry, her eyes not seeing through the blackness that surrounded her. Her clothes were drenched with sweat, and her heart raced in what was now a much too familiar cadence. The air was saturated with the smell of mildew. Where was she?

She looked around and saw the ancient motel-issued alarm clock next to the bed. It was three in the morning. As her eyes adjusted, she could make out the gently swaying curtains in front of the window she had opened the night before. She recognized the room, with its late Twentieth Century décor of plaid bedspreads and mass market cityscape artwork. It was the final stop before she returned home after being briefed for days in Coronado, California, following her flight back from the Middle East. It was her last chance to pull herself together before facing her family and moving back into the home she left at the tender age of eighteen, over sixteen years ago.

Now, at thirty-four, she looked back on the day she left home as having been so full of promise despite the many emotions she felt as she climbed onto the bus. It was a thirty-four-hour ride from Fayetteville, near her home in Buffalo Springs, Arkansas, to the elite Academy on the shores of the Chesapeake Bay in Annapolis, Maryland. Like most incoming freshman, she felt excited, nervous, apprehensive, and downright scared. Unlike most freshman, who would be looking forward to four years of college life, Andi prayed she could just make it through the first week. Being at the Naval Academy was all she ever wanted. It was what she'd been working for since she was nine years old, and she could hardly believe it was happening as she watched the Ozarks fall away through the bus window.

Andi knew her parents never understood why she wanted that life, what drove her and the small handful of other young women heading to the Naval Academy that week, but she knew it was where she belonged. *Was* being the operative word. It *was* where she belonged, until she failed her country, her unit, her platoon, and the best friends she had in the world. The day the helicopter that carried Seal Team Three went down over the dry and rocky terrain in the war-torn province, was the day Andi's entire world shattered. The Navy may have forgiven her, but she would never forgive herself for the part she played in the deaths of the men who meant the most to her.

Sleep was not going to come again that night; Andi knew that from experience. The Navy therapist told her that the best thing she could do was get out of bed, write down her feelings, and focus on getting through the next day. She laughed at the thought of writing down her feelings. What good would that do? What she needed was something to focus on, something to help her stop seeing her friends every time she closed her eyes, something to make her believe that life was still worth living. She hoped that being with her family would help, but she wasn't sure even her loving parents would be able to make things better. How was she supposed to go on with her life when she had caused the death of her entire crew?

As the officer in charge of intelligence, it was her responsibility to keep them safe, and she had failed. What had she missed? How could she have prevented their deaths? Why wasn't she able to stop them from being shot down? These were the questions that plagued her every day and every night. No matter how often she was told it wasn't her fault, she could not get past the feeling that she had failed them. Someone had to be at blame. The only person she could point a finger at was herself.

Andi dragged herself from bed, used the toilet, brushed her teeth, and splashed cold water on her face. With the aid of the dim lamp on the nightstand, she changed into leggings and a t-shirt. She pulled a windbreaker over her head, grabbed the key card and her phone, and headed out into the moonlit night.

The motel was in the middle of nowhere in the panhandle of Texas, a little more than halfway between Coronado and Buffalo Springs. The highway that ran alongside the motel was well traveled by eighteen wheelers as it stretched through miles of nothingness punctuated here and there with small towns before it reached the suburbs of Oklahoma City.

Andi's feet pounded on the pavement, kicking up the dry autumn dust, and the music blared through her earbuds. She paid little attention to the dusty, brown fields on either side of her but kept her eyes ahead on the flat stretch of land that seemed to have no end as it reached toward the horizon. She knew better than to run alone, in the middle of nowhere, near a truck stop, but she no longer cared about what was dangerous or smart. She no longer cared about anything, and she knew that was a problem.

A horn blasted as a truck rolled by, and Andi felt the vehicle-created draft push her toward the grass that ran along the shoulder. She was just warming up, her legs beginning to feel their power, her lungs filling with the clean air of the countryside and occasional exhaust from the passing trucks. She ran at a steady pace until her heart and muscles began to protest, and then she turned to head back to the motel, pushing herself harder and faster as her legs burned with growing fatigue.

When the motel sign came into view, she imagined a finish line waiting ahead. She was transported back to her days on the track team, when she helped the Academy achieve victories on the track. The more her legs burned and the more her lungs ached, the faster she was compelled to run. When she slowed her pace in the parking lot, her calves and glutes were on fire, her breathing was labored, her clothes were drenched, and her heart felt like it would burst, but her mind was empty. The many images it was prone to conjure, of the falling chopper, the frantic scramble to take cover, and the mangled, bloody bodies had been erased from her brain. For now.

***

Empty. Dreary. Sad. Desolate. Broken. Depressing. Unrecognizable. Dying. Those were the words that tumbled through Andi's mind as she drove past the town's main square. The thought occurred to her that the words could be used to describe them both— Buffalo Springs and Andrea Nelson.

What happened here? The town was always so vibrant, so alive with community pride. The last time she'd ridden down this street, it had been in a convertible with confetti flying in the air and people cheering for her.

For her.

She dismissed the thought of shedding tears as she remembered the way they hailed her as a hero. It was 2011, and Andi was among the last troops withdrawn from Iraq. She had yet to tell her parents that she was only home for a short period of time and would be taking a position with the elite Navy SEALs.

The entire town had turned out to welcome her home. Though she had taken course after course of military history and served time in Afghanistan and Iraq, she was still naïve enough to believe that the good guys always won, and she let herself think that she was special, above the crowd, in the know, and willing to defend her country at all costs. Now she knew the truth—she was a failure, and those costs were a price too high to pay, or repay. From the looks of things in the town, the disease that rotted inside her mind and heart was contagious, and she had brought it home with her.

Andi shook her head as her gaze wandered around. Almost all the storefronts were empty. Windows were smashed, the sidewalk was cracked and broken, and the beautiful fountain in the center of the square that represented the many springs throughout the Buffalo River watershed was dry. The once thriving community was little more than a ghost town of empty buildings with red bricks and paint-peeling siding.

When Andi pulled up in front of the white two-story house on one of the side streets, she realized that the sickness had spread there, too. The house was in desperate need of paint. The front porch railing was falling apart, and the screen door had been patched in several places; but the fall foliage in her mother's exquisite gardens brought a rainbow of color to the street, and Andi couldn't help but feel like Dorothy, emerging from the black and white surroundings of Kansas into the technicolor hues of Munchkin land and its yellow-brick road.

As she put her car in park, the door opened, and her mother walked out onto the porch. Andi sat in the car for a moment, looking at her mother through the windshield, and her heart sank even lower. The woman standing on the porch was not the mother she knew. This woman looked old, tired, and worn. Andi could have wrapped her arms around her mother's waist twice. Her face was aged from years, sun, and worry. Her hair, pulled into a tight bun, was as grey as the fictional Auntie Em's, and Andi felt a wave of sadness at the comparison between her mother and Dorothy's aunt, both trying to survive in a place forged by hopes and dreams but reduced to a landscape of despair.

Andi exited the car and forced a smile. "Hi, Mama."

"You're home," the familiar voice said.

"I'm home," Andi said quietly.

"Do you need help? I can call your daddy to come get your things."

"He's not at work?" Andi looked around and saw her father's old, beat-up pickup truck in the yard.

Grace Nelson shook her head. "He's been out of work for six months now. Hardware store laid off almost all the employees."

"Hardware store?"

Andi opened the back seat and retrieved her Navy sea bag—a large green duffel-backpack combo—and her purse. She hoisted the heavy pack onto her back and picked up her purse before scanning the backseat once more and slamming the door with her hip.

Her mother answered Andi's question. "He took a job there when the paper mill closed. Imagine a world without paper. Hmph. Dang technology is ruining everyone's lives if you ask me."

Andi suppressed a grin. If only her mother knew how much she relied on technology to keep her crew... The thought died before she finished it, and she swallowed back the bile in her throat. Technology is only as good as the person using it. She had the blood on her hands to prove it.

"That bag looks awfully heavy. You sure you don't want your daddy to help?"

She shook her head as she walked up the steps. "I've got it. Why is the store laying people off?"

"Same reason all the other businesses are laying people off. They don't have any money. The whole town's shutting down."

"I noticed."

Grace opened the door and held it for Andi who gracefully maneuvered past her mother and into the turn-of-the-century house with the skill of a sailor used to carrying a sizeable load without assistance. She slid the bag from her shoulders and placed it onto the floor at the base of the stairs, dropping her purse on top of it, before looking around. How the house had remained standing for over a century was beyond her, but despite the disrepair of the outside, the inside was as warm and cozy as she remembered it. The furniture wasn't the same as when she was a child, but the style was similar, a blue and white plaid pattern that always said 'home' to Andi. There were throw blankets and pillows on every cushioned surface—invitations to sit down, put up your feet, and get cozy. On the mantel, stood a graduation photo of Andi in her uniform at the young age of twenty-two, still idealistic about her future.

"Come here and give me a hug," her mother admonished.

Andi smiled and turned to her mama. She melted into the woman's bony arms.

"We've missed you so much."

"I've missed you, too. Mama. Where is everyone?"

The house was quiet, and she didn't see anyone else.

"Helena's got her own place now—the old Peterson house over yonder. Remember that one?"

"I do. I was friends with their daughter, Emma. I knew Helena lived there. I just thought…"

"Oh, don't you worry your little head. She'll be along after work. She's the only one left at the library now. Not sure how long she can keep it open. The county's just about dried up her funds even though nobody can afford to buy books. Without the library, this whole town would become illiterate."

"How's Jackson doing?"

"He's working, too. He'll be home for supper."

"Working? I thought he was away at school."

"He was, but he quit. With your father being laid off, we needed Jackson to move back home and help with the bills. Plus, his tuition was, well, you know."

"Mom, why didn't you tell me? I would have helped."

Andi looked at her mother and wondered how there was so much she didn't know. How many things weren't they telling her?

Grace shook her head. "We didn't want to worry you. You were always so busy protecting our country. We didn't want the problems here at home interfering with your job."

"My job? You were worried about my job? But you're my family." Andi wanted to chastise her mother, but in her heart, she knew the truth. They hadn't told her because she hadn't asked. She spent her entire life trying to leave this town behind. Once she was gone, she never looked back. Whatever problems her family and friends faced back home paled in comparison to the things she and her crew faced on every mission.

She felt ashamed. She didn't know how bad it was because she didn't care. She was too wrapped up in her own world.

As if Grace could read Andi's mind, she waved her hand in the air and said, "Well, all of that's in the past now. You're home, and we can all be happy that you've returned safe and sound and that we don't have to lie in bed at night wondering if you're dead or alive."

That hurt. Was she really that out of touch? Did her job worry her mother that much?

"I'm sorry, Mama. I always meant to call more." It was a lie, and Andi was sure they both knew it.

"Bless your heart, child. You got out, saw the world, served your country, and did some good. Now you're home. That's all that matters. God took care of you, and he's been taking care of us."

Andi looked around the old, drafty house. *This is how God takes care of people?*

Ever since the crash, Andi doubted there was such a being as an all-powerful creator. Where was he when her platoon needed him? Where was he when her father got laid off? Where was he when Jackson had to quit school? So much for taking care of his flock.

"Is that my brave girl I hear?" The voice boomed from the kitchen door. Andi turned to see her father, also older and greyer than she remembered, but with the same piercing blue eyes. He opened his arms to her, and she went to him.

"Daddy," she whispered into his chest. She always was daddy's girl, and just the warmth of his arms around her comforted her. He was a big man, strong and big boned but also on the heavy side. A hug from him was like being hugged by a friendly bear—soft, warm, and all-encompassing.

"We're so happy you're home. Though I'm not sure what kind of home you're returning to. Not much opportunity in this place for a woman of the world like yourself."

Andi pulled back and looked at her daddy before turning back to her mama. Grace bit her lips and worried her hands. Their faces hid nothing. They looked as nervous as a cat in a room full of rocking chairs, fully prepared for her to tell them that she wasn't staying, that she was going back to the Navy or moving to another town, perhaps another state.

"I, uh, I'm not sure what this place has to offer me, but I'm not planning on going anywhere."

Her mother breathed a noticeable sigh of relief. "You're really done with the Navy?"

Andi held her breath and swallowed back the urge to cry. She nodded. "I'm done."

"Lord, have mercy," she said, raising her eyes upward as if her prayer had been answered.

Whether Andi wanted to be done or not, she was. That was the reality. Her bag contained a stamped paper giving her an honorable discharge which she didn't feel she deserved. What was left to go back to?

But as she thought about the dilapidated town and this house frozen in time, she couldn't help but wonder, what on earth was left in this town to keep her here?

***

The library, a converted two-story house, was small, but Helena used the space well. It had a tiny office in back with just enough room for a desk, a couple comfortable chairs, and a book cart. It had a gutted and restyled upstairs, opened wide to accommodate the many tall shelves that loomed over a spiral staircase. The first floor had a cozy reading corner along with three long tables with several computers and removable wooden dividers between them for privacy. The first time Andi saw them, she recognized her father's handiwork.

"So, what now?" Helena eyed her sister over the stack of books on her desk.

Andi felt rested after her first night in her own bed, but now that another day had dawned, she had no idea what to do with herself.

"Honestly? I have no clue." She sat in an overstuffed chair in the small office. "I kind of hoped that I'd get home, and things would just fall into place."

Helena raised an eyebrow and sighed. "Really? That was your plan? Move back into your old bedroom in a dying town, and your life would automatically 'fall into place'?" She used air quotes, a gesture that Andi always found annoying.

"I didn't really have a plan," Andi said defensively.

"Obviously." Helena slapped another barcode on a book, deposited it onto the cart, and reached for the next one in the stack.

Andi felt her ire ratchet up. "It's not like I wanted this, you know. I didn't plan on coming home at all. I thought I'd serve my platoon until I was too old to do so." She looked away, clenching her cheeks in her teeth so tightly she winced in pain.

Helena took a deep breath. "Are you going to tell me what happened, or are we going to keep playing this game where I try to read your mind?"

Andi sighed. "I'm not ready to talk about it." She knew she sounded like a petulant five-year-old, but she couldn't help it. Her sister was beautiful, smart, popular, and the apple of her parents' eye. She was always doing things for others, volunteering for this or that, and living her perfect life. Andi couldn't bear to admit that, unlike her perfect sister, she had failed those who counted on her the most.

"Please tell me you got kicked out for seducing your commander and carrying on a torrid love affair behind enemy lines while rockets lit up the sky above you."

Andi gave a quick shake of her head and reached for one of the books on the desk. "What the heck kind of books have you been reading? Is that really your idea of romance?"

Helena shrugged. "I'll take whatever I can get. Don't you remember the slim pickings available around here?"

"Hey, you're the one who moved back here right after you finished your master's. You could have married that guy you dated as an undergrad. What was his name? Bif? Bart? Barf?"

"Don't be ugly," Helena said with a laugh. "It was Brett, and we had a great time while it lasted, but the truth was, it wasn't going anywhere. We came from vastly different worlds, and neither of us wanted to give them up."

Andi looked around the cramped office. "So you opted for this? Life in a struggling library in a decaying town, with no prospects for love?"

Her sister frowned. "I didn't say it was the best decision I've ever made." She dropped the last of the books on the top of the pile and clapped her hands together. "I have the best idea."

"Oh, no, kill me now," Andi groaned.

"Move in with me."

Andi sat up and narrowed her gaze on her sister. "Are you kidding? We'd kill each other."

"No, we wouldn't. We lived together for fourteen years before you left for the Academy."

"And nearly killed each other."

"Oh, come on. It wasn't that bad. I remember plenty of good times."

Andi thought about the late-night chats, giggling about boys, gossiping about the other girls they knew. Though four years apart, they both discovered boys around the same time—early for Helena and late for Andi. She smiled as she recalled the many times their mother called to them to quiet down and go to sleep. Then she reminded herself about all the other times.

"You're a slob. I could never live with a slob."

"I'm not that bad anymore. Kind of." Helena smiled and lifted her shoulders. "I mean, I do know how to clean house. I just don't always get around to it."

"There is no way I'm moving into your house."

"Suit yourself. Just let me know in about a week how it's going, living with Mom, Dad, and Jackson. I'm sure you'll have a load of fun."

Andi let her head drop back against the chair. "Why do I torture myself? I'm so going to regret this."

Helena squealed and leapt from her seat. She ran around the desk and grabbed Andi by the hands, pulling her to her feet. "I knew you'd say yes. It will be just like when we were teenagers."

Andi found herself being dragged into a hug. "You mean with dirty glasses on every surface and your underwear in the middle of the floor?"

Helena stepped back and gave Andi a mock glare. "Ha. Ha. I promise, I'll clean up after myself. But you need to promise not to bounce quarters on my bed or inspect my closet."

Andi laughed. "Yes, Ma'am." She gave her a mock salute as she turned to leave. "I'll be over after you're off from work. And Helena…" She stopped and looked back at her sister. "Thank you."

"Thank you," Helena said with a grin. "I can't remember the last time I was this excited about having a roommate."

Two

The monuments were all but abandoned to time, the elements, and fading memories. Once an inspiration to Andi and others who hailed the Greatest Generation as heroes, the WWII monuments were almost hidden behind overgrown bushes and low-hanging tree limbs. Andi stood on the brick walkway outside the town hall and reverently bent back the branches so that they hung behind the tall, concrete monuments. On one, the war years were carved into the stone above the often-seen words, 'In Memory of…' followed by the list of men who sacrificed their lives in the European and Pacific Theaters so that others could be free. On the other, was a depiction of a soldier holding a fallen brother-in-arms. Beneath the soldiers were the words, 'Saying goodbye to a brother and friend' and below that line, 'Do not forget me lest I die in vain.' At the bottom, the acronyms of each of the armed forces completed the tribute to those who gave all.

A sob caught in Andi's throat, and she lifted a balled fist to her mouth, fighting the tears. She could smell the woodsy scent of the tree branches on her hand. Her heart ached as she thought of the many men and women throughout her country's history who had lost their lives. She pictured herself as the living soldier, or sailor in her case, holding the bodies of not one man but sixteen. She reached out and touched the cold, stone face of the man who had gone to his eternal rest. She blinked twice and took a deep breath before turning away from the too familiar depiction.

Andi followed the brick path back to the sidewalk and stood gazing at the buildings across from her. It was the first chance she'd had to walk around the town since coming home. She had spent time catching up with both her parents and her brother, helping her daddy, and settling in at Helena's, but she still didn't know what she was going to do with the rest of her life.

She put her hand over her eyes to block the sun and looked at the buildings, standing like soldiers at attention across the street. Some were brick buildings constructed for the purpose of housing business. Others were turn-of-the-century homes, like the one she grew up in, that had been rezoned as commercial properties. She gazed at the red brick saloon, Rick's Place, one of the few businesses still surviving. She took in the boutique that used to cater to the wealthier women in town but likely no longer had the same clientele—the fashions in the windows looked like they hadn't been updated in years. The fire station still stood tall and proud, and the post office hadn't changed with its row of blue mailboxes and tall flagpole waving Old Glory. The antique store, a two-story white house with a second-floor balcony, also looked the same, but she doubted it boasted too many customers these days.

She followed her gaze to the buildings on the other end of that row, all of which were now abandoned—the little Italian restaurant where her family had celebrated many birthday dinners, the chipping white paint of the bakery that made the best cinnamon buns far and wide, the once-grand movie house where she spent many a rainy day, and the cracked, peeling pink and white siding on that was once a colorful, cheerful cafe but was now a bleak, empty house with a sagging porch.

Andi crossed the road that circled around the fountain. She turned back and let her gaze move from one end of Main Street to the other on the opposite side of the street. In the center of that side of the street stood the town hall with the council chamber on the first floor and the mayor's office on the second. An American flag flew proudly in front of that building, too, as it did in front of the bank, two doors down. In between was the fledgling hardware store where her father apparently worked before being laid off, and she wondered how many employees continued to work inside its brick walls.

On one end of the street was the old, now empty, laundromat, a victim to modernization as well as the fleeing from town of those who found a way out. Next to it was the town drug store. Andi assumed it had only survived because the Walgreens and CVS stores of the world had overlooked the decaying town. At the other end of the street, on the far left, was the original jail which once held within its walls the infamous Jesse James. A few other buildings, including the barbecue joint and the library, filled in the other spaces, some open and some closed up tight. The toy store, once a beautiful Victorian home, was boarded up. Small parking lots and empty grass lots dotted the map here and there on both sides of the street. Down the side streets were the police office, grocery store, and hair salon. On one side of town was the quaint, white Baptist Church, and on the other was the red brick Catholic Church with its colorful stained-glass windows, where she spent every Sunday morning as a child. More buildings stood here and there, some open and some closed.

Andi turned and moved toward the white-brick building. She looked through the broken window of the once beloved bakery. The peeling paint on the interior walls was pink, and Andi thought it was a nice color for a bakery. She put her head close to the crack in the window and inhaled. She thought she could still smell the faint scent of cooling croissants and apple strudel. She shook her head as she strolled down Main Street.

Andi stopped in front of the one-theater movie house, now out of business, with a For Sale sign hanging in the box office window. Andi stood, looking at the beautiful, historic building, once home to a live stage show, known far and wide, before being converted to a modern movie theater.

"It's for sale if you're interested," a voice said from behind her.

Andi jumped and caught her breath in her throat. Resisting the instinct to maim the person who snuck up on her, she turned to see a man, nearly six-feet tall, with a neatly combed head of short, blonde hair and a friendly smile. He looked familiar, but she couldn't place him.

"Sorry to scare you."

"It's okay, but I'm not in the market for a theater. I wish I was though. It's my old stomping ground. I swear, I spent half my childhood in this place." She sighed and shook her head. "I can't believe everything is shutting down."

"Yeah, it's pretty sad." He reached his hand out to her. "I'm Wade Montgomery. And you're Andi Nelson, right?"

Andi felt taken aback. She must know him. She tried to make the connection as she took his hand. "Yes, how did you—"

"I remember you. From the parade way back when, I mean. My mother sent me the newspaper clipping. She likes keeping me abreast of the goings on in town. Besides, I make it my business to know when someone new comes to town, or when someone returns. I think you might have been a freshman when I was a senior."

"Wait a minute. You're Wade Montgomery. You were Valedictorian of your class."

"Wow. You actually remember that? I didn't think stuff like that mattered after high school." Wade laughed, and Andi enjoyed the cadence of the light-hearted sound.

"It does to those who aspired to do the same."

Wade's bright green eyes widened. "Oh, and did you aspire to that Andi?"

"I did. Like you, back when I thought it mattered. It was all I wanted besides an appointment to the Academy." The truth escaped too easily from her mouth.

"So, you got all you wished for in life?"

Andi sighed. "I suppose I did." *Be careful what you wish for indeed.* "And so did you if I remember right. Didn't you go to college on a full scholarship?" She smiled, shifting the subject away from her Naval education and career.

Wade scoffed, and Andi noted a shadow cross his face. "Yeah, I went to Notre Dame. It was quite a change from little old Buffalo Springs High. I was a very small fish in a pretty large pond." His smile returned as he leaned closer and whispered, "My dream was to be a basketball star, but I'm a bit lacking in the height department."

His comment surprised her since his height didn't seem lacking to her. Andi knew that she was quite tall compared to most of the women she knew, but he bested her by about an inch or so.

"And now?" She wanted to keep him talking. She liked the sound of his voice and the way his eyes sparkled when he laughed and smiled, like emeralds in the sunlight. He had an easy way about him, despite his button-down shirt, khaki pants, and dress shoes. He didn't dress the way she remembered most of the guys around here dressing —in flannel shirts, faded jeans, and cowboy boots. So far, his smile was the only bright spot in her otherwise dismal three days back home.

"I recently moved back to town. My mama needed help with the sale." He gestured toward the theater.

"Oh, my gosh. Of course! Your family owns the theater. Wasn't it your grandparents who renovated it back when it still a stage theater?"

"My great-grandparents, actually. Way back in the 1940s, after the war, when movies were really gaining in popularity."

"And now? Not so popular anymore?"

"Not here. Folks can't afford to spend that kind of money on a night out. Lombardi's is closed, and The Smoke Pit is struggling. The theater was bound to be next."

Andi looked across the street to the barbecue joint she and her friends liked to frequent when they came home on college breaks. Disappointment filled her. Her friends hadn't kept in touch once they got married and started having babies, and now her one connection to them was on the verge of closing.

"I don't understand. Is all of this because the paper mill closed down?"

Wade shrugged. "That mill employed a lot of people for a long time. Well over a century. When it was gone, people thought they'd just find something else, but there weren't really any other jobs to be found. Most people our age got out while they could. The rest of the population is dying out as quickly as the town is. Smoking takes a lot of them, drug addiction is starting to take its toll, but I think the majority of folks just die of boredom. They've got nothing to get out of bed for."

"There must be something that can be done." Andi felt a wave of desperation wash over her as she thought of how much her parents had aged, her father out of work, her sister's struggling library, and her brother having to leave school.

Wade lifted his shoulders again and let out a long breath. "I don't see what. We don't have the tourists flocking to us like up in Branson. Eureka Springs has become rejuvenated as a hippie kind of town, but I don't see that going over very well down here. I think the best thing folks can do is pack up and move on."

"You're not very optimistic." She looked around. "I see so much potential here." At least, she assumed there could be.

"I don't know where or what or how. Anyway, it was nice talking to you. I've got lots of paperwork waiting for me up in the office."

Andi said goodbye and watched Wade disappear into the dark theater. The wide white marquee read 'CLOSED" in large black letters, and the movie poster boxes mounted on the walls were empty, one of them shattered.

She furrowed her brow as she made a three-hundred-sixty-degree turn. Was Wade right? Was this the end of the town? Growing up, Andi couldn't wait to leave, but now she had nowhere else to go. She guessed she had no choice but to watch her family and her hometown fade away just as Jeremy's voice had done during his last radio transmission.

***

"So, what's his story?" Andi asked as she put her clean laundry away in the dresser in her sister's guest room.

Helena twirled a strand of curly blonde hair. "I'm not really sure. He's a lot older than I am."

"But you're a librarian. Aren't you supposed to be able to find out anything about everything?"

Helena ran her hand over the cream-colored crocheted bedspread, handmade by their grandmother, and wrinkled her brow in thought. "I suppose I might know a little more. Why the interest?" Suddenly the blue eyes that matched her sister's lit up. "You like him."

"Stop. It's nothing like that. I'm just wondering what he did that allowed him to leave wherever home is now and move back here to help his mama sell the theater. I'm curious, that's all. I mean, I just got back here myself. It's like we're, I don't know, kindred spirits or something."

"He's single. I know that. And he's—"

"Knock it off," Andi said with annoyance. "He seemed nice, but so does the Ayatollah until you're facing his military in the desert."

"I hardly think the two compare."

Andi closed the drawer and neatly folded a pair of jeans. "I'm just saying, not everyone is what they seem. Just because someone looks nice doesn't mean they should be trusted." She opened the closet and hung a pair of pants before closing the door and turning to face her sister.

"Wow. You sure got jaded. What happened to that good, old-fashioned Southern hospitality?"

"I left it in the Middle East." Andi sighed and took a seat on the bed next to Helena. "Look, he seemed decent, but I'm not interested in him that way. I enjoyed talking to him, but I can't..." She hesitated. "I'm not looking for a relationship."

"Why not? You're a free woman now. You're no longer married to the service. You're still young. You've got years ahead of you. Why wouldn't you be interested in him or any other guy for that matter?"

Andi debated within her own mind. Helena had tried for three days to get the details of leaving the Navy out of her. How much was Andi willing to share? It helped a little to talk to the therapist on base, but there were things she didn't even tell her. She couldn't.

Okay, here goes.

"I was in love with someone, but it didn't work out. I'm not sure I can go there again."

Helena grabbed her sister's hand. "Oh, Andi, I'm so sorry. Did he break your heart?"

"Hmph." Andi gave Helena a wry smile. "He never had the chance. He wouldn't, we couldn't...It was complicated."

Helena gripped Andi's hand tighter. "He's in your platoon, isn't he?"

Andi swallowed and bit her lips. She nodded, holding herself together and fighting back the forbidden tears. "It wasn't allowed. We would have been separated. Every mission would have been compromised. We would have been putting our platoon in danger. We decided it was best to—"

"Oh, sweetie, I'm so sorry." Helena pulled her sister into a hug before suddenly pushing her away. "But, Andi, you're out. You're not part of the platoon anymore. You could call him. Tell him you want to give it a try. What's stopping you?"

Andi looked up at the ceiling where the fan lazily circled above a bright bulb. She blinked, steeling herself against the flood of tears she refused to shed, but the words she couldn't even say to her therapist banged at the door, demanding to be released.

"I killed him," she whispered. "I killed them all."

***

One hour, a few shots of whiskey, and a pot of reheated spaghetti later, Andi had regained control over her emotions.

"Never," Helena said, her chin set like stone and eyes fierce. "Never, ever again say that you killed your platoon. Do you hear me?"

"You don't understand. It's not that simple."

"Stop. Did you have all the intel that was available at the time?"

"Yes, but—"

"Did you relay all of the info to the platoon?"

"Of course, but—"

"Did you have any way of knowing there would be an accident?"

"No, but you make it sound so—"

"And was your mission successful despite the crash?"

Andi nodded. That one was easy to answer even if she couldn't share the covert details. The kidnapped daughter of a Middle Eastern prince, and little Amira had been rescued and returned to her family. The press was none the wiser. The crash had been reported as a helicopter malfunction during a routine test run.

"Then what are you blaming yourself for?"

It was too hard to explain. More than losing Jeremy, more than answering to the Navy, more than wondering if she might have done something—anything—to have prevented the crash, Andi had failed. Maybe it was survivor's guilt, like her therapist said. She was alive while the rest of her platoon was gone. She knew they would want her to live, to have the life they wouldn't, to carry their memories into the future; but all Andi could think of was how she had failed her country, her service, her friends, and herself. It was her job to read the intelligence and relay it to the team. She knew she had missed something, but she was tired of arguing the point.

"I guess, you're right," she told her sister with a half-hearted smile. It was easier than trying to explain.

Helena's tight lips and narrowed eyes told Andi that she wasn't convinced, but she didn't press the subject any farther. After a moment, Helena sighed and stood.

"I better head to bed. I've got to work tomorrow. What are your plans for the day?"

Andi shrugged. "I have no idea. Any suggestions?"

"Well, if you're looking for a job, I'd drive to Branson or Harrison, maybe even up in Fayetteville But if you're wanting some relaxation, and you deserve it, you should go hiking. The weather will be perfect, and you won't get too many perfect days once the temps start dropping."

"Okay, thanks. I'll think about it. I'm going to run in the morning, so if I don't see you, have a good day."

The sisters said goodnight, and Andi told Helena to go ahead and turn off the lights, but Andi didn't move from the couch. She sat in the dark, thinking about her talk with Helena, the plight of her parents and brother, the things Wade said about the town, and her own prospects for the future. It was all too much to take in her first week back, and that, along with the whiskey, was making her head spin.

When she finally dragged herself to bed, Andi fell asleep wondering what she was supposed to be doing with her life.

Three

"Boomer, come back! Boomer, dadgummit!" Wade ran through the thick forest of trees, mindful that he was breaking every rule in the national park. Boomer had gotten free of his leash, they were off the trail, they were running at break-neck speeds, and the abandoned mines were up ahead. If Boomer chased the rabbit into one of those, Wade would have to follow.

He temporarily lost sight of the dog amid the oak and hickory trees but then recognized the golden fur flying through a patch of steaming sunlight up ahead, dodging a sugar maple. Wade pushed through the brush, stumbling out onto a trail and into a hiker.

Completely unaware of the man racing into her path, the hiker went down hard onto the dirt trail but jumped up in a flash and swung her leg in an arch so that the leg wrapped behind Wade's knees and sent him spiraling to the ground.

Wade saw stars as he fought to catch his breath. A voice came from beyond the pounding in his head and the throbbing of his startled heart.

"Oh my gosh. I'm so sorry." The woman yanked the earbuds from her hears and reached for his hand. Recognition slowly dawned on him.

"Andi?" He breathed heavily as she helped him up. He shifted his gaze back to where he last saw Boomer.

"Are you okay?" she asked.

"I think so." He managed a slight smile. "Man. I'm not sure who was more surprised there, you or me."

"I'm really sorry. I reacted out of instinct."

"It's fine." He brushed himself off and reached his hand to the back of his head. He pulled his hand away and held it in front of his face. He didn't see any blood, and his heart rate was slowing down. "I think I survived the assault in one piece."

Andi frowned. "You ran into me, you know."

"I did. That was a bad joke. I'm sorry. About the joke and running into you. I was in a hurry. Are you okay?"

"I'm good. Where's the fire?" She looked around, and Wade remembered Boomer's hasty departure on the heels of a rabbit.

"Nowhere. I'm glad you're okay. Again, I'm sorry. I've really got to go. " He started moving, picking up his pace as he called his dog's name. He didn't see Boomer anywhere.

When he stopped to catch his breath, he heard another voice. "Boomer! Come on, boy!"

Wade looked around and spotted Andi's bright blue jacket several yards to the east. "What are you doing?" he called.

"Looking for your dog. What do you think I'm doing?"

They began walking toward each other, his labored breathing beginning to ease. When they were about ten feet apart, Andi pointed to her left. "You want to go that way while I circle around back toward the entrance? Maybe he headed back on another trail?"

Wade was surprised she was willing to jump in and help. It wasn't what he was used to around these parts anymore and especially not what he'd grown accustom to in the city.

"Why are you doing this?"

Andi shot him a look that he could only describe as extreme bewilderment. "Why wouldn't I? You seem to need help, and I'm offering."

"Why? What's in it for you?" Maybe she was trying to be nice, but after years of city-living, Wade was suspicious of anybody who seemed too friendly or too helpful.

"Nothing. We're neighbors, I thought maybe friends. Why wouldn't I want to help you? Wouldn't you do the same for me?" She shifted her weight and crossed her arms in front of her chest.

"Yes, but you don't even know me. Not really."

Andi tilted her head and raised her brow. "So? That means we can't be nice to each other and lend a hand?

If that's how you treat would-be friends, I'd hate to see how you treat enemies."

Wade could feel heat flood into his cheeks. "You're right. I'm sorry. I guess I'm just worried about Boomer. He doesn't usually act this way. He's actually really well-behaved. I was trying to put his leash on him when a rabbit ran by, and he was gone, just like that."

"Well, do you want my help or not?" She cocked her head to the side, looking askance at him.

"I could use your help. Thanks. How about—"

Andi's face lit up as she looked past him. "Boomer!"

Wade turned around and saw the dog happily heading their way, tongue hanging out and tail wagging. The dog bounded over a fallen log and skirted a sugar maple before stopping happily at Wade's feet.

"Boomer," he said sharply. "Bad dog. You're a very bad dog. You can't just run off like that."

Boomer put his head down and tucked his tail between his legs for a split second before raising his eyes to Andi. Obviously sensing an ally, he bounded past Wade and jumped up to greet her.

"Down, boy, down," she said through laughter. "I can see just how well-behaved he is." She bent to one knee and gave Boomer more loving than he deserved.

Wade frowned at his dog. "Well, that scolding did a lot of good."

"He's a dog. He has an attention span of about five-point-three seconds. Give him a break."

Wade ran his fingers through his wind-blown blonde hair and heaved a long, exasperated sigh. "I guess our leisurely walk in the woods is over. I've used up what little time I had chasing this beast."

"Don't listen to him, Boomer," Andi cooed to the dog. "Daddy just didn't like the workout you gave him. He's used to sitting in an office all day, isn't he?"

"What's that supposed to mean?"

Andi stood and faced Wade. "No offense. You seem a little winded, that's all. I assumed you don't get much exercise now that your basketball days are over."

Wade couldn't tell if that was an honest observation or a dig. He might not have six-pack abs, but he worked out. When he could. On occasion.

"And I guess you're the epitome of good health?"

Andi laughed, and the sound completely wiped away his irritation. "I wouldn't go that far. I run every day, lift weights a few times a week, play tennis when I can, but I have a weakness for cookies. And pie. And ice cream. Oh, and whiskey."

"Whiskey? Not fine, white wine?"

Andi wrinkled her nose. "Mercy, no. Do I give off that vibe? I must be getting soft."

This time, Wade laughed. "You do not give off the vibe that you're soft. From what I've heard, you could take me out in a split second."

"What have you've heard? What does that mean?"

"Oh, you know, the word on the street. The big, bad Naval Officer is back in town after serving time fighting the Taliban. People tend to exaggerate about people like you. I heard you killed at least half a dozen people."

Andi's face went ghost white, and she took a step back. The change in her was so sudden and drastic, Wade worried she might pass out.

"Andi." He reached for her. "Are you okay?"

"I have to go," she said, her voice clipped. She turned on her heel and began quickly walking away.

"Andi, wait!" She kept going, and Wade looked from her to Boomer. The dog sat watching her as if wondering whether to follow. "Was it something I said?"

***

It was an offhand comment, a joke, a reference to her military career. He hadn't meant anything by it. She tried to tell herself that she was upset over nothing, but it wasn't nothing. He was able to laugh about killing people, but it was no joke to her. It was the life she had lived for the past twelve years. And it ended with her being responsible for the deaths of sixteen people even if the Navy and her sister disagreed with that assessment.

Andi was just beginning to think Helena was right, that she should forgive herself and move on, but Wade's comment brought it all back.

She'd been looking forward to a quiet walk in the woods, maybe some hiking up to a higher elevation, but all she wanted to do now was go back to the house and crawl into bed.

She fumbled with the handle that automatically unlocked when she neared the car. She swung it open, got inside, and slammed the door shut. Jeremy's last radio communication played over and over through her mind. She rested her head on the steering wheel and closed her eyes. They were just words now. His voice was already fading in her memories. Soon, his face would begin diminishing in her thoughts and dreams. Just like with her grandparents, to whom she was so close, eventually, she'd have a hard time conjuring Jeremy's smile, his big brown eyes, and his dimples.

The knock on the window made her jump. Her heart beat frantically in her chest. She looked over and saw Wade, peering at her through the glass, his green eyes narrow and his mouth tight with worry. She jabbed at the start button and rolled down the window but didn't say anything. She didn't want him to hear the quiver in her voice.

"You okay? If I said something to upset you, I'm sorry."

"It's fine. I'm fine. No need to worry." She forced a smile. "I just remembered I told Mama I'd help her today. She's canning." Andi had no idea what her mother was doing that day.

"Are you sure? You looked upset."

She waved him away. "All is good. Gotta go. See you around." She looked down at the dog sitting beside him. "Goodbye, Boomer. You be good."

Before Wade could say anything else, Andi closed the window and put the car in reverse. She waited for him to step back before backing out. She avoided looking back at him as she drove away, leaving him standing in a whirl of dust.

***

Andi filled the shopping cart with everything she needed: fresh blueberries—as fresh as they could be seeing as how they came from Mexico—flour, butter, sugar, a handful of spices, a half-gallon of vanilla ice cream to go with the already purchased bottles of Bailey's Irish Cream and Jameson Irish Whiskey.

Before she reached the checkout lane, she spun around and headed back to the frozen food section. She selected a pizza with everything and then remembered Helena only liked pepperoni. She switched the boxes, put the pizza in her cart, and went to check out.

She had no idea how to cook a real dinner, but she could manage a pizza. Thanks to her mother, she had mastered the art of baking pies before she was thirteen. And who could eat pie without coffee? Irish coffee, that is.

"I heard you were back in town," the cashier said with a smile. "Are you here for good?"

Andi looked at her name tag and then at the bottle-blonde hair and baby blue eyes. "Betty Jean? Betty Jean Thomas?"

Betty Jean beamed. "Hi, Andi. It's Betty Jean Jefferson now. Are you back for good?"

"For now, at least. Not sure what the future holds." She loaded her groceries onto the belt.

"Are you making one of your prize-winning pies?"

"How'd you guess?"

"I was always so jealous of you every year when you beat me in the county fair, but everyone knew your pies were the best in three counties."

"Oh, come on now, Betty Jean. I don't think you have a jealous bone in your body." It was true. Betty Jean was the nicest girl in school. "What are you doing these days? I mean, besides working here."

"Davy and I live in the same house where I grew up. Mama and Daddy moved to Florida years ago. Got out when the getting was good, if you know what I mean."

Andi was pretty sure she knew what Betty Jean meant. "You're still with Davy, huh?"

"Of course, sugar. Who else would I be with? We've got us three little ones, though they ain't so little anymore. Davy Junior is almost sixteen, Katie's twelve, and Billy's ten."

"Wow, time sure does fly." Andi bagged her things as Betty Jean rung up the total.

"Well, you've been gone a long time, Andi. Things change." She smiled, and Andi thought, *and some things never do*.

Betty Jean read the total as Andi reached into her pocket for her wallet. She double-clicked her phone inside the leather case and waved it over the payment pad.

"Oh, we don't have that fancy phone payment thing here. Do you have a card? We can take cash, too, but no checks." She looked apologetic. "Too many bad ones floating around these days."

Andi nodded and took out her credit card, sliding it through the reader. After signing, she looked back at Betty Jean. "It was nice seeing you. I'm sure I'll see you around."

"Don't be a stranger, Andi. We've all missed you. Maybe I'll see you at church on Sunday."

Andi doubted she was missed, but it was nice of her to say. As far as church, fat chance. She said goodbye and headed to her car.

Once back at Helena's, Andi threw herself into making the pie. It was an easy chore, one she could do without even thinking about it. As she rolled out the pie crust dough, she tried to come up with a plan. She couldn't spend all of her days hiking in the national park and baking pies. Helena suggested getting a job in one of the nearby towns, but what could she do? She could do darn near anything with a computer, but the thought of sitting at a desk all day made her want to throw up. There must be something she was good at besides deciphering intelligence, plotting military missions, and firing a gun. But even if there was, what could she possibly do here?

"Dadgummit," Andi said, the familiar word slipping through her lips. She set aside the rolling pin. The dough was as thin as a sheet of paper. She huffed out a breath and began gathering it all back into a ball. She kneaded it a little, re-floured the surfaced, and rolled the dough to a perfect eighth-inch thickness. Once the pie was in the oven, she sat at the table with her laptop and began researching local jobs.

Lyft driver, postal worker, lots of physicians, painter, truck driver, waitress—all noble professions, but nothing that inspired or applied to her. Park ranger. That sounded interesting, but would it be boring compared to what she was used to? She supposed everything would be. She'd just have to get used to it.

When the clock on the wall said five-fifteen, and the pie had just ten minutes left, Andi opened the oven. Mingled with the heat that escaped from the oven was the tantalizing aroma of blueberry pie, pouring into the already scent-laden air. Andi carefully switched the pie to the top rack of the oven and slid the pizza on the rack underneath. Helena would be home by five-thirty. Andi hoped she wasn't looking for a more substantial dinner than a couple slices of pizza and a piece of pie. All of a sudden, Betty Jean's words came back to her, *everyone knew your pies were the best in three counties.*

Andi pictured the bakery with the teal walls and the broken window and remembered how much she loved going in there as a child. The pastries were good, but Andi always knew hers were better. At least, her pies were. If she could cook pies, why not other baked goods? She'd never tried anything else. After particularly hairy missions, she often went home and baked pies, sometimes as many as four or five of them. The guys said those pies made every frightening endeavor worth it. All the wives wanted her recipes or begged her to bring homemade pies whenever one of them had a dinner party or a cookout. She went crazy at Christmas time, baking everyone's favorites, unless the Team was away on a stealth pursuit in some Godforsaken land.

No, she shook her head. It was a crazy idea. To open a bakery in a town where nobody had money, and everything else was being sold or shutting down. It was absolute idiocy. She'd have to be out of her mind, or suffering from extreme PTSD, which she felt were one in the same sometimes as she definitely suffered from both.

She reached across the table for her laptop and began researching possibilities. She may be crazy, but what if she wasn't? What if this was just what she was meant to be doing.

Four

The familiar denim coveralls and beat-up work boots left no doubt as to the identity of the man working under the rusty, blue pickup truck. Andi smiled as she stood over Joshua Nelson's legs and listened to the sound of his tinkering.

"Daddy, are you busy?"

Joshua rolled the trolley out from beneath the vehicle and smiled up at his daughter. "Never too busy for you, sweetheart." He pushed himself off the ground and held up his grease-stained hands. "Let me wash off, okay?"

"Sure." She followed him into the garage where he used a handful of citrus-smelling grease soap to wash his hands in the utility sink. He looked over at Andrea as he scrubbed.

"Everything okay?"

"Getting there, I guess. I had an idea, and it's probably a crazy one, so I figured I should talk to you about it. You could tell me if I'm barking up the wrong tree."

"Well," he said, reaching for a towel hanging over the sink. "This sounds interesting. Want to go sit on the front porch for a spell?"

The front porch was the go-to place for everything. It was where Andi spent hours as a child, coloring on the wooden plank floor or reading on the porch swing her grandfather made. It's where she and her siblings were allowed to be 'alone' with dates, knowing their mother could see through the gauzy curtains. It's where dessert was often served, birthday cakes were cut, and neighbors were invited to visit. It served as a respite after a long day of work, with its inviting cool, evening breeze, and a place to sit and watch the world go by.

As Andi sat on the swing, her feet automatically put the swing in motion as if the gentle swaying was a condition of sitting there. Her father took a seat in one of the padded, faux wicker chairs.

"So, what's this crazy idea you've got?"

"You know the bakery shut down, right?"

Her father nodded slowly. "Almost a year ago. Has been up for sale for longer than that. Seems like the whole town has been for sale for quite some time."

"Yeah, I noticed, which is why this might be the worst idea ever conceived."

"And the idea is?" He raised his brow and leaned forward, elbows on knees, to give her his full attention.

Andi gazed at the house across the street where her childhood best friend lived. They hadn't spoken in years. Next door to that house was, at one time, the home of the high school principal. Most of the teachers lived on this street or the next, their kids in the same classes as the Nelson kids. The town was so different back then, when neighbors were also friends, children played outside until well after dark, catching fireflies and paying manhunt, and everybody worked hard all week and went to church on Sundays.

Andi's daddy cleared his throat, bringing Andi back to the present.

"I'd like to buy the bakery. Maybe sell pies, cakes, cookies, and other pastries. Maybe sandwiches, too. Might even put in an ice cream counter. Make it a real, old-fashioned shop where people would buy stuff but also stop and take a break for a bit."

She stopped and looked at her father. He sat unblinking, as if stunned into an irreversible stupor. He opened his mouth as if to speak but then closed it again.

"Well?" she asked tentatively.

"If you had asked me this five years ago, heck, maybe even two years ago, I might have said, it's a fine idea. But now…I'm afraid that dog just don't hunt, sweetheart. Just the investment to get it up and running would be enormous. And then you'd have to be able to pay the mortgage and the bills, and folks around here don't have the money to spend on extras like ice cream and pie."

Andi felt her heart sink. Though she knew this was exactly what he would say, she had hoped that her father would offer her some kind of encouragement.

Andi sighed. "I guess you're right. Another time, another place, perhaps." She shook her head. "It just doesn't seem right to let the town die, though, without even trying to make things better."

"Andi, people tried for a long time to make things better. But there comes a time in every life when all the medicine in the world isn't going to prolong the inevitable."

"So, we just let it all go? Let whatever hopes and dreams people might have had fade to black? Let Buffalo Springs become another ghost town like Rush and Eros?" She felt her heart constrict at the thought. When Andi left home, she didn't care two cents about the town. She never fit in—too smart, too tall, head too far in the clouds. But Buffalo Springs was her home, the only one she'd ever had, especially after years of being a Navy nomad, her bag always packed in anticipation of the next mission. Though she had been based in Coronado for the past nine years, it always felt like no more than a place to stow her things. She never realized until this very moment how much she longed for home and all that the word means.

"Andi, I understand how this all comes as a shock to you with you having been gone all these years, but there's nothing anybody can do. Eventually, we'll have to leave for greener pastures. Unfortunately, our properties are worth so little now, I'm not sure where anyone can afford to go. We just have to put our trust in the good Lord and hope he shows us the way."

Andi pressed her lips together. The town was lost, the people were defeated, and life as she knew it in Buffalo Springs was gone forever. There was nothing she or any fictional supreme being could do to change it.

"Okay, then. I guess that's it." Andi stood and headed toward the door. "I'm just gonna go in and say hi to Mama before I leave."

"Where are you going?" Joshua asked, standing from the chair.

Andi shrugged. "Not sure. To find a job somewhere, I suppose." She thought he might try to stop her, encourage her to keep thinking of what kind of work she could do around here, but she saw the look in his eyes and the sorrow that told her he knew there was nothing to keep her there. Sadly, she was beginning to see that he was right.

Andi went in search of her mother. She found her in the laundry room at the back of the house.

"Laundry never ends, even when it was just the two of us." Her mother shook her head.

Andi followed her mother out the back door to the clothesline and started helping her hang the wash on the line. The fragrant scent of fall mums, Russian sage, and hydrangea filled the air.

"So, what brings you here this morning?"

"Just an idea I wanted to run by dad. Nothing special."

"Do I get to hear the idea?" Grace pinned a nightgown to the line, and Andi recognized it as one she had given her mother for Christmas several years back. She looked down into the basket and realized that many of the clothes were ones that her parents had been wearing for years. She wondered when the last time was that they had something new. Though she wore a uniform more than anything else, even Andi had a somewhat decent wardrobe.

"I'm thinking about buying the old bakery and starting up a new one, but Dad disagrees. He says it's time to let the town go and move on."

Grace turned to face her daughter. "I wish I could say he's wrong, but others have tried to come in and make something work, and they've all failed."

"It's too bad. I wish there was something we could do."

"There is." The voice came from her brother, and Andi turned to see Jackson, sitting on the picnic table in the middle of the yard.

"Hey, Jackson. You still sneaking up on people? At twenty-one, I'd have thought you would've grown out of spying on me by now."

Jackson smiled and shook his head. "It's the only way to learn anything around here. As the youngest, I'm always shielded from all the family secrets."

Andi laughed and threw a shirt at him. "Get over here and help us. Half these clothes are yours."

Jackson sauntered across the green grass to the line and pinned up his shirt.

"So, what do you mean, there's something we could do?"

"I've been doing some research since I got back home, and there are lots of towns that have made miraculous comebacks. We just need a gimmick."

"Don't listen to him," Grace warned. "He came back from college with a head full of big ideas. He doesn't realize that all these things he thinks will work require money, and that's something people around here don't have."

"Go ahead, Jackson, I'm listening."

"Towns are dying all over the country with the rise of urban city centers and bustling suburbs, but here's the thing: there are a lot of people who think they want the city life, and then they miss life in a small town and come out for vacations or even move back.
What are suburbs other than small towns linked together by roads? Everyone thinks they want the city, but what they really want is community. They find that the lure of the city doesn't live up to their expectations. For some, it's too loud, too dirty, too crowded. Those people want a place for their kids to play and roam free. They want what we have and don't even know it.

"Statistics show that Millennials, especially, start out in the city, but then want their kids to have a more rural upbringing. However, they're doing it differently than their parents. They want a smaller house in an eco-friendly environment, with fewer things and more experiences. They can have that here."

"A bunch of falling down old buildings and people of all ages strung out on meth and prescription drugs? I don't think so," their mother scoffed.

But Andi was intrigued by her brother's assessment and had questions for him. "You might be right, but how do you propose we lure them here? How are they going to realize this is what they want? And why would anyone move to a place where there aren't any businesses or any jobs?"

"Once we have the people, the jobs will follow. That's the way it's always been. Look at the settlement of the Old West. First, there were the people, those looking for the American dream or gold or buffalo. Whatever. They moved out west, and they needed housing, schools, churches, grocery stores, banks, and all the stuff that makes a town. That's how the jobs are created."

"But we had those things, and everyone left. Now there's nothing to draw anyone here," Grace told him.

"Then we find something that will. A gimmick. Something that will make people want to come here for a weekend but puts a bug in their ear that this would be a great place to live."

Andi put her hands on her hips and looked at her brother. "Jackson, this isn't a Hallmark movie. You can't just make those things happen?"

"You can if you do it right. I'm telling you, I've thought about this a lot. Look, we have a great national park nearby with fishing, canoeing, and hiking. Adventure seekers as well as bird watchers would love it here. Families who like to camp, guys who like to fish. We've got the town infrastructure that just needs to be updated. A main highway runs nearby. There's a wooded lot for sale a few miles from here that could be bought and turned into a zipline course. Do you know how popular those things are today?"

Andi felt dizzy. "Take a breath, Jackson. I get it. You've really thought about this."

He nodded. "I have. All we need is to bring in some impact investors who run endowments and foundations. They would back business owners financially. I just don't know who to talk to around here who can see the potential I see and get the ball rolling."

Andi turned toward her mother. She could feel her own excitement building. "Mama? Any ideas?"

"Lord have mercy, child. Are you not listening to me? There's man's plans and God's plans, and I think the almighty has already let it be known what his plans are for this town."

"Mama, please. Let's look at this rationally. There must be somebody I could talk to."

"Have you tried talking to the man upstairs?"

"For Pete's sake, Mama. I mean a real person."

She huffed in exasperation. "I guess you could start with the mayor."

"Who's the mayor these days?"

"Well, you might remember him though he was a few years older than you. His name's Wade Montgomery."

***

Andi slammed the library door. "Why the—"

Helena shushed, and Andi noticed the few patrons staring at her, wide-eyed. She lowered her voice.

"Why the heck didn't you tell me that Wade Montgomery is the mayor? I thought he was only here temporarily. How did he get elected mayor?"

Helena grabbed her sister's elbow and led her into the office. She closed the door and spun around to face Andi, her blue eyes full of sparks.

"First of all, you can't come in, slamming the door, raising your voice, and using that kind of language."

"What kind of language?"

"I know what you were going to say before you realized you had an audience. I watch movies. I know how SEALs talk."

"Really?"

Helena smiled. "Yes, miss smarty pants."

Andi smirked at her sister. "Okay, I'm sorry. Now, what about Wade? He's the *mayor*?"

"I tried to tell you that the other day, but we got off topic. It's not a big deal. I mean, it's not like a mayor really does anything. Not here, anyway. We're not New York or Washington."

Andi dropped down into the chair. "I just feel so foolish. He must think I'm an idiot."

Helena looked sympathetically at her sister. "I'm sure he thinks you're just returning to town after many years and don't know everything that's going on."

"Well, he can't be that great a mayor if he's helping his mom sell the theater. Shouldn't he be encouraging her to find ways to make it sustainable? He should be doing that for everyone, but least of all her. She's his mom for heaven's sake. What kind of son is he?"

Helena flinched, then looked away and bit her lips.

"What?" Andi asked.

Helena took a deep breath before speaking. "Look, there are things you should probably know."

"Like what?"

There was a knock at the door. "Come in," Helena called.

"Ms. Nelson." A little girl with a blonde ponytail pushed open the door. "Can I please check out a book?"

"Of course, Sami. I'm coming out right now." Helena looked at Andi. "We'll talk later, okay?"

She was gone before Andi could ask what she meant. What things did she need to know?

Andi stood and headed out the door. She left the library and hurried next door. She knew exactly who could answer her questions. The only person who would know what was going on was the mayor himself.

***

"Trudy, can you hold my calls, please? I need some time to work on paperwork."

"Yes, sir."

Wade thanked his office manager and closed himself in his office. He sat in the rolling, black desk chair, flanked by flags—the American flag on one side and the Arkansas and Buffalo Springs flags on the other. Blue curtains hung at the window behind him that looked out at the fountain in the middle of town. The theater was directly across the street. On his desk was a picture of Wade and his parents after his law school graduation.

A large bronze county seal adorned the front of the desk, and a tall plant stood to the left of it. A lamp glowed on the right side of the desk. Two high-back, red-padded chairs faced the desk, a red and blue Oriental rug beneath them. A small seating area had been arranged in the front, right-hand corner with a leather coach, two matching chairs, and a small coffee table. The office wasn't fancy, but it more than served its purpose, and Wade was kind of proud of the way it looked. He didn't have the stellar view of the Empire State Building that his office in New York had, but this would do for now.

Wade sat at his desk. There was always something that needed his attention, and it was always just as important as the other ninety-nine things that pulled him in every direction, or not. In reality, nothing he did in this job seemed important.

What had he been thinking when he decided to become mayor? It wasn't anything he was ever interested in doing. He had no political aspirations. He just wanted what was best for his family and their community. That's what they all wanted, after all, to unload and move on in whatever way was best for everyone.

Before Wade could pick up the first document in front of him, his intercom buzzed.

"I'm sorry, Mr. Montgomery, but there's someone here to see you. Shall I have her make an appointment?"

"Trudy, how many times do I have to tell you to call me Wade?" He snickered and shook his head. "Who's here?" Wade had to work at keeping the annoyance out of his voice. It seemed to be his natural inclination to take out his frustrations on Trudy from the minute he stepped into this dreaded office, and he adored Trudy. She was his only cousin, and she'd worked in the mayor's office longer than he had.

"It's Andi Nelson. Remember her? Her mama and daddy—"

"Yes, Trudy, I know who Andi is." He sighed and pushed aside the stack of papers. "Go ahead; send her in."

Andi opened the heavy mahogany door and stuck her head inside. "Are you sure it's okay? If it's a bad time, I can come back later."

Wade smiled and gestured for her to enter. "No, come on in. No time like the present."

She wore jeans and a long-sleeved US Navy shirt. He gestured to her footwear. "You can take the girl out of the Arkansas but not the Arkansas out of the girl?"

Andi looked down at her cowboy boots and smiled. "Believe it or not, I found these in the back of my closet at Mama's. I can't imagine how old they are, yet they're still the most comfortable things I can put on my feet other than running shoes. What about you? Did going to school up north take the Arkansas out of the boy?"

Wade stood, walked around the desk, and hiked up his pants leg to reveal his favorite pair of Justin boots. He rarely wore them, to tell the truth, and he wasn't sure what inspired him to put them on that morning.

Andi laughed, and Wade pointed to one of the cushioned chairs in front of his desk. "Is this official business?" He then turned and gestured toward the seating area in the corner of the office. "Or a social chat?"

Andi hesitated, and Wade got the feeling that she wasn't here on a social call. "Um, maybe you should sit here." He pulled out a cushioned chair and offered it to her. Andi took a seat and waited for him to circle the desk and settle in his own chair.

"You didn't tell me you'd moved up in the world," she said, waving her arm to indicate to the office.

"Who said it's moving up?" Wade leaned back and gazed at her. She had something on her mind. What was it?

"Why are you helping your mama sell the theater?"

"Because she's my mother. Do you want me to hand her off to someone else who won't have her best interests at heart?"

"Of course not, but why aren't you helping her keep it? I'm guessing you can afford to help with renovations or whatever it needs."

"That's getting a little personal, isn't it?"

He watched her inhale and clench her teeth.

"I mean," she said testily. "Why not try to salvage it? Why not try to salvage everything?"

"And by everything, you mean…?"

"Everything. The businesses, the town, everything. You're the mayor. Shouldn't you be looking at what's best for the town?"

Wade felt his irritation grow. He leaned across the desk. "Look, I don't know who you think you are to leave town for all these years, and then waltz back in one day, out of the blue, and presume you know what's best for this town. You don't have a clue what's going on here."

Anger flashed in her eyes as she leaned closer to the desk as well and spoke in a clipped, irritated tone. "What I know is that, as *mayor*, you should be trying to save this town, not destroy it."

Wade sat up in his chair, trying hard to contain his anger. "I think this meeting is over."

Andi stood, hands on her hips. "If you can't take the criticism, you picked the wrong profession." She turned to go but spun back on him. "By the way, just what is your profession? I mean, your real one. Before you decided to masquerade as the town's hero and savior."

He'd had just about enough of her attitude. "Not that it's any of your concern, but since you're a citizen of this town, I'll tell you. I studied both law and finance. I've worked for almost fifteen years as a mergers and acquisitions attorney. I have more than enough education to stand up to your privileged, military degree. Just because you went to Annapolis—"

She was around the desk and in his face before he knew what was happening.

"Don't. You. Ever. Say that my experience at the Academy or the years I served were entitled. I put my life and the life of my team members on the line every day so that people like you could sit in your cozy classrooms, smoking pot, drinking beer, and chasing girls. You think because you have a few more framed pieces of paper on the wall that you're better than me? Smarter? Maybe you have more schooling, but I learned everything I know in the oppressing heat and humidity of the desert and in the frigid, snowy mountains, in the belly of a relentlessly rocking ship, and in planes and choppers and command centers where you learn lessons nobody should ever have to learn. You think you're better than the rest of us because you went to a highfalutin school, but you have no idea what the real world is like."

Her anger was palpable, and Wade found himself taking a step back, but she moved forward.

"The real world is one where people have to fight to survive, where they have no idea where their next meal is coming from, where they don't know if they will die in the night from an aerial attack or a suicide bomb. The real world is where people like me have to come to the aid of people like you, where your very existence is dependent upon my skills and knowledge. The real world, Mr. Mayor…" She took a step back, inhaled, and tossed back her long, brown hair. "The real world is one where we help each other survive, not cut and run like a pitiful deserter."

Wade swallowed his rage as he watched her turn and leave the room, slamming the door behind her. She was fierce, formidable, and even frightening, and he was furious. However intrigued he might be by her, she had no right to waltz into town and speak to him that way. Whatever it was she wanted, there was no way on earth she was going to get it.

***

"How'd it go?" Helena asked when she got home that night.

"How'd what go?" Andi asked, her anger still emanating from every part of her being. She had baked two pies and a batch of cookies and had tried a new scone recipe. And that was after a five-mile run.

"Don't play coy with me. I know you. You went to see Wade, didn't you?" Helena looked around the kitchen. "And from the looks of things, it didn't go well at all."

Andi slammed a platter of barbecued chicken on the table.

"Hey, be careful. Those are my dishes you're throwing around."

Feeling penitent, Andi looked at her sister. "I'm sorry. I'll rein it in." She placed the blue and green patterned bowls of coleslaw and potato salad on the table and poured each of them a drink—wine for Helena and Jameson and diet ginger ale for herself.

"Smoke pit carry-out?"

"Yeah. I hope that's okay. I can bake, but cooking... Well let's just say, I don't want to kill you."

Helena grinned. "It's okay. But you know, you don't have to have supper on the table every night when I get home. It's not like we're married."

"But I'm living here for free. I have to earn my keep somehow."

Helena took her seat at the oak four-person table and imbibed a healthy sip of the wine. "Good choice."

"Thanks." Andi sat across from Helena, and they bowed their heads to pray.

"Anyway, you're as neat as a pin. You vacuum. You dust. You do the dishes and the grocery shopping. I think you are more than earning your keep."

"Well, someone has to do those things. Do you know the size of the dust bunnies I found under the couch?"

"Watch it now. Those are household pets. Can you pass the coleslaw, please?" Helena accepted the bowl and then returned to her previous question. "So, how'd it go? I know you went to the mayor's office."

"That man is an egotistical, self-centered, piece of...work." Andi raised her eyes to her sister.

"Nice choice of words. Now, tell me how you really feel about him."

Andi sat back in her chair. "He had the nerve to act like he knows everything, and I know nothing. He had no desire to hear anything I had to say."

"What did you say?" Helena eyed her sister with suspicion.

"I set him straight on the real world, that's all. He's been living in some fancy ivory tower and has no idea what it's like to suffer, to work hard, to spend every day making sure the people you love are taken care of. He doesn't even care that his mother has to give up the family business. He'd rather just sell everything off without a second thought." Andi stopped and met her sister's worried gaze. "What?"

"Did you say that to him?"

"Not in those words, but I told him what I think of him and his highfalutin ways. I even used that stupid word to describe them. What does that even mean? *Highfalutin*?" Andi continued to shovel in her meal, but Helena had yet to move. Her eyes were wide, and Andi knew she had missed something. "What? Why are looking at me like that?"

"Oh, Andi. Please tell me you didn't tell Wade that he doesn't live in the real world and doesn't know suffering and he doesn't care about his family business."

"Of course, I did. Something like that anyway. He's nothing but a self-serving politician, just like all the rest of them."

Helena shook her head. "Oh, Andi."

"Will you stop saying that? 'Oh, Andi,' what?"

"Wade's mother has Early Onset Dementia. She's really in a bad way. Wade has tried really hard to take care of her. That's why he came back, not to sell the theater, but to care for his mom. About a month ago, she got lost on her way to church. She drove clear out to the forest and was missing for hours. Wade had to hire round-the-clock help."

Andi put down her fork. "And his dad?" She said through a mouthful of potato salad she could barely swallow.

"He died two years ago. Lung cancer. He fought hard, but it beat him in the end."

"I had no idea."

"I know. I didn't have a chance to tell you."

"You told me you didn't know anything about him. You made it sound like it he had just breezed into town one day, and you didn't have a clue about his life at all. Why?"

"I don't know anything about him other than that."

"Well, he had to run on some kind of platform. What did he say about his background."

Helena took a long drink of her wine and placed her glass gently on the table. "Well, you see, there wasn't actually an election."

Andi looked at Helena, trying to read between the lines, but comprehension refused to dawn. "What do you mean, there wasn't an actual election?"

"Nobody wanted the job. That ornery old Mrs. Baker finally retired, and Wayne Pritchard was elected, but he stepped down, and the town council appointed

Wade. Then everyone on the council quit, and Wade was all that was left."

"Everyone on the council quit?" Was this really the type of democracy she had fought for? What was wrong with this town?

"Apparently, they just wanted out. I guess they all want to sell off and move on. They couldn't do that as elected officials."

"Has this whole town gone crazy?" Andi pushed her food away. She no longer had an appetite. "No wonder the town is falling apart."

"So, now you see why everything is shutting down. Nobody wants to deal with a lost cause."

"What if it's not a lost cause?"

"Andi, I appreciate what you're saying, but that dog don't hunt."

"You sound just like Daddy. And what if you're wrong? What if Jackson and I can find a way to save the town?"

"If that's what you really want, then I think you have some crow to eat in front of Mr. Mayor Montgomery."

Five

"Any chance he'll see me?" Andi smiled sweetly at Trudy, hoping things weren't as bad as she thought they were between herself and Wade.

"I'll ask, but honestly, Andi..." She leaned across the light brown desk and lowered her voice. "He was pretty ticked after you left here yesterday. He slammed the door, worked for a couple hours, then headed straight to Rick's Place across the street." Trudy pointed behind herself toward the saloon across Main Street, opposite Wade's office. It had been there for years, long before Andi was alive.

Andi grimaced. "I guess that's not his normal behavior?"

"Indeed not." Trudy smiled. "But if I'm right, and I usually am, I smell a pie in that bag. That might be enough to entice him into forgiving you. Let's see." She picked up the phone but stopped the motion in mid-air to look up at Andi. "You're not going to make him mad again, though, are you? He's got an awful lot of things piling up on his desk."

"I promise. I'm here to try to smooth things over." She held up the bag as a reminder.

"Okay, then. In that case, I'll ask." She pushed a button and put the receiver to her ear. "Wade, Andi's here to see you. She's brought a peace offering." Trudy winked at Andi. "He'll see you now," she said in her most professional tone.

Andi pushed open the door and took a deep breath before going inside. She closed the door behind her and held up the bag with a smile. "As Trudy said, I've brought a peace offering."

Wade didn't return her smile.

"And an apology. I should not have said the things I did. I had no right to make assumptions about you or the life you've had. It was wrong of me, and I'm sorry."

Andi stood by the door, waiting for some sign that she was forgiven and an invitation to go further into the room. Instead, Wade wheeled his chair around so that his back was to her, facing the window overlooking Main Street.

What an immature jerk.

Just as Andi was about to sit the pie down and leave, Wade turned the chair around.

"Forgiven. Is that all?" There was no warmth in his tone, and his eyes remained clouded. Gone was the friendly smile from the day they met. She didn't detect a bit of the concern she had seen at the park.

"I, uh, I…" Andi debated whether to say more, but she knew what a dismissal felt like. "I guess not." She laid the pie on a nearby table and straightened herself up. "Enjoy the pie. If you don't want it, give it to Trudy. I have more than I need right now." She hurried out of the office, closing the door quickly behind her.

"I didn't hear any shouting this time. That's progress, right?" Trudy smiled from behind her desk.

"I'm not sure about progress, but what's done is done." Andi headed for the door.

"Andi," Trudy called, and Andi turned back to look at her. "He's not that bad. He's under a lot of stress right now. Work, home, you know."

"I know. I just didn't know before. Not that it excuses my behavior. I just…didn't know."

Trudy lifted one shoulder and gave a lopsided grin. "We all make mistakes. And that includes Wade. He'll cool off."

"It doesn't really matter, but thanks."

Andi headed outside and looked up and down the street. Jackson was right. There was potential here. Maybe they weren't going to get any help from the mayor, but did that mean they should give up?

She marched across the street and took a picture of the phone number on the FOR SALE sign in the bakery window. She had enough money for a down payment and probably enough to pay for most of the updating. She had good credit and could qualify for a loan for anything else. She scrolled through her phone and tapped on the number of a former Navy friend, now happily living as a civilian with a house full of kids and a jewelry business on the side. As the call was going through, Andi peered through the window, trying to figure out exactly how much work would have to be done.

The call connected, and Andi's friend, Monica, cheerfully answered. "Hey, Andi, how's it going?"

"Great, Monica. How about yourself?"

The friends chatted for a few minutes, catching up on babies—Monica now had two—and husbands—zero for Andi—and life outside of the Navy.

"Question for you," Andi said. "Didn't you get some kind of small business loan for women entrepreneurs? How can I get one of those?"

Monica explained the process and program run by the U.S. Small Business Administration. Andi listened carefully, asking Monica to hold on now and then so she could make a note in her phone. She asked some questions, giving Monica a bit of insight as to what she was thinking.

"Thanks so much. I'm going to see what I can find out."

"Good luck, Andi. Let me know when it all comes together. I'm willing to make the three-hour trip for one of your pies." Monica's words sparked an idea.

"What about putting in an online order? Would you do that? I mean, if I had a website and took orders, do you think people would buy them?"

"Andi, people will buy anything online if the price is right and the product is good. And believe me, your product is better than good."

Andi told her friend goodbye and walked to the next empty shop. It was in pretty good shape—nothing that a coat of paint couldn't fix. She walked a bit farther and stood outside the movie theater. She looked up at the marquee. Theaters were probably big money to renovate these days. While the basic technology had gotten smaller and less expensive, theaters-goers today were after the in-home experience with recliners and sushi bars, and Andi assumed that was a big expense. She'd have to give some more thought to that one.

On the corner, stood a small shop, not much bigger than Wade's office. There wasn't a lot of retail potential there, but what about an information center? She could picture a rack of brochures about the area on one wall, a counter at the back, and a small sitting area with a table and chairs for planning one's trip. She frowned as it occurred to her that the Internet made everything so much easier these days. Did people still go to information centers anymore? What if it was high-tech? Scan your phone to check-in for your tour, take a virtual reality tour of places in the Ozarks that can't be reached by the average visitor, sign up for a walking tour or rent a bike, plan your day using an interactive map of the area.

Andi thought about a trip she made to Wellington while visiting a classmate stationed in the South Pacific. Helena asked her to go the National Library of New Zealand which had just reopened to the public. After reading an article about it, Helena was dying to know what the newly renovated library was really like. Andi was amazed at the high-tech building. Her favorite part was the interactive map of New Zealand, spread across an entire wall on the first floor of the building.

She could picture something similar here, but on a smaller scale. Visitors could see everything offered in Buffalo Springs as well as nearby attractions such as hiking trails, waterfalls, and boat ramps. A tap on the map would bring up the ability to find out more information or book an activity.

"Whoa, Andi. Slow down," she whispered. She was getting way ahead of herself. Still…she smiled as she turned to look across the street.

There were three other empty spaces as well as two businesses up for sale. One was the old Lombardi's, and she wondered if there was anyone who would have the desire to reopen the Italian restaurant or try a new cuisine in its space.

Then reality set it. This was going to be so much work, and the townspeople were broke, tired, and feeling defeated. The only way to make this happen was to find a way to light a spark in the town or bring in new blood. Andi feared that both options were impossible.

***

Wade watched from his office window. What was she doing? Part of him wanted to go down and find out, and part of him wanted to turn away and forget he ever met her. But he couldn't. She was trouble, and he knew it. Andrea Nelson was a know-it-all who embodied everything Wade had ever heard about Naval officers—opinionated, self-inflated, and self-righteous.

Only, she hadn't seemed that way when they met on the street and certainly not when she fled from him at the park.

Wade hit the button on the intercom and asked Trudy to come into the office. Trudy entered, closed the door behind her, and took a seat in front of the desk. "Yes, boss?"

"Knock it off. You've been bossing me around since we were kids."

"I know. That's why I say it. I have to remind myself that you're in charge here."

He smiled in spite of himself. "What do you know about Andi Nelson?"

"Other than she's older than me, an ex-Navy officer, darn beautiful with the most intense blue eyes, and really gets under your skin?"

Wade rolled his eyes. "She doesn't get under my skin."

"Then how would you put it?" Trudy leaned forward, giving him her full attention.

"She's exasperating. Sweet and funny one minute, moody the next, and downright spitting nails the next."

"But she doesn't get under your skin at all, I see."

"Would you stop saying that?" He huffed out a breath and ran his fingers through his short, wavy hair. "She's up to something, and I can't figure out what it is.

All she does is walk up and down Main Street, looking in and out of the empty store windows. This is the second day I've seen her doing it since she got back in town."

"Maybe she's thinking of becoming a real estate agent."

He shook his head. "I don't think so. She berated me for helping Mom sell the theater."

"So, you sold it?"

"Not yet; I'm still trying."

She frowned. "Any bites?"

"No." He sighed as he twirled a pen between his fingers. "I can't get anyone interested in it. Everyone says it's a bad investment. Heck, this whole town is a bad investment. I don't know what I was thinking, taking this thankless job. I should be back on Fifth Avenue. Do you know how much money I was making?"

"I have a pretty good idea. So, why not go back? Nothing is keeping you here. I mean, don't take this the wrong way, but if you move Aunt Blanche into one of those homes up there, she won't know the difference as to where she is. You could close up the house, sell it, level it, whatever. I'd leave if I could. And I'd never look back."

"Why haven't you? You're young. You've been working here since you were sixteen. You must be ready to move on."

"And where would I go? I don't make enough to buy a house or even rent an apartment. You know what this gig pays."

"Why don't you date?"

"For the same reason you don't. Look around."

Wade nodded. He got it. Just about everyone he'd gone to school with had left and never come back. Trudy's friends were the same. They were either gone or popping out babies or fighting drug addiction. The town was nowhere to find one's future.

"Andi's sister runs the library. Doesn't she have a brother? What's he doing now?"

"Not sure. He quit college, though. I don't think it was his choice, but he's back home. Not sure what he studied. Business? Marketing? Something like that."

"Huh."

"Huh, what?"

"Nothing." He stood and looked out the window again. Andi was staring at the movie theater. "What would you do with the theater if you were in my shoes?"

"Hmm...I'm not sure. It's such an icon around here. I hate to see it closed, or worse, torn down. Mama likes to talk about how she and Aunt Blanche used to sneak around behind the old stage and smoke cigarettes and share bottles of Boone's Farm."

Wade turned to face her. "Really? My mother smoked and drank?"

Trudy shrugged. "I guess there wasn't much else to do. I think they were good kids though. They obviously turned out all right. And they made great babies."

He laughed. "I guess they did." Wade clapped his hands together. "I should get back to work."

Trudy stood and stifled a yawn. "Want me to find out what Andi's up to? It's not like I have tons of more exciting or pressing matters on my desk."

Wade thought about it. "How 'bout you keep your ear to the ground. Let me know if you happen to hear anything. But don't go asking questions and stirring things up."

She gave him a mischievous grin. "Little ol' me? Stir things up? Why, when have I ever done anything like that?"

"You forget who you're talking to. There aren't many secrets in our family."

Trudy threw her head back and laughed. "Oh, cousin, dear, you don't know the half of it." Wade smiled as he watched her leave. Nothing she said surprised him. He knew his cousin was a wild child at one time. She got in big trouble one night back in school and was ordered to do community service at the mayor's office. She'd been there ever since. Wade also knew, as office manager to the mayor, a lifelong resident of Buffalo Springs, and the prettiest and most popular girl in town, she had her ways of finding out exactly what she needed to know about everyone and everything.

***

"An information night." Andi explained the plan as the family feasted on spaghetti with meatballs, salad, and garlic bread. "Jackson and I will make a presentation and offer some ideas and see if anyone is interested in giving this a try."

Helena took a long drink of iced tea. "I guess I could do that. I've got the room, and it would be after hours. I can put up signs and hand out flyers to my patrons. I'll put it on the website, too. Oh, but you can't do it on Tuesday because of book club or on Wednesday because of Girl Scouts. Oh, or Monday because if you're going to have it at the library, I have to be there, and I volunteer for bingo at the retirement home—"

Andi interrupted her. "How about Thursday? Jackson, does that work for you?"

Jackson nodded in agreement, his mouth full of food.

"Then, it's settled." Andi reached for another piece of bread. "Town meeting, next Thursday, to discuss how to rejuvenate Buffalo Springs."

"Now hold on there, missy." Joshua waved his hands in the air. "Just where do you think everyone is going to get the money for this rejuvenation project of yours? Not everyone just got out of a life of no rent, no bills, and no mortgage, with a nice sum in their savings accounts. These are people who can barely put food on the table each night."

"He's got a point there, Andi." Helena gave Andi a questioning look.

"Honestly, Dad, I don't know. I'm trying to take this one step at a time. I guess some will have to take out loans, depending upon what they want to do business-wise."

"That's not going to be possible, honey. These people are tapped out, and the bank is already knocking at the door. They don't have any collateral. Look at your mama and me. I'm out of work, the car and truck are over ten years old, the house is falling apart, and the property isn't worth a thing. And we're doing better than most."

"Then what do you suggest?" she asked, feeling cornered and defensive. "There's got to be something they can do, someone who'd be willing to invest in the town."

"Actually…" Jackson finished swallowing and wiped his mouth. "There are real estate investors who do this sort of thing through grants and foundations. They help small businesses get off the ground. We'd just have to find the right company or companies to come in and invest. Ones who would rent out the spaces at reasonable prices."

"But how are people going to afford to pay any rent before their business is up and running?" Grace asked. "Isn't that putting the cart before the horse?"

Andi hadn't realized how complicated this was going to be. She sat back against the chair and heaved a long sigh. "I don't know how to answer any of these questions."

"Well, you'll have to know the answers before you can hold a meeting," her father said.

"He's right, Jackson. What do we do?" She looked at her brother for reassurance, but he lifted his shoulders and dropped them down as a frown formed on his face.

"I don't know either."

"Here's the issue I see," Helena chimed in. "Who's going to trust a woman who's been gone for almost twenty years and a twenty-one-year-old college dropout? Andi, they're going to see you as having no stake here and no understanding of the region; and Jackson, you've got no credibility as a seasoned adult. I'm not trying to offend either of you, but facts are facts."

"She's right," their father agreed. "You're going to need to show them a lot more than fancy ideas from two people who have never done this themselves."

Andi put her elbow on the table and rested her forehead in her palm. She took a breath and looked up. "So, what? We just give up?"

Everyone looked around the table at each other, but nobody spoke. Andi took her napkin from her lap and tossed it onto the table.

"I'm full." She stood, picked up her plate and scraped the rest of the food into the trash before putting her dish in the sink. "It was good, Mama. Thanks. I need some air." Without waiting for a response, she walked through the house to the front porch and took her usual place on the swing.

After a few minutes, Jackson joined her, sitting on the swing and pushing it back and forth with the toe of his boot. "They're just trying to help, you know."

"I know. It's not them." She picked up the throw pillow in the corner and hugged it like she did as a little girl when something was bothering her. "Jackson, I'm just so lost. I don't know what I'm doing with my life.

For the first time in weeks, I felt like, maybe, I had a purpose. If this isn't it, then what is?"

"I know how you feel, sis. I felt like that when I got back from school."

She turned to look him in the eye. "And you don't still feel that way? I mean, what's here for you? Are you content to stay here forever with no prospects for the future?"

"No way. I mean, I don't care if I stay, but I'm not giving up on my future. I'm taking classes online. It's cheaper than going away. I'm going to get my degree and figure out how to put it good use."

"And then what? What will you do when you graduate?"

Jackson continued to push the swing, and Andi found the rhythmic swaying still held a nostalgic, comforting feeling for her.

"Believe it or not, I think I want to get into real estate investing. Maybe for a bank or a corporation. Those were the classes that interested me the most, maybe because I knew what was going on back here. Anyway, when I moved back home, I started thinking, maybe it's time to put what I've learned to good use. I was afraid everyone would laugh at me, but then you got home and started talking about the bakery. The problem is, I don't know what I don't know. And I definitely don't know any real investors."

"And that's not quite the kind of circles I ran around in either."

"Sounds to me like you need a connection with someone who has some Fifth Avenue experience." Helena pushed open the screen door and walked to the swing. "Make room."

Andi slid one way, and Jackson slid the other, making a spot for Helena in the middle.

"Like I know anyone with Fifth Avenue connections," Andi said. "My military experience didn't quite put me in touch with the high-finance crowd."

"Lucky for you, there's someone right here in Buffalo Springs who has those very connections."

"And who might that be, miss smarty pants?" Andi asked, echoing her sister's assessment of her.

"His Honor, The Mayor, that's who."

***

The smell of coffee mingled with the morning sunlight that beamed into Helena's blue, green, and yellow kitchen. With a lifelong dream of visiting Italy, Helena had attempted to bring a little bit of Tuscany into her home, and Andi admired the handiwork in the tiles. Today, however, Andi was in no mood to think about Italy or kitchen décor.

"I told you no, and I meant no," Andi said over her bowl of Wheaties. She'd gone over it with her brother and sister until she was blue in the face, and she was tired of telling them no.

"Then you might as well forget your idea of opening a bakery because by the time you get it up and running, there won't be anybody left in town to buy anything you're baking."

"He's a pompous, self-righteous, know-it-all who holds a grudge. I'd have to get down on my knees and beg just to get him to listen to me, and I'm not going to do that."

"Then, let's do this. Let's hold your meeting. You and Jackson put together your presentation, lay it all out there—how you propose to reinvent the town, what shops you think would work, what kind of jobs it would mean both during and after the renovations, how much time and money would have to be invested, etcetera. Then wrap it up by saying, we just need an investor or two to believe in us enough to help make it work. Get people more than interested. Get them excited. As mayor, Wade will have to be there, and as mayor, he will have to at least try to see how he can help."

"Or he can show up and break the news to everyone that it's a terrible idea because nobody will want to pour money down the drain."

Helena shook her finger at her sister. "Do you believe it's a good plan that will work?"

Andi didn't have to think about her answer. "Darn right, I do. It's a great plan. I can already envision it. We could be on that list of top small towns in America. We're in the perfect location, with the national park nearby and Branson just an hour away. Jackson's right about all the outdoor activities that could be offered around here, and I think, the old Jefferson farm would make a great Christmas tree farm. Then Betty Jean wouldn't have to work at the Shop-a-Lot, and she and Davy would have a steady income and something real nice to leave to their kids."

Helena put her hand up, her eyes sparkling with excitement. "Andi, you just solved part of the problem!"

"I did?" Andi squinted as she looked at Helena. "How?"

"Everything doesn't have to be dependent upon selling or buying the places in town. There are plenty of places to start." She took her phone from her pocket and started typing on it. "Look, here. Christmas tree seedlings start at thirty-five cents per tree. It takes six to eight years to grow the trees, so it's not a quick turnaround, but it's a lifeline for a farmer on the brink of having to sell his farm. Oh!" She nearly jumped from her seat. "And there's a Christmas tree organization that helps people get started."

"Okay, that's one business, but what about others?" Andi reserved her excitement, waiting to see what else her sister had on her mind.

"The other day, you mentioned a tourist information center. That could be set up pretty quickly. If the town is willing to invest just enough money to pay the rent and hire someone to man the storefront, they could start advertising on social media. Maybe partner with the hotel. Social media is free, so there's no extra costs there. They could advertise rooms in the hotel and a world of activities within less than a ten-minute drive. Oh! And a farmer's market! I'm only open every other Saturday, so the library parking lot could be used on the off weeks, and people could sell seasonal produce plus handmade, folkcraft kind of items."

Andi laughed. "Okay, okay, I get it. We start with local resources. If we start pulling together some ideas before the meeting, we can open up people's minds to a whole realm of possibilities."

"I'm going to be honest with you, sis. I didn't believe this was going to work, but the more I think about it, the more I think it just might be possible."

"So, you don't think everyone will say I'm crazy?"

"I didn't say that. It's going to take a heck of a lot of convincing, but Mark Twain once said, 'Every inventor is a crackpot until his idea succeeds.' We'll just have to prove to everyone that you're a crackpot whose ideas have a really good chance of succeeding."

"I'm going to assume there's a compliment in there somewhere," Andi said, rising to rinse her cereal bowl.

"If not a compliment, at least some encouragement. After all, behind every crazy idealist is a loved one who believes in the ideals."

"And who said that?"

"Me, and I'm behind you one-hundred percent."

Andi had never loved her sister as much as she did at that very moment.

Six

"What's this?" Wade stood in the doorway to his office, holding the flyer that Trudy had put on top of his mail.

"I believe it's a call for a town meeting."

"Shouldn't I be the one to call for a town meeting?"

"I suppose that depends. Perhaps if you had listened to this particular citizen rather than shooing her away, you would be the one calling the meeting. Turns out, she had to take matters into her own hands."

Wade scanned the leaflet and felt his blood pressure rise when he saw the contact name at the bottom. "This is Andi's doing?" He fixed his gaze on Trudy, wondering how much she knew about this. She'd been quiet for the past few days despite her promise to keep him in the loop about what Andi was up to. "Did you know about this?"

"Not much. Just that she was out and about, talking to some of the building owners and local farmers."

"And you didn't tell me?" Wade's irritation with Andi and the whole situation returned. He was beginning to feel the pressure of the job he had accepted, one that went far beyond being mayor.

"There wasn't much to tell until now. The flyer was under the door this morning when I arrived."

Wade slammed the paper down on her desk, causing Trudy to jump. "Darn it, Trudy, you knew something was going on. You knew she was up to something. I asked you to find out what. Why did I not know about this?"

If the mayor had been anyone else, Trudy may have reacted differently. Then again, maybe not. Wade had seen her stare down more than one guy who thought she wasn't as smart or able as she was. When she stood and glared at him, returning the accusation in his own stare, he almost recoiled.

"I told you I would find out what was going on. I never said I would relay it to you. You're the mayor of this town. Maybe it's time you started acting like one. Andi was right the day she let you have it, and she's right on this. I know things are hard with Aunt Blanche. I get it. I remember how much it hurt all of us when your daddy suffered, and now your mama's suffering, too. I get that you never intended to give up your life in the city and move back here, but dadgummit, Wade, you agreed to this job, and you've got to step up and do something."

"And what am I supposed to do, Trudy? We both know they gave me this job so that I could help put this town out of its misery."

"Maybe some did, maybe some are ready to give up, but I'm willing to bet that most of the people around here were hoping you'd see things differently. Come on, why do you really think they gave you the job? They wanted fresh eyes, a new perspective, someone with ideas that might just save everyone and everything they all love."

"Well, I'm not that guy." Wade regretted shouting at Trudy the instant the room became silent.

"Well, that's too bad," Trudy said quietly. "Because the guy I grew up with was that kind of guy." She picked up her jacket and purse and headed toward the door without looking back. "I'm taking the day off. You don't seem to need me or my opinions around here. You seem to know everything."

"Trudy, wait, I'm sorry." He started to go after her, but she closed the door soundly and left him standing in the middle of the room. After a moment, he went back to the desk and picked up the incriminating piece of paper.

What was Andi thinking, riding into town and stirring everything up like this? She had no idea what she was doing. They'd all had all the heartache they could stand, and here she was, aiming to get everyone's hopes up. And where would she be when everything crashed and burned? Not here, he was sure. Nobody in his life ever stuck around when there were rough waters ahead. He was certain she would prove to be no different.

Worse than that, Wade would have former Council President, Ted Mitchem, breathing his neck, demanding answers. Wade had taken this job with the understanding that the town was to shut down. He was told over and over by Mitchem and the rest of the council that giving up and giving in was best for everyone. Wade didn't look forward to hearing the tirade he was going to have to endure. Never one to back down from a fight, Wade would prefer to steer clear of Mitchem. That man had a mean streak a half a mile wide, and Wade had no desire to be on his bad side.

***

There was a pulse in the air, but Andi couldn't get a feeling as to whether it was a good pulse or a bad one. She wasn't used to speaking to crowds. In her job as mission intelligence commander, she typically answered to one person—the chief intelligence officer of her division. She didn't give speeches or rally the troops, so to speak. Her job was to relay intelligence and keep her platoon safe.

She felt so out of her league as she watched the large crowd gather into the tight space in the library's main reading room. Every chair was occupied, and a few dozen people leaned against the walls and shelves. Andi was no stranger to speaking in front of people and giving reports, but she was used to small intelligence gatherings and intimate briefings. She hadn't spoken to a crowd of this size since her high school valedictory speech, and she threw up beforehand. The thought caused bile to rise in her throat, and she swallowed it down as she looked over at Jackson. How did he look so poised and confident?

Just when she thought it couldn't get any worse, Mayor Wade Montgomery walked in and took a place against the wall by the door. His face was etched in stone, his green eyes clouded, his brow furrowed, and his mouth tight. The man she had hoped to have as an Allie looked anything but.

Jackson smiled as he waved his hands to stop the pockets of conversation around the room. "Hey, everyone," he said casually from the small, makeshift stage their father had constructed to elevate him above the crowd while speaking. "Thanks for coming."

He waited for the room to become silent, save the ticking of the clock on the wall and the nervous shuffle of some of the attendees.

"Some of you know that my sister, Andi, has just returned after sixteen years of service to our country." He paused as a few people stood and clapped, prompting the rest of the room to follow suit. Andi felt embarrassed by the display and hurriedly motioned for them to sit back down. "Andi has come home, but not to the same home she left." Jackson looked around the room, making eye contact with as many people as he could. Andi saw a few heads nod in agreement.

"Ever since the mill closed down, we've seen businesses close, people lose jobs, houses foreclosed upon, property values plummet, and our friends and neighbors pack up in search of something better. A sense of hopelessness has taken hold here. We've let others tell us that we aren't good enough, don't have the smarts to turn this around, and can't make a living in the place we all love."

Andi saw more heads nodding and heard murmurings of agreement.

"Andi and I think we are good enough. This town is good enough. We can make this town into something bigger than it was before, a place where people will not only want to visit but live. We can do what other towns in places like Georgia and Kansas, and even here in Arkansas have done. We can create a place that embodies the American Dream—a place to visit, work, raise your kids, and not worry that the bank is going to come in and take it all away."

A few cheers went up from around the room, and Andi felt like she was at a political rally rather than a town meeting in a cramped library. She looked at her baby brother in amazement. He had them captivated, practically salivating, and he hadn't even begun to tell them what the plan was they had all come to hear about.

"Tonight, Andi and I are going to present some ideas to you, some things for you to think about, talk about, and decide if our town, our future, our children are worth taking a chance." His voice rose as he spoke, and he became more animated as he sailed to his big finish.

"We want you to know that we are one of you! we are walking in your shoes! Our family shares your burdens, and we are not ready to give up the fight!"

People rose to their feet. Cheers and applause filled the building. Andi was dumbfounded.

She looked around, taking in all of the faces. She noticed a line of men leaning against the wall at the back of the crowd. They wore hardened expressions, and their arms were crossed in front of them. She recognized one. What was his name? Mr. Mitchell? No, Mr. Mitchem. He lived down the street from her parents. He had a bunch of sons, all of them meaner than snakes from what she remembered.

Perhaps sensing her stare, the man turned toward Andi. Before she could look away, he nodded at her, but his expression was anything but friendly. She thought of the old adage, if looks could kill, and a chill ran down her spine.

"Andi, Andi now!" Helena prodded her, and Andi became aware that Jackson was trying to get her attention. She flushed as she went to stand by his side on the small stage. Her hands shook as she opened the paper in her hand. She cleared her throat, and the room quieted down. With a trembling voice, she attempted to summon some of her brother's eloquence.

"Good evening," Andi said quietly. She took a deep breath, slowly let it out and raised her voice. "I've spent the past few days speaking to some of you." She looked for a reassuring face in the crowd and settled on Betty Jean's broad smile and encouraging nod. She breathed again and looked down at the quaking paper in her hands.

"We've come up with some ideas that we think would be positive for our town's future. Things like, turning Betty Jean and Davy's farm into a Christmas tree farm and turning the old laundromat into a tourist information center to capitalize on all that the Buffalo River area has to offer." She cleared her throat again and continued. "We think there's real potential in creating a folk arts group to sell locally made art, handicrafts, honey, and jams. The old jail would be a great escape room, drawing people in with its history and architecture. Who wouldn't want to relive one of Jesse James' greatest escapes, right?" She gave a nervous chuckle and was relieved to hear others laugh as well. "There are so many things that can be done with the empty buildings. I'm planning on reopening the bakery, and I'd love to see Lombardi's back in business." She felt more confident as she came to the end of her speech. "We have a great community here in what was, at one time, a bustling little town. We live in one of the most beautiful parts of our nation. We have the ability to show others how great Buffalo Springs was and can be again." There was more applause, and Andi felt herself relaxing until a shadow fell over the stage.

"And who's going to pay for all this?" An older man she remembered as Shane Callahan stepped forward. The stony-faced men along the wall backed him up with shouts of, "Yeah, who?"

Andi looked to Jackson who nodded and smiled. "We thought you might ask that. There are investors who do this sort of thing, look for towns with potential, buy the buildings, pay for the startup costs, and help the new businesses get set up."

"Investors who are looking to make money, not lose it." Andi had wondered when the mayor would speak up. He pushed his way through the crowd. "Investors who have the assurance that their money is going to be returned to them, that they're going to make a profit." He looked at Andi. "Can you promise them that?"

She felt the intensity of his gaze. Her mind fogged, and she struggled to remember how they agreed to handle this exact question. She fumbled for words. Jackson came to her rescue.

"Can anyone promise them that an investment isn't going to tank? It's part of the risk they take as investors, and there are endowments and foundations who are on the lookout for just this kind of investment."

She watched Wade's eyes move slowly from her to Jackson. Her brother continued to speak.

"What we can promise is good, hard, honest labor from people who want their town and their neighbors to succeed. Isn't that what we all want, *Mayor Montgomery?*"

All eyes shifted to Wade, and Andi saw the color of his neck turn red as his Adam's apple bobbed. "What we all want is to be able to take care of our families in the best way possible. We want to ensure a future for our children and not repeat the mistakes of the past."

Jackson smiled at the mayor. "Then we all want the same things, don't we?"

It was as quiet as the dawning of a snowy morning as the two men stared each other down, Wade's stony expression acting as a fun-house mirror's morphed reflection of Jackson's wide grin.

Finally, Betty Jean's shout from the back of room broke the silence. "I say we give it a shot. It's either that, or we tuck our tails between our legs and get out of dodge. I, for one, think our community is worth saving."

Slowly, like the rising of a wave on the Atlantic, a fervor spread through the room until it built into a wall of excitement that cascaded around them, wetting them all with the hope for something better.

Wade turned back to Andi and leaned in close, whispering words only she could hear. "I hope you know what you're doing because every person in this room has even more to lose now than they did an hour ago. If this fails, you and your little brother will be held personally accountable."

He turned and quietly made his way back through the crowd. Andi watched him leave, his words echoing in her mind until the enthusiasm of the crowd took hold and swept her up in the tsunami she and brother had just created.

***

"She's not wrong, you know. To give them hope." Blanche Montgomery's frail voice floated across the room. She'd been quite lucid upon Wade's arrival home from work on Friday. Her caregiver, a local part-time nursing student named Melanie, told him they had read the newspaper together, and Blanche had many questions about the proposals of the 'Nelson kids,' as she called them.

Wade shook his head and took a seat on the leather couch across from his mother's armchair. The large room was chilly, and Wade glanced at the immense brick fireplace to make sure he had wood to make a fire before it got too dark. "Hope is a four-letter word."

"Is that how you were raised, Wade? To think that having hope is a bad thing? When did you become so cynical?"

"I'm not cynical, Mama. I'm being realistic. They're getting everyone excited about something that can only end badly."

"And why is that?"

Wade stood and began pacing on the Oriental rug. He drew the dark green drapes across the wall of windows to conceal the inhabitants of the room though there was little chance anyone would be looking into the room from the backyard of the two-hundred-acre family farm, a property that could easily be called an estate. Wade faced his mother.

"Mama, nobody is going to invest in a town that's this far gone. Who wants to visit or live in a place that has one restaurant, a library, a single bank, and a convenience store that poses as a supermarket?"

"Do you know, when your great-grandparents bought the theater, the only place to eat in this town was a saloon with a questionable 'hotel' above it that rented rooms by the hour? There was a mercantile that sold a little bit of everything, a jail, and a loan office. At one time, there was more, but the itch to move farther west, the loss of lives in the wars, and the rise of academia caused a lot of changes here. Young people left and never came back."

Wade glanced at the wall of books before turning back to his mother. "What made them buy the theater?"

"That little four-letter word you refuse to put any stock in. They had hope. And they saw potential there. They knew that vaudeville was on its way out and movies were on their way in. *Gone With the Wind* and *The Wizard of Oz* had captured the attention of the world. Giants like Humphrey Bogart, Greta Garbo, Katherine Hepburn, and Jimmy Stewart were making people laugh and swoon and, yes, giving them hope, not unlike Andi and Jackson are trying to do for this town."

"I don't see the comparison," he said wryly.

"Because you don't want to, and I'm sorry for that."

Wade frowned. "Sorry for what?"

"I'm sorry for making you come here, for being the reason you stayed, for taking you from your world. You never wanted to settle here. You were always looking for the next great adventure. You wanted the big city, the bright lights, the glitz and glamor of high finance. You were railroaded into taking that job as mayor that you hate so much."

"I never said I hated it." He went to the fireplace and began building the fire, not willing to look his mother in the eye.

"But you do. And I understand that. It's not what you thought you'd be doing when forty is just around the corner. You wanted to be rich and successful and call your own shots. I get it. Funny, when you think about it."

"Think about what?" He sat back on his heels and turned toward her.

"You had pretty high hopes. Hope in the future, hope in your success, hope in something bigger and better than what we could give you. It's that hope that spurred you to work so hard in school and look to a bright future. You hoped for a scholarship, and that hope lead to Notre Dame and law school, then hope led to a career in mergers and acquisitions. I guess it's not such a bad word after all."

Wade wasn't sure he'd give that much credit to a single word. After all, where had all that 'hope' gotten him?

He struck a match and watched as the paper and kindling caught fire. "And what about you Mama? What about your hopes? You had to have wanted more than sitting in a movie house all day."

"Oh, Wade, I got all I ever hoped for. I had fifty wonderful years with the man of my dreams. I had a son I am immensely proud of. I have too many friends to count. And you know what? I loved sitting in that movie house, watching stories about hopes and dreams and pain and agony and everything else life has to offer, but I had something else, Wade, something you seem to have lost along with your sense of hope."

"Oh, yeah? What's that?"

"Faith. I have faith that people are good, that communities are meant to support each other, that nothing is ever lost completely, that there is always another chance, and that God does not forsake those who believe."

"You know I'm with you on that, Mama, but I don't see how that helps us right now." He stood, satisfied that the fire was lit. "I think I'll go see what Melanie left us for supper."

"Wade…"

He stopped in the doorway and turned to her. She seemed so small in the big chair, surrounded by floor-to-ceiling bookshelves and massive windows with elaborate custom-made treatments.

Blanche started to say something, but her expression abruptly shifted, and she looked confused.

"Is your father home from work yet?"

Wade's heart broke a little more as his mother left him once again. "No, Mama. Daddy's not coming home tonight, remember?"

She gave a slight shake of her head. "I, I don't feel so well."

"It's okay, Mama. You'll feel better after you've eaten."

Wade made his way to the large kitchen with a wall of glass cabinets, a butler's pantry, and a wine cooler taller than he was. He leaned his palms against the granite counter. The time was coming when he'd have to move his mother from the house she loved, and it broke his heart. He thought about what she'd said.

Hope and faith. Two things Wade hadn't given much thought to since coming home. Maybe that was his problem.

***

The evening was quiet. Grace and Joshua tried to outdo each other on Jeopardy while Jackson worked on his online course at the kitchen table.

Suddenly, the peace was broken by the sound of shattering glass. A fireball of some sort sailed through the window. The room filled with smoke, and Grace screamed as she leapt from her chair. Jackson ran into the living room as Joshua picked up the fire extinguisher next to the fireplace and aimed it at the flames on the rug.

"What was that?" Jackson asked, watching his father put out the small fire.

"Whatever it was, it about gave me a heart attack," Grace said through panting breaths, looking at the charred object with her hand on her heart.

Joshua bent closer. "It's a rock with a rope tied around it. The rope was on fire." He grabbed the fireplace poker and prodded the rock that was now covered with white bicarbonate residue.

"Why on earth would someone do such a thing?" Grace asked.

"I don't know," Joshua said as he walked to the end table where the house phone sat. Fury radiated from him as he looked at his wife, pale and trembling beside her chair. "But I'm calling Earl. If we hadn't been home, our whole house could have burned to the ground."

He hastily paged through the ages-old leather-bound book next to the phone and dialed the number for the chief of police.

Seven

They were the last ones left in the Buddha Bar, one of the few bars in Bahrain. The rest of the platoon had gone to bed, mired in the exhaustion brought on by a long, tedious day of waiting. Some missions were executed with the speed and power of a raging fire. Others were carried out with the slow, careful collection of intelligence and the necessary good fortune of being in the right place at the right time.

"Any closer to pinpointing his whereabouts?" Jeremy asked in a hushed voice.

"We're getting there. Hopefully, by morning. I know how the waiting eats at the Team. "Andi ran her finger around the rim of the glass, wishing it was stronger than soda but knowing she was on the clock with a long night ahead of her.

"They can't help it. The race to the finish line is in their blood. It makes them who they are."

"We're doing the best we can," she told him. "We're already closer than we've ever been to ferreting him out. We'll get him this time. I know we will."

Jeremy finished his drink but made no attempt to leave. He watched her for a moment, his stare penetrating, as if he could see into her soul. "You know what you are? You're like a fire in the desert. Once lit, there's nothing around that can put it out. It feeds on the brush and the heat surrounding it until there's nothing left to consume, and it dies out."

Andi snorted. "Is that right? What makes you say that?" In the dim light of the bar, the gold flecks of his eyes burned like embers, punctuating his description of her, and she realized they were exactly alike, she and Jeremy.

He continued. "You won't stop until you achieve your goal. To you, the mission is sacred, surpassing all else in scope and importance. It consumes you and pushes you. You'll never give up, and you'll never give in. I don't know if everybody in your position is like that, but I know that our Team is lucky to have you as one of us."

His gaze was intense and her hand that lay on the table near his itched to reach out to him. She knew it was wrong. They both did. So far, neither had made a move. She was sure that neither of them ever would even though she sensed that his feelings for her were as strong as hers were for him. And the knowledge kept her up at night, longing for an end to the masquerade in which they both participated. Then morning would come, and she was reminded that their work was far greater than their own individual needs or desires.

"Thanks," she said breathlessly, her eyes still locked with his. She saw the muscle in his jaw twitch, and she read his thoughts. A chill ran down her back, breaking into the moment. "I'd better get back to command." She stood and left without looking back.

This time, when Andi woke, her breathing was even, and her pulse was normal, but it wasn't sweat that ran down her face and wet the pillow under her cheek. She sat up and wiped the tears from her face. It was only when she dreamed that she allowed herself to feel, to cry. The question was, why that dream? Why that memory? Why now?

Not that she could ever decipher when her dreams would come nor whether they would be memories or convoluted creations of things that never happened, and never would. She supposed her dreams came when and how they wanted, unbidden by her thoughts and unwelcome by her heart and mind.

She reached for her phone. Four A.M. She'd almost made it through an entire night, but she wouldn't sleep any more.

Once dressed in her running gear, she silently slipped out of the house. There was no moon that night, but the streetlights were on.

Andi enjoyed the quiet of the pre-dawn morning, not even putting her earbuds in to listen to music. She allowed herself, for the first time in many weeks, to recall Jeremy's face, his voice, the way he took her in his arms that one time.

He had known. He told her that he didn't have a good feeling about the mission. He was worried somebody was going to be hurt or that something was going to go wrong. She had assured him that everything was going to be okay. Instead of saying more, he reached for her and pulled her toward him. No matter how wrong it was, Andi couldn't resist. The kiss was all that she imagined it would be, and then it was over. When she opened her eyes, he was gone.

Maybe she'd been distracted by the kiss. Maybe she'd felt guilty, knowing she was betraying the Team. Maybe she was not in the right head space. Whatever the reason, she'd missed something. Maybe her superiors were right, and it wasn't a piece of intelligence or an undetected movement. That didn't mean it wasn't her fault. Maybe it was a glitch in her instinct, her keen awareness of every vibe, every current that she felt during a mission... If she had only been more focused, not thinking about the kiss or the implications of admitting their feelings or how they'd have to change their assignments—no, how she'd have to change her assignment. Jeremy would never, could never, leave his platoon.

Andi stopped running and bent forward, breathing in the cool air. She saw a raindrop hit the dirt between her feet and looked up at a cloudless sky. Where had the rain come from? She felt another drop on her cheek, and another, and another. She stood in the middle of the street, illuminated by the streetlight, and tried to tell herself that it was okay to cry. She was no longer in uniform. She no longer had to hold it together for the enlisted sailors. She didn't have to hold everything inside anymore. She was allowed to be human, but the tears did not come.

Standing straight and looking around, Andi realized she was on Main Street. She studied the buildings, the waterless fountain, and the broken sidewalks. Her eyes strayed to the dark windows of the mayor's office.

She wrinkled her brow, wondering what compelled a man like Wade. How could she get him on their side?

Unlikely to find the answers then and there, Andi began a slow, steady jog toward the edge of town where the sidewalks ended but the shoulder was wide.

She and Jeremy never had the chance to date, the chance to share secrets, dreams, hopes, and plans, but they knew each other in ways more intimate than most married couples. They knew each other's fears and drives and those things that were never spoken out loud. If he were still alive, he'd be behind Andi all the way, feeding the fire, fanning the flames, and pushing her to increase the heat until the entire town was roaring with an overpowering sense of purpose and life.

***

Like clockwork, Boomer was breathing in Wade's face, whimpering to go out.

"For once, I'd like to see you sleep until six." Wade sat up in bed and forced his eyes to open. He smacked his lips a few times, craving water and a dollop of toothpaste, but Boomer was insistent.

He stood at the back door and waited for his dog to finish his business as the soft glow of the dawn appeared over the trees. He was about to call Boomer inside when the dog stopped, snapped her head to attention, and raced off down the long, gravel driveway.

"Oh, no. Not again." Despite what he'd told Andi, Boomer had a bad habit of chasing after anything and everything. What was it this time?

By the time Wade reached the front yard, Boomer was completely out of sight. Frustrated, Wade looked down at his white t-shirt, flannel lounge pants, and bare feet. He quickly ran back inside and reached for his long, beige raincoat that hung on the coat rack. He secured the belt around his waist as he reached the top step of the porch. His shoes were upstairs, and he didn't want to waste time getting them. He looked down at his feet and sighed as he went back outside, his heels scraping the front walkway as he made his way toward the driveway.

He called Boomer and cursed out loud as the gravel dug into his cold, bare feet. He moved over to the grassy strip along the drive, searching for Boomer in the fields, hoping he hadn't run into the street. His toes sank into the wet grass, and he cursed again as his feet grew cold.

When he reached the end of the driveway, he saw Boomer, standing on hind legs, bathing Andi's face with his slobbering tongue. Andi looked up as he approached, her expression unreadable.

"I'm sorry," Wade apologized. "He thinks he's made a friend."

"He has. It's his master I'm still on the fence about."

Wade rubbed his unshaven chin. "Yeah, I guess he hasn't been the most welcoming neighbor."

"You might say that." She pushed Boomer down. "No jumping, Boomer."

He took in her leggings, performance T, and running shoes. "You were serious about running every day."

"It helps clear my head." She gave him her own once-over. "Judging by the raincoat and footwear, you aren't a run-first-thing-in-the-morning kind of guy."

Wade looked down and wiggled his cold, wet toes. "Not really. Once upon a time, I suppose. Besides, it's barely morning."

"It is for some of us. Go home, Boomer." She turned to leave.

Remembering his mother's advice, it occurred to Wade that he was running into Andi an awful lot since her return to town. Maybe God was trying to tell him something. Perhaps he should give her and her a brother a chance.

"Andi, would you like a cup of coffee?"

She stopped and faced him. Her puzzled look gave way to a hesitant smile. "What would your constituents say if I followed you inside at this time of 'barely morning' with you being half-naked?"

"There aren't too many other houses around to see what we do. What are you doing running all the way out here anyway?"

Andi shrugged. "Just taking the scenic route, I guess."

Wade looked around and saw that the road was empty in both directions. "You sure you don't want to come in? You really shouldn't be running out here alone, and it's starting to rain."

She shot him a look of annoyance. "I think I can handle myself, and I'm not going to melt, but thanks for the advice. And thanks for the invite, but I've got to get back."

"Then how about later?" he called as she started to jog away. Boomer sat in the street, swinging his head back and forth between the two of them. "I think we have some things to discuss. Like, how much is the town supposed to put up for this information center of yours?"

"Have your people call my people," she called back with a grin. "I'll see if I can fit you in."

Wade couldn't help but smile as he watched her go.

"Boomer, come." Thankfully, the dog listened. For once.

Wade didn't agree with Andi and Jackson's plan, but he was the mayor. He supposed he should hear them out. What could it hurt to entertain their ideas for a bit? Maybe even call some of his friends in New York? After all, if it worked, and the town rallied, they could elect a new mayor, and he could get on with his life. And maybe Mitchem would be okay with it after all.

***

"Everyone's okay?" Andi was frantic, listening to her mother's recount of the events of the previous night.

"Yes, we're all fine. We'll have to replace the rug when we can, but for now, we've put a chair over the burn."

"Does the chief have any idea who did this or why?"

"No, but he said he'd let us know if there are any other reports of this happening."

Andi couldn't help but wonder if it was related to the meeting, but why target her parents? Just because Jackson lived there didn't give someone license to go after the rest of their family. Maybe it was just some kids playing a prank. Only there was no humor in trying to set someone's home on fire.

"Let me know if you hear anything, Mama. Okay?"

"I will, Andi. Come on by sometime. Now that you're home, don't be a stranger."

"I will, Mama. Love you."

Andi disconnected the call and hoped this wasn't an omen of things to come.

***

Andi was nervous as she waited by Trudy's desk.

"Don't worry. He won't be long." Trudy smiled at Andi. "Mrs. Baker doesn't stay long. She just likes to check in once a week."

"Check in?"

"To make sure he's doing his job. She was mayor for a long time before her doctor told her it was time to retire. The last guy didn't do so well, in case you hadn't noticed. She wants to make sure Wade isn't as derelict in his duties."

The door opened, and Mrs. Imogene Baker, all four-feet-two of her, said her goodbyes to Wade and Trudy.

She turned to Andi and looked her up and down. "You're really shaking things up around here."

Andi wasn't sure how to respond. "I didn't mean to."

"Sure you did," the woman said. She broke into a wide, toothy grin. "It's about time somebody did. Come by the house sometime. I think you and I have a lot to talk about." Without further ado, she was gone. Trudy, Wade, and Andi stood transfixed by her lingering presence.

"How old is she?" Andi asked in astonishment.

"Ninety-six last month," Trudy answered. "And still going strong."

"Wow," was all Andi could say. She turned to Wade. "Is this a good time?"

"Trudy, what's on my schedule for the next hour?"

"A meeting with Andi Nelson, according to the calendar." She smiled at Andi. "Keep to your own corners in there. I'm not playing referee."

Andi followed Wade into the office and was surprised when he settled into one of the armchairs in the corner seating area. "Have a seat." He gestured to the other chair.

"Okay. Does this mean that this isn't an official conversation?"

"Yes and no. I'd like to talk person to person rather than mayor to constituent, or whatever you want to call it."

Andi took a seat. "Okay, then. What do you want to talk about?"

"Let's talk about this plan you and your brother have for the town. Lay it all out for me, step by step. Let's see just how feasible all of this is."

Andi was stunned. Why the sudden change? Was he serious, or was this a trick of some kind?

"You don't trust me." He cocked his head and squinted as if trying to read her mind.

"Honestly, I'm not sure. Last Thursday, you were dead set against this. What changed?"

"Maybe nothing. I just decided to hear you out, that's all."

Andi was suspicious, but she began telling him her plans, hesitantly at first, but then with all the passion she'd felt each time she and Jackson discussed the possibilities. Once she started, she found it hard to stop. After a while, she glanced at her watch and gasped.

"I've been going on and on for almost a half hour. Why didn't you stop me?"

"You were on a roll." Wade smiled. "I have some questions. And some concerns, but I think I might also have some suggestions and ideas of my own."

Andi didn't know how to respond, but she couldn't continue to sit there with her eyes bulging and her mouth hanging open. "Okay, then. Go ahead."

An hour after her arrival, her head was spinning. *Wait until I talk to my brother.*

"I'm afraid I've got to put an end to our discussion," Wade told her as he stood. "I've got a phone call in about five minutes that I have to take." He reached to shake her hand once she was on her feet.

"Thank you, Wade, for meeting with me. I appreciate you taking the time to listen, and I think your ideas are going to work out perfectly with our plan."

She realized they were still shaking hands, and she pulled her hand away, feeling a bit awkward in the ensuing silence. They both spoke at once.

"Thanks for coming in, Andi."

"Thanks again, Wade."

They laughed despite the strange tension that enveloped them. Andi searched Wade's eyes, not trusting that his show of support was real, but she couldn't see anything discernable in his gaze. Still unsure about the declared truce, Andi moved toward the door, and Wade followed.

"I'll get back to you when I know more," he told her.

Andi agreed to do the same and started to leave, but Wade called to her.

"Andi, wait. Your parents. Are they okay?"

Andi turned back toward him. "How'd you know…?"

"Mayor, remember?"

"They're fine. Shaken up, but fine." She relayed her conversation with her mother. "It's just a hateful thing to do."

"It is, and I'm sorry I didn't ask about it as soon as you arrived. I should have."

"It's okay. You have a lot on your mind." Andi tried to shrug it off, but Wade took a step closer and laid his hand gently on her arm. Andi's arm tingled at his touch.

"Andi this is serious. The whole house could've burned down."

"I know. I can't imagine who would have done that or why." She had her suspicions and tried to read his gaze to see if he shared them, but his face gave nothing away. He removed his hand and ran his fingers through his hair. Andi recognized the gesture as something he did when he was bothered or perplexed.

"The police are asking around, trying to determine if anything like this has happened before and went unreported, but…"

"But you think it's related to what we're doing, don't you?" Andi didn't like beating around the bush.

"I think it's possible, but let's not make assumptions."

"What should I tell them?"

"Nothing. Let's see what the investigation turns up. No need to worry them. But I'm going to ask that a patrol be assigned to their street at night just to be safe."

"Thanks, Wade. I appreciate that." Andi offered a small smile as she opened the door. She waved goodbye and closed the behind her.

Once in the outer office, she expelled a deep breath.

"How'd it go?" Trudy's eyes blinked.

"It went…well. Really well, I think." Andi gave a nervous laugh, feeling a bit blindsided by Wade's turnabout. "I don't know what made him change his mind, but he seems on board."

Trudy clapped her hands. "I knew he'd come around. It's a great plan, Andi. We're going to make this town the talk of the Ozarks."

While Andi appreciated Trudy's enthusiasm, she hoped Wade was sincere. The town had a lot riding on this plan, and Andi's future depended upon its success.

*****

Wade stood at the window and watched Andi cross the street. She stopped in front of the closed-down bakery again, and he wondered why a former Naval officer was so hung up on opening a bakery. It seemed strange to him, but then again he didn't know Andi very well. And who'd have thought a New York City attorney would take a job as a mayor in a town that was barely holding on.

Wade turned from the window and sat at his desk. He gazed around the room and wondered, for the thousandth time, just what the heck he was doing here. He had always hated this town, he hated the job, and he hated feeling like every little move he made was being scrutinized by unseen eyes. Sometimes he wondered if his office was bugged, but that just made him seem paranoid.

Andi was the first bright spot in his life since his return to town. He'd spent the past year counting down until he could leave. All he had to do was find his mother the right place to live out the rest of her days— somewhere close to him preferably—sell the farm, pack up, and head back to New York. It was simple, or so he thought. Then he suddenly found himself agreeing to be mayor, and all of his plans were derailed. Sitting there in the office, still smelling the lingering scent of Andi's shampoo, he wondered if he took the job to prolong leaving. Because the truth was, he didn't want to sell the farm. If he ever had kids, he'd want them to experience life in the Ozarks. He wanted them to understand how things grew, to see a foal being born (which he'd seen at his best friend's house when they were just eight), to be able to count the stars in the sky. He thought he missed the bright lights of the big city, but then he'd find himself gazing at the night sky and think, *this is one of the things I missed the most about home.*

Wade thought it would be easy to move his mother to New York, but no matter how hard he tried, he couldn't see her anywhere else but here. Her husband was buried here. Her beloved movie theater and the farm she cherished were here. Her friends were in this town.

As for Wade, he had many colleagues but few friends. He'd lost touch with the people back home and hadn't reconnected with any of them since returning. In the city, he worked too long and too hard to have a social life outside of business dinners and charity affairs. He hadn't dated since he lost Pam, and he hadn't wanted to. Work consumed him, and he was okay with that. Until now.

This town that he always thought he hated and couldn't wait to get away from had slowly begun to take hold of his heart. The people were genuine. They smiled at each other on the street. Everyone knew each other's name, address, and every detail about their personal lives. The lack of privacy used to rankle him, but then he realized how lonely it was to go home to an empty high-rise apartment every night, eat every meal alone, and stare out the window at a city that never sleeps but never truly opens its eyes either. There were so many nights he longed to sit on someone's front porch and wave at neighbors or sit in a church pew and actually know the person sitting beside him. In the city, people walk around all day with earbuds in their ears, sunglasses shielding their eyes, and tunnel vision, never even acknowledging the world or lives around them. Here, there's a sense of community, of looking out for each other, of working together to make life better.

At least, that's the way he remembered it being before… before the mill shut down, before businesses began closing, before Ted Mitchem and the rest of the town council threw in the towel and thrusted to power a man with no vision, no plans to stick around, and no desire to help makes things better. And then Andi walked into town.

Wade sighed. This new way of thinking, this introspection that Wade didn't have before, this sense that he was screwing up everything and had been since day one—it all led back to the first time he saw Andi in front of the movie theater two weeks before. What was it about her that made him take a long, hard look at himself and not like what he saw? And how could he become the man she and this town needed him to be, the man his mother assured him he was and is? And why did it even matter to him at all?

Because it's what God wanted, a nagging voice said from inside his head. God put him on the path back to Buffalo Springs. God led him to take the job, and God brought Andi into his life. Nothing was coincidence, and nothing was random. Wade firmly believed that even though things like his father's death, his mother's illness, and losing Pam seemed to have no rhyme or reason, no good consequences or redeeming value. Still, Wade knew that God had a plan for everyone and everything. He just had to figure out how all of this featured into God's plan and what he was supposed to do next to fulfil his part in it.

Wade looked at his watch and hastily reached for the phone. He was ten minutes late for his call with Ted Mitchem. Why he continued to check in with the man was a mystery even Wade couldn't answer. Perhaps it was time to let the former council president know that he was no longer calling the shots.

Or not.

Wade had a feeling that it was not smart to get on Mitchem's bad side. Instead, Wade would bide his time, see how Andi's plan unfolded, and then deal with the fallout. In the meantime, he thought there were a few ways he could discreetly help Andi with her endeavor.

***

"I don't understand why you're so nervous," Helena said as they ate. "He heard you out, offered ideas of his own, and said he'd support you."

Andi took a bite of the roasted venison she had cooked in the slow cooker. It was better than she thought it would be, which she assumed was due more to her mother's recipe than to her own culinary skills. "He didn't exactly say he was supporting us."

"Well, he's not trying to block it. That's a good start."

"I suppose." Andi picked apart a brown n serve roll and popped a piece in her mouth.

"What did Jackson say?" Helena asked.

"He didn't have much time to talk. He was in the middle of unloading feed at the Tractor Supply, and he's taking an exam this evening. He was happy though. As happy as he can be after what happened."

Helena frowned. "Daddy says Chief Manning wasn't much help."

"Sounds like it. Who would do such a thing?" Andi couldn't shake the feeling that the incident was a sign of foreboding.

"I wish I knew. At least nobody was hurt, and the house is okay."

"You got that right." Andi picked at the food on her plate. "Do you think it was meant as a warning?"

Helena's fork stopped in front of her mouth. "The rock?"

"Yes. Do you think it was meant as a warning to Jackson and me?"

Helena laid the fork on her plate and took a deep breath. "I can't deny that the timing makes it seem so. And we've never had anything like this happen here before."

"I'm worried that I might be putting Mama and Daddy in danger. Maybe you and Jackson, too."

"That's ridiculous," Helena said, but Andi could see in her sister's eyes that she'd had the same thought.

"Do you think we should stop? Just let the town continue to die and stop stirring things up?"

Helena reached over to lay her hand on top of Andi's. "Andi, what I saw at that meeting the other night was just short of a miracle. People had hope. For the first time in ages, they could see a better tomorrow. If someone is trying to stop you from making people's lives better, are you really going to let them win?"

Andi thought about it for a moment. "Maybe you're right."

Helena patted Andi's hand and picked her fork back up. "Of course, I am, sugar. I'm always right."

Andi smiled. She loved her sister dearly.

"Now, let's get back to your problem at hand. What can I do to help?"

Andi took a long drink of her iced tea as she thought about where to begin. She felt overwhelmed by everything and worried she'd bitten off more than she could chew.

"I'm not sure. I'm going by the bank tomorrow to see about a small business loan to buy the bakery. I asked if the owner of the building might be willing to lower the price a bit, but Rudy says he won't go any lower." Andi wished the real estate agent had at least asked, but she'd let that go for now.

"You should be able to get a loan, right?"

Andi shrugged. "I don't know. I don't have any capital. I own a car, but it's not worth much. I don't have a house or any other holdings. And opening a bakery in Buffalo Springs is a big business risk."

"What about that women's business group? Can they help?"

"I've filled out all the paperwork, so we'll see." Andi stabbed a carrot with her fork and chewed it slowly before she spoke again. "I'm not sure I can do this."

"Get the loan?"

"Get the loan, renovate the bakery, run a business, kickstart the town, any of it."

Helena put down her fork and folded her hands in front of her. "That's not the sister I know. Do you remember how shocked Mama and Daddy were when you told them you were applying for the Academy? And how much more shocked they were when you actually got accepted and headed to Annapolis? Remember how many people told you that as a girl, you'd have to work harder, dig deeper, and push yourself more than the guys just to make it through the first month? Remember how hard it was to get through the first few days and how each day, week, then month got better and better? And later, you got accepted into the intelligence sector of the SEAL program. Not many women can say that."

"Well, I wasn't exactly boots on the ground, you know."

"Still, you proved everyone wrong, including that upperclassman who berated you all through your plebe year. He tried his hardest to break you."

Andi knew that her sister was right. When she graduated, Glen—her senior Midshipman—surprised her by coming back and attending the ceremony. Afterward, he sought her out, congratulated her, and told her he was hard on her at first because he didn't want her there, but he eventually came around and continued to be hard on her because he knew she had it in her to make it. Boy, how she hated Glen back then, but after she graduated, he became one of her most trusted confidants. He'd give her h-e-double-hockey-sticks if she backed down from this challenge.

"Look, I appreciate all this, but it's not the same."

"You're right," Helena said with confidence. "This time, you've got a whole town who believes in you and wants to support you. Nobody wants this to fail. Everyone needs it to succeed, not just you."

"And what if I fail them all?"

"You won't unless you've already decided you will. I have a sign hanging up in the library. It's a quote by Theodore Roosevelt, 'It is hard to fail, but it is worse never to have tried to succeed'."

Andi closed her eyes and took a deep breath. She opened her eyes and smiled at Helena. "Thanks, Helena. I'm going to need your enthusiasm and encouragement to help me get this done."

"I knew there was reason I put up with the other girls and the skimpy costumes and shedding pom pons for four years. It was all leading to this moment."

"Yeah, well I hope you still have those poms somewhere because we may need a cheering section."

Eight

When Andi left the bank the following day, she headed right to the real estate office. She was dumbfounded that her loan had been approved so quickly. The loan officer barely looked at her application before giving it a stamp of approval, but she wasn't going to question him. She rushed out as quickly as she could, certain he was going to realize his mistake and revoke the approval. Once the settlement date was confirmed, she would be on her way to owning a bakery.

She stopped in front of the broken window to peek inside. Thirty days from now, assuming the seller would agree to the short contract time, Andi would be unlocking the doors to her future store. To say she felt overwhelmed was an understatement.

"Any news on your status?"

Andi jumped at the sound of the voice behind her.

Wade looked repentant. "Sorry, it seems I have a habit of doing that to you."

"I'd have thought you would've learned your lesson that day in the park."

"You're right. I need to start giving you some warning when I'm approaching."

"Maybe you could walk a bit louder, or whistle as you get close. Any kind of notice would be nice." She let out a breath as the shock of his sudden appearance wore off.

"I'll remember that," he said with the same smile he had worn the day they met outside the theater.

"So?" He looked at Andi expectantly, and she raised a brow in question. "The bakery? Where are you with that? Did your loan go through?"

Andi narrowed her gaze on him. *How did he know about the loan? Had he been keeping tabs on her?*

"It did go through." She smiled despite her puzzlement at his question.

"Congratulations!" He gave her a friendly pat on the back.

"Thanks. I'm on my way to see Rudy to let him know he can tell the seller." She frowned. "I'm not sure who actually owns the building. In fact, I'm not sure who owns any of the buildings that are closed. Apparently, they were all bought up by the same person and never reopened. Any idea what that's all about?"

"None. I could look into it though."

She searched his face but couldn't detect any deceit. Maybe he really didn't know.

"That would be great. Thanks. Maybe whoever it is would rather see the businesses up and running than cut his losses. Jackson says he or she might like the idea of a higher return on his investment."

"Makes sense to me. Hey, how are your folks? Any news on the rock throwing?"

"None. I guess you didn't find out anything."

"Nothing. No other reports about it happening to anyone else, but I'll keep my ear to the ground," Wade assured her.

Andi still wasn't sure how she felt about him. Was he truly on their side or not? Other than sharing some ideas about the town, he never seemed to have much to say, and she felt that he was a difficult person to get to know. After a few moments of silence, both of them staring into the empty store, she decided she had too much on her mind to worry about trying to get him to open up or to stand around and engage in idle chit chat.

"Thanks. I guess I should get on over to see Rudy."

"Of course. It was nice talking to you. I'll let you know what I can find out about the owner."

"Thanks, Wade. I appreciate it."

She smiled and headed toward the real estate office, wondering what his story was despite telling herself she didn't care.

＊

Wade watched Andi walk away. What was her story? He still didn't understand her desire to open a bakery.

Not after the life she'd led up to this point. From what he knew, she was pretty successful in her job with the Navy. She was known as a tough, confident, take-no-prisoners kind of person. But that's not what he saw.

When Wade looked into Andi's eyes, he saw sadness, distrust, and, unless he projected too much, loneliness. Why had she left the Navy? Why had she moved back to town? Why did he have the impression that she was as broken as the town was, as broken as he was?

Wade unlocked the movie house and started to climb the stairs to the office, but he hesitated halfway up. Making his way back down the steps, he went into the theater and stood looking at the torn screen. When the beam fell, taking half the screen with it, his mother believed it was sign. Rather than have the falling beams and screen repaired, she started talking about selling it. His father had just passed, and Blanche claimed it was too much for her to take care of alone. When Wade came home and started looking at the books, he was amazed at the mistakes he found, the unpaid bills, and the thousands of notes she had pinned everywhere to remind herself how to do things that should have been rote tasks. Wade refused to consider there was more to her forgetfulness than just missing her husband. She was only fifty-five at the time, much too young to have serious cognitive health issues. And then the doctor broke the news to him. Young or not, her mind was betraying her.

Wade sat down in the last row and recalled his childhood, what it was like to grow up in the shadows of the old movie house. Like Andi, it was his old stomping ground. He hated to sell it. If his sister had lived, maybe she could have…No, he wasn't going to go there. Jolene had been the first person he lost, and her tragic death, at the age of ten, was not something he was going to think about.

What he wanted to think about was Andi. Well, not her specifically, he told himself. He wanted to think about her plan to revitalize the town. Was there a way for the movie house to be a part of that, or was it too late for the grand old building? With the opening of the megaplex in Harrison, was there even a reason to consider letting the old place stand?

His phone vibrated in his pocket, and Wade reached for the device, grateful for the reprieve from his thoughts.

The text was from Trudy. His buddy from New York had emailed the information Wade requested about impact investors interested in rebuilding small towns. Wade replied that he would return to the office soon and forced himself to stand. He took one last look at the screen, the stage beneath it that still retained much of the original oak floor, and the velvet curtains that hung on each side. It was once the crown-jewel of the town.

Saddened by the loss his parents, his sister, the theater, the town, and the loss of Pam, whom he refused to think about for so long but was now finding on his mind more and more, Wade made his way back out into the lobby. He knew God was trying to tell him something, but he still didn't know what it was.

He trudged up the stairs and retrieved the box of papers he kept putting off going through. Despite his desire to help Andi, he felt discouraged. Because he knew that all things came to an end. He might be showing his support for the town and his neighbors and this crazy plan of theirs, but he knew the truth that they all refused to face. There came a time when everyone had to accept that nothing lasts forever. No matter the age, the grandeur, or the amount of love poured out, death always came knocking, one way or another. Maybe that's why he kept thinking of Pam. It was a reminder that nothing in this world lasted.

That left Wade two choices—sit back and wait for death to claim the next victim or do his best to trust in God's mercy and forgiveness and find a way to bring life back into the town and maybe into his heart.

***

The caller ID read, *Number Blocked*, and Andi considered not answering it, but it might have been somebody calling about the town. It was her number on all the flyers after all.

"Hello."

"Is this Andi Nelson?" The voice was mechanical sounding and immediately gave Andi the creeps.

"Yes, who's this?"

"You've gone too far. Lives are in danger. Stop this foolishness now before things get out of control and people get hurt."

The line went dead. Andi shivered. She was now even more convinced that what happened at her parents' house was her fault.

**

The next morning, Andi received a text from Wade asking her to meet him at the old laundromat. She waited on the sidewalk in front of the empty storefront on the corner and debated over telling him about the call. Still unsure if he could be trusted, she decided to keep it to herself for now.

Andi watched with interest as a couple she did not recognize stood outside the Italian restaurant and gestured through the window. The man backed up into the street and pointed toward the upper level, and the woman nodded. Her animated gestures peppered her speech. Andi could see her mouth moving and wondered what she said.

She was pulled from her thoughts by the sound of the *Jeopardy* tune. She smiled and shook her head as Wade approached, and the whistling subsided.

"Your warning of impending arrival?"

"I wouldn't want to scare you again."

"Well, I'm grateful for that. At least I won't have to be on constant alert, waiting for you to sneak up behind me or tackle me on my morning run."

"I'm trying to fulfil my promises," he said. "Speaking of which…" He turned toward the building. "I've got a contractor meeting us here in fifteen minutes. I figured we should make sure we're on the same page before he shows up."

"A contractor?" Andi tried to hide her surprise and her confusion.

"I've managed to isolate some funds to create the tourist information center. One of the perks of not having to answer to a town council. We can go inside, and you can tell me what you have in mind. But first, tell me about the call you got last night."

Andi blinked. "The call?"

"Come on, Andi. The call you reported to the police. There's not much that goes on in this town that I don't hear about."

She repeated the words of the caller.

"Is that it?"

"That's it. Short and not so sweet."

"Okay, let me see about putting a—"

Andi raised her hand to silence him. "I don't need a patrol on my street. I'll be careful."

He opened his mouth to protest, but she shook her head. "I mean it. The force is small, and you've already got them keeping an eye on my parents. I'll be fine."

She could tell by the look on Wade's face that he disagreed, but he didn't argue.

Wade let out a long sigh. "Fine. For now." He turned toward the door and unlocked it while Andi stood silent.

He held the glass door open, and she followed him inside.

"Okay, what's your vision for this space?"

"Well…" Andi hesitated as she turned in a slow three-sixty, carefully examining the space. She told him what she had in mind for the room.

Wade was silent for a minute before knitting his eyebrows together. "You want us to create a wall-sized, interactive map?"

"I know it sounds like a big project, but I think, with the right technology people, we could make it work." She held her breath as she watched his expression change from confusion to disbelief to annoyance.

"Are you crazy? Do you know how much that would cost? How much work that would entail? I was prepared for a few thousand, but that would be…I can't even voice it. This town is on its way to becoming a ghost town, and you want to do what?"

Andi squeezed her eyes together. His reaction was slightly worse than she thought it might be. She looked at Wade and sighed. "I know it sounds a bit over the top—"

"A bit? Have you looked into the cost at all?"

"Actually, we would start with basic Google satellite mapping on a giant interactive white board. It's not the endgame I envision, but it's a start. We tweak the protocol to give us the ability to map only within the area radius we want, then we allow users to access national park information, booking sites, interesting facts. There are ways to manipulate the software so that it brings up only what we want it to bring up. We start small, maybe a four-by-six-foot board, and progress to a wall-sized map as we are able, using money we make through bike rentals, walking tours, and partnering with local artisans to buy and sell their products: jewelry, soap, jams and jellies, that kind of stuff. Jess Swanson makes amazing blown glass ornaments, and Richard Mackenzie makes beautiful wood carvings. Have you seen them? Oh, and there's the quilting association—"

"Slow down. I thought we were talking about the map."

"We are. We start small and use the money we make selling local souvenirs to eventually go bigger."

"That all sounds great in theory but selling ornaments and grape jelly won't pay the kind of costs you're talking about." Wade blew out a frustrated breath and shook his head. "I just don't see how this is going to work. I thought, maybe we could try, but this seems already out of hand."

Andi felt her face grow red. "Didn't you listen to anything I just said? I know it's going to take time, but we can make it work. The technology is there and getting less expensive every day."

"And who's going to create this manipulated software you mentioned? Last I looked, we don't have any MIT graduates banging on the door to do it for free."

"Well, I know how to do it. It's simple html, stuff anybody who understands coding can do—"

Wade put up his hand. "Andi, stop. How are you going to renovate your own store, start up a business, and take on this center while helping everyone else in town plan their own endeavors? We need more know-how than just you. We need expertise that we just don't have here in Buffalo Springs."

"I think you're wrong about that. Heather's a librarian. She understands coding. Mabel Henry's son is studying computers at the University of Arkansas. I bet he'd help us out. And I bet there are more people with the exact skill sets we need for all of these projects." Andi pulled out her phone. "Look at this list I've created." She held it out to him.

Wade took the phone and scrolled down the list she had compiled. "How did you find out all of this?"

"I asked. I've talked to nearly every citizen of the town. I've listened to them, their ideas, their concerns, their skills, their hopes and dreams, and their thoughts about what jobs and other enticements would lure their grown kids back to the area. Who have you talked to, *Mayor*?"

A knock and the opening of the door kept Wade from answering. "Wade, are you ready for me?"

Wade looked from the contractor to Andi and back to the contractor before exhaling and waving the man inside. "I guess so, Stan. Come on in."

The man entered and reached for Wade's hand. "Good to see you Wade. Thanks for calling me."

"Who else would I call?" He turned toward Andi. "Andi, do you know Stan? We went to high school together."

"I don't think so." She turned to Stan. "I was a few years younger than you."

"I know. I remember you. Thanks for you service?" He reached for hand, and Andi gave it a good, hearty shake.

Wade addressed them both. "Stan, Andi's got some ideas for this space. I'm going to let her tell you what she has in mind, and you let me know how much it's going to cost."

"I can't give you a quote today, sir. I'll have to go back and figure up all the costs."

"A guess, then?"

"As best I can."

Wade shook his head. "I suppose that's a start. Andi, take it away."

Andi began with the simple things—wall paint, basic construction of shelves and counters, carpeting and electrical wiring. She moved on to her bigger ideas—the map, a shopping area, and a coffee bar. She glanced at Wade every now and then as Stan audibly calculated costs. Wade listened intently, sometimes nodding in agreement, and other times, hardening his jaw in irritation. After she finished, she braced herself while Stan worked up a quote.

"That's all?" Wade asked after hearing the projected cost.

"Well, like I said, it's a guess, but the construction and wiring stuff is pretty easy, especially since this was a laundromat at one time and outlets are everywhere. As far as the map, I know of a school warehouse place that sells used supplies at pretty good prices. I bet I could find a smart board there. They're pretty old technology these days."

Andi shot Wade a look, but he averted his gaze from hers.

"So, you really think we could do this without much overhead?" Wade asked.

"Yeah, I know we could. And honestly, Wade, I need the business. If I do a good job here and ask a decent price, then others will hopefully hire me for their jobs. From what I heard the other night..." He turned toward Andi. "This place could be a haven for construction in the near future."

"That's the plan," Andi said with a smile. As soon as she settled on the bakery, she'd ask Stan to give her an estimate on her renovation.

"How soon can you give me a real quote?" Wade asked.

"As soon as tomorrow morning."

Wade reached for the man's hand. "Thanks, Stan. I look forward to hearing from you. Give my best to the family."

"You're welcome, Wade. Thanks for thinking of me." Stan turned to Andi. "And thank you, Andi. You've got a whole lot of people feeling hopeful again. It means a lot to us all."

As she watched Stan leave, Andi felt really good about the prospects for the future. She almost congratulated herself, but she felt the intense stare of the mayor and turned toward him.

"I hope he's right about the cost and that we don't find anything that causes the bottom line to escalate. It seems the whole town has their hopes and dreams tied to your shirttail."

Andi swallowed. "It does seem that way. Thank you for giving us a chance."

"I just hope we don't all regret it."

Wade walked to the door and held it open for Andi. After he locked up, he stood and looked up and down the street, and Andi wondered what he was really thinking.

"You know, Wade, I've come to believe that we only regret the things we do not try." She turned and walked away, her trepidation growing with each step. She had a lot of people depending upon her. If they only knew what happened to the last group or people who put their lives in her hands, they might feel differently.

***

"What's this I hear about you turning that laundromat into a tourist center?" Ted Mitchem looked down his nose at Wade.

"And good morning to you, too, Ted. How are you on this fine day?"

"I'm not here to chat, boy. I'm here to give a warning. We had a deal. You're supposed to be convincing people to leave town, not hunker down and give the American dream another worthless try."

"What's so wrong with giving people hope?" Wade asked, echoing his mother's sentiment.

Mitchem turned red in the face. "Everything! Now, you listen here, put an end to this madness before it's too late."

The former town council president fled the room, slamming the door behind him, and Wade wondered why he could finesse million-dollar deals and forge outrageously overpriced contracts but not stand up to a small-town bully. He was getting tired of being that man's punching bag. He had a town to run whether Mitchem liked it or not.

Nine

Over the next two weeks, Andi made sketches for the bakery, compiled a list of things she would need to ask Stan, formed a list of things to be ordered, and met with family after family, business after business, hooking them all up with investors that Wade had convinced to take a chance on the town.

Betty Jean and Davy had contacted the Christmas Tree Growers Association and were preparing their land for their first delivery of saplings.

The couple Andi had seen outside of the restaurant lived a town yonder. Children of Italian immigrants, Antonella and Leonardo Russo, wanted to take a shot at opening an authentic Tuscan restaurant, a dream they'd had for several years, but they didn't think they could afford the real estate until they read about the town meeting in Buffalo Springs in the county newspaper.

Helena had used her contacts to have an article printed in all of the surrounding counties' publications, from newspapers to attraction magazines to organizational newsletters.

Ally Michaels and Paige Albrecht, best friends since elementary school, were interested in a small storefront for a t-shirt shop that would specialize in tees, sweatshirts, sweatpants, and loungewear depicting Ozark lore and local sayings. Their first batch would feature Bigfoot and Gowrow, the Ozarks fabled wingless dragon said to prey on livestock and small animals.

Angela Taylor planned to spruce up her hair salon, and Paul Logan began talking about expanding the Shop-a-Lot. There were just two more empty buildings on Main Street as well as the original jail and the movie house. Wade never mentioned it in the few meetings he and Andi had about the developing tourist center, and Andi got the feeling that talk about the family theater was off the table as was the rest of Wade's personal life. Still, Andi was fascinated by the building and often found herself standing in front of it, remembering the movies of her childhood.

"Excuse me. Are you Andi Nelson?"

Andi tore her gaze from the theater and turned toward the voice. She blinked as she stared at the man before her, and her throat went dry. Jeremy? Her legs wobbled, and she reached for the brick building for support.

"I'm sorry, I didn't mean to startle you. I should have warned you I'd be coming to town."

"You're..." She couldn't say the name out loud.

The man nodded. "Joseph Blake. But, please, call me Joe."

Andi pushed down the sour taste in the back of her mouth. "Joe," she repeated. "I'm sorry. I didn't expect to see you. For a minute, I, uh, I mean, well, what are you doing here?"

"Maybe we should find a place to talk."

Andi nodded but didn't move.

"Is there some place we can go?"

"Oh! Yes, sorry. How about Rick's Place? It's kind of a bar, but it's quiet this time of day." And she could use a drink right about now.

"That's fine. Lead the way."

Andi wasn't sure she could take a step, but thankfully, muscle memory moved her legs even though her brain could barely signal to them to walk. As they made their way across the street, Andi stole sidelong glances at the man she'd only heard about from his brother.

Once they were seated and drinks were on the way, Joe spoke. "Jeremy said you were pretty. He undersold you."

Andi blushed, reaching around to tug on her messy ponytail, conscious of her faded jeans and dingy SEALs sweatshirt. Her wardrobe was passable but limited, and she regretted not choosing a different shirt that morning when Joe's blue eyes dropped to the SEAL emblem on her chest. His eyes clouded over, but he blinked it away. Andi came to her senses.

"He talked about me?" she asked in a hushed tone.

Joe locked eyes with her. "All the time. I often wondered if there was something my brother wasn't telling... Never mind. It's none of my business."

Andi debated filling him in but thought it best to let bygones be bygones. "He was my best friend."

Joe studied her eyes for a moment before giving a slow nod as if he understood she didn't want to say more. "Mine, too."

"What brings you to town?" Andi asked, taking a sip of her beer, resisting the urge to down the entire bottle in one gulp.

"I've wanted to reach out for a while, but I wasn't sure if I should." He looked away but turned back to her. "It's been hard, knowing he's gone." She focused on the movement of his Adam's apple as he swallowed, unable to meet his eyes.

"Yes, it has been." Her voice was almost a whisper.

"Anyway, I wanted to let you know that we, our family, appreciates you being there for Jeremy when we couldn't be. It meant a lot to know that he had a, um, a friend he could count on."

Andi nodded and took a swig. She didn't know what to say. If his family only knew the truth.

Joe took a long drink and put the bottle on the table. "I was wondering, I mean, I read online..." He looked away and turned back to her. "I read that your town is trying to get some businesses to move in and take over the empty storefronts. I did a little research and it looks like you don't have any type of clinic in town."

"Clinic?"

"Yeah, doctor's office, urgent care, that kind of thing."

"No. The closest one is a good thirty minutes away."

"Yes, I know. I'm thinking, maybe I could help with that?"

Andi didn't understand what he was saying. Perhaps it was the beer that she was drinking way too fast, or the way he fidgeted, seemingly unable to find the right words, or the fact that his eyes were Jeremy's eyes. Maybe the combination of all three. She motioned for another beer.

"I'm sorry. Can you explain what you mean? How can you help?"

Joe played with a sugar packet as he spoke. "Ever since the accident, I've felt kind of lost. Like I said, Jeremy was my best friend. Back home, everywhere I go, I see him. I think about him all the time. I can't get away from my grief."

Andi wasn't sure where he was going with this. Was he just opening up to someone else who loved Jeremy, or was he saying what she prayed he wasn't.

"Anyway." He looked up at her. "I thought, maybe you could use a doctor. You know, to help revitalize things and bring more people into town. I'm a general practitioner, so I can do just about anything. Other than surgery. I mean, I could if I really had to, in a dire emergency, I guess, but it's not in my training. Anyway, I'd love to get out of Houston and help you out here."

Andi's breath caught in her throat. This could not be happening. She could not spend every day for the rest of her life knowing that at any minute, she might have to look into those eyes. She could not live the same existence that Joe was living now—seeing Jeremy all around town. And she could not take a chance that he would learn the truth, that he would know the crash, the 'accident' as he called it, was all her fault. She wanted to scream, to shout at him to get out, leave town, and never come back. She wanted to hurl her fists at him and pound his chest and take out all of her fury, her sadness, her guilt on him.

"That would be great." She heard the words, not more than a whispered voice she didn't recognize, and she reached her hand to her throat as if to stop herself from saying more.

His face lit up, and his eyes—Jeremy's eyes—sparkled with excitement and with relief. He reached for her hand and shook it.

"Thank you, thank you. I'll take a look at the downtown and see what's available and have my accountant start the necessary steps to rent space or buy a building, or whatever I need to do." He kept shaking her hand as he stood, and Andi thought he might pull her arm right out of the socket. Good thing he was a doctor.

"You're welcome," Andi said, managing to break the hold he had on her hand.

Joe thanked her again and left the bar, leaving Andi in a state of shock. She looked down at her trembling hands, chastising herself for not telling him no. But a doctor would be so good for the town, and he seemed as lost was she was, which was saying a lot. Who was she to tell him he couldn't start over. After all, that's what she was doing, wasn't it?

A shadow fell over the table. Andi looked up and immediately clenched her hands, trying to stop the shaking.

"Friend of yours?" Wade asked, motioning to the door through which Joe had exited.

"Not exactly." She motioned to the now empty chair across from her. "Want to join me? I'm having another beer." She raised her bottle and gave the waitress the universal signal for, 'bring me another.'

"A little early in the day to be drinking, isn't it?"

Andi lifted her shoulders. "It's five-o'clock somewhere."

"In that case…" He signaled for the same. "Want to tell me what that guy wanted and why you're so upset?"

Her head shot up. "Who says I'm upset?"

Wade looked her up and down. "Your hands are shaking, you're pale, and you just ordered your third beer in the past half hour."

She narrowed her eyes at him. "How do you know I've been here a half hour." *Or how many beers I've had?*

He gestured to the outer wall. "My office is right across the street, remember?"

So what? She wanted to challenge him. Did he spend all day looking out the window to track the movements of everyone in town, or just her?

"There's nothing wrong with having a drink now and then."

"As long as it's now and then." He leveled his gaze on her, and she shot daggers at him with hers. "Okay." He raised his hands as if to ward off the weapons in her eyes. "None of my business."

Their beers arrived, and Andi raised hers, tapped his, and said, "To bringing in new business," before taking a large sip.

"Is that what that was? A business deal?"

"You could say that. His name's Joe Blake. We share a mutual friend. He's a general practitioner and thought we might like a clinic opened here in town."

Wade's eyes widened. "Really? He's going to open a clinic?"

"Looks that way." She took another drink.

"Hey, I know I said it's none of my business, but are you okay?" The concern in his voice was off-putting and caused Andi to feel defensive.

"Of course, I'm okay. I just found us a doctor. I'm celebrating." She took another long drink.

"Andi, why don't you let me give you a ride home?" He signaled for the check.

"You think I can't take care of myself, Wade? That because I'm a girl, I need someone to protect me or something?"

"I never said that, Andi. I'm just trying to be a friend."

"I've had enough friends. You know what friends get you? Heartache, that's what. And guilt. And feeling sorry for yourself."

"Sounds to me like you've been making the wrong friends." When she stood, he stood and gently took her elbow, but she yanked her arm away.

With a clipped, even tone, she bored her gaze into him and said, "I had the best friends on this earth. The best. They were there for me. Always. And I was there for them. Until it really counted."

With that, she grabbed her purse and stalked out of the bar. She arrived at her car and fumbled with her keys, but her hands were shaking. Wade reached her and put his hand on her arm.

"Andi, stop. I can't let you do this."

"I had three beers, Wade." She glared at him, her pulse roaring in her ears. "I think I can handle more than three beers."

"Maybe you can, and maybe you can't. Maybe you're just having a hard day and drank a little faster than you normally would. Maybe you're just fine and can drive without a problem, but I won't be responsible for you killing somebody."

Andi's hand froze, and the keys fell from her grasp. She suddenly felt foolish, sick even. She stared at the keys, lying in the dirt between her feet, and fought back tears. She'd spent her entire adult life holding back tears, and she was good at it. Whether she was attending a funeral or watching a heart-wrenching movie, she kept her emotions in check. Even if she was dying on the inside, she was stoic on the outside. But feeling Wade's hand on her arm and seeing the concern in his eyes, she began to feel herself shake. Before she could stop it, the dam broke, and she found herself convulsing in his arms, surrendering to sixteen years of pent-up emotions.

***

Wade wasn't sure how it happened. One minute, he was trying to convince Andi not to drive, and the next, he was pulling her to his chest, running his hands down her back, letting her cry against him.

When her trembling seemed to be subsiding, and her gulping eased, he whispered, "Feel better?"

She nodded, and he felt her raise her hand to wipe away her tears.

"I guess if I was a real gentleman, I would have a handkerchief to offer you."

She leaned back and looked at him with a slight smile. "If you were a real, *old* gentleman." He could tell that she was embarrassed and was trying to make light of the situation.

"Now, that's the Andi I know." He looked at his watch. "It really is almost five o'clock. Want to get something to eat?" He started to say, *I think you could use something besides beer on your stomach*, but he thought better of it.

"I have to get home and make supper for Helena."

"Helena's a big girl. I bet she's quite capable of making food for herself."

Andi seemed to think about it for a moment before she gave a slight nod. "Let me text her."

Wade waited while Andi sent a message to her sister.

"Where do you want to eat?"

Wade looked around. "Not too many choices, are there?"

Andi shook her head.

"Let's go to my place. My mother's caregiver always makes something good, and she cooks enough to feed an army. Besides, she'll be ready to head out soon."

Andi looked horrified. "Oh, no, I could never do that. I can't eat your mother's food."

"It's my food, too." He took her arm again, giving her a gentle tug. "Come on, I promise it's better than barbecue or frozen pizza."

Andi gave him a suspicious look before she said, "Okay." She bent to pick up her keys.

"I'll take those." Wade took the keys from her hand and pocketed them before she could protest. "I'll bring you back after supper." He expected an argument, but she just sighed in acquiescence and followed him to his car.

She was silent on the five-minute drive to his house. Unlike Andi, Wade lived on the very edge of the town limits. In fact, he was pretty sure the house was outside of the town proper, but nobody brought it up when the mayor position was offered to him, and Wade didn't volunteer the information.

As Wade turned onto the long, tree-lined driveway, he saw Andi sit up and take notice of the landscaped gardens and the rolling fields that she hadn't been able to see weeks ago from the road.

"What does your family do? Besides run the theater, I mean."

"Nothing these days."

"Those fields aren't planted with nothing."

"They're rice fields. We have people who tend to them."

He kept his eyes on the house ahead, but in his peripheral vision, he saw Andi turn and look at him.

"Arkansas's cash crop, huh? You didn't need a scholarship to go to Notre Dame, did you?"

Wade didn't answer. He knew what she was asking, and frankly, his family's wealth wasn't any of her business any more than her friendship problems were his business. He was grateful when they reached the end of the driveway. He turned off the engine and opened the door without a word, unsure as to why he had invited her to dinner.

**

Andi followed Wade up the steps of the wraparound porch, neatly painted, with a swing similar to the one at her parents' house, and real wicker furniture, not the fake plastic kind they had.

The foyer they walked into was grand, with a marble floor, rounded staircase, and the biggest chandelier Andi had ever seen inside a house. Without warning, Boomer bounded into the room and slammed his giant paws into her chest. Andi grabbed his legs and used his weight as a counterbalance to keep herself from toppling over.

"Hello there, good boy." She laughed as he licked her face.

"Get down, Boomer." Wade pushed him aside. "Mama?" he called. "We've got company."

Andi heard the frail voice call from another room. "Company? Why didn't you tell me?"

Andi followed Wade into what she would call the parlor, with its enormous brick fireplace, wall of books, expanse of windows, and large, plush furniture. Boomer was at her heels.

"I'm sitting here in my loungewear. I would have changed."

Wade bent down and kissed his mother on the cheek. "You look beautiful, as always."

Mrs. Montgomery peered around her son. "Who do we have here? No, don't tell me. Andi Nelson. My how you've grown, and you're so pretty, too."

Andi blinked a few times, staring at the woman, until she remembered her manners. She went closer and took her hand. "It's so nice to see you, Mrs. Montgomery. I'm surprised you remember me."

"You're Grace's daughter, and you like horror movies and action-adventures. No chick flicks for you."

Andi smiled. "How do you know that?"

"My dear, one always remembers what genres their patrons lean toward. If I didn't know what people liked,

I'd never be able to order the right movies." Mrs. Montgomery looked expectantly at her son. "Is your father home?"

Andi saw Wade's jaw tense and his green eyes glaze, but he gave his mother a compassionate smile. "Dad won't be home tonight, Mama. It's just the three of us for supper."

"Mr. Montgomery?"

Andi turned to see a young woman in the doorway.

"Is it okay if I leave? There's chicken and dumplings on the stove, and I made it with extra green beans and carrots, the way your mother likes it. And there's carrot cake for dessert."

"Thank you, Melanie. How were things today?"

Melanie glanced at Andi and then answered Wade. "Not great, I'm afraid. I had to keep a close eye on her today. She kept wanting to go to the theater. She said she needed to open up and get the projector going. I had hoped she might be a bit better by the time you got home."

"Not your fault, Melanie. Thanks. You may go."

"Thank you, sir. I've got a date tonight." She smiled, and Andi admired her youth and enthusiasm.

"No class?"

"Not tonight. And I got my homework done while your mother took her nap."

"Well, have fun tonight. I'll see you in the morning."

"Jolene, dear? Make sure you wear a jacket. It's getting chilly out there."

Wade froze, and Andi saw the pain in his eyes.

"Wade, why don't you get supper together? I'll stay here." Andi took a seat on the footstool in front of his mother's chair, and Boomer collapsed by her side. "Mrs. Montgomery tell me more about the movies. What's your favorite one?" Wade hesitated for a moment but then nodded and disappeared through another doorway.

"Oh, there are too many to pick just one. Of course, my parents loved movies, and I was raised on the classics—*Casablanca*, *King Kong*, *The Godfather*, and Hitchcock, but I love *Sleepless in Seattle*. Wade's father took me to New York City once, and we went up to the observation deck in the Empire State Building. It was so romantic."

Afraid she would ask for her husband again, Andi asked more questions about movies. She sat and listened, prying for more information now and then, and realized she could sit and listen to the dear woman forever. She told such fun and interesting stories, including an old family tale about John Wayne attending the premiere of *True Grit* at the Buffalo Springs movie theater in 1969.

"My mother thought he was the nicest looking man she'd ever seen, other than Daddy, of course."

"Of course," Andi said.

"You two hungry? It's on the table." Wade leaned against the doorjamb, and Andi wondered how long he had been standing there.

Mrs. Montgomery looked around. "Are your Daddy and Jolene home?"

Andi patted her hand. "They're not here tonight, Mrs. Montgomery, but I'd like to have supper with you and hear more about the theater if that's okay."

"Oh, yes, dear, but please call me Blanche. I've always hated being called Mrs. Montgomery. It makes me feel old."

"Well, Blanche it is. Let's go eat." Andi stood and reached for Blanche's hand.

***

They ate and cleaned up the kitchen and then talked for another hour in the parlor. While Wade put his mother to bed, Andi perused the titles on the shelves. It was almost an hour before Wade returned, apologizing for keeping her waiting, but Andi said she hadn't minded. While she waited, she reacquainted herself with Jane Eyre and found that she felt quite content in the big, old house. Wade assured her that his mother would be okay for the short time they'd be gone.

"Thank you," Wade said in the car on the way back to town.

"For what?" Andi asked.

"For being so kind to my mother, for helping with the dishes, and for waiting patiently for me to return."

"You don't have to thank me. I enjoyed being with your mother. She's quite the character."

Wade chuckled. "She is."

"If you don't mind my asking, how old is your mom?"

Wade took a moment before answering. "Fifty-six."

Andi gasped. "Oh! I thought…"

"She aged quickly once she was diagnosed last year."

"She's so young," Andi said in almost a whisper. She thought of her own mother, just fifty-four.

"I never imagined I'd lose them both at such young ages."

Andi couldn't imagine how it felt to lose both parents, but she knew how it felt to lose someone you loved. "I'm so sorry, Wade. Please believe me when I say, I know how hard it is to have to say goodbye to someone you love."

Wade glanced at her, and though it was dark, she saw something pass over his expression, a silent agreement, perhaps? Maybe an acknowledgement that they shared something that not many people their ages could relate to?

Wade took a deep breath before he spoke. "Who was it?"

Andi wasn't sure she correctly heard what he said. "Excuse me?"

"Who did you have to say goodbye to?"

Andi looked at her hands folded in her lap and pondered his question. She looked out the window into the dark night.

"My best friend." She hesitated but continued. "Friends. All of them."

"What do you mean, you lost all of them?"

She braced herself, unsure as to whether she was ready to share what happened with anyone other than

Helena, but especially with Wade. She barely knew him. But she found herself wanting to tell him. Maybe it had something to do with his mother or with him losing his father and his little sister Andi vaguely remembered.

"My platoon. They were my best friends. I lost them all. All at the same time, in the same instant. One minute, they were there, and the next, all I heard was radio silence. Jer—" His name caught in her throat. "Jeremy radioed that they had been—he said they were going down, and…that was it. Everything went silent."

The same type of silence engulfed the car. The kind of silence that signifies unfathomable loss and grave sadness. They both understood that type of silence. Wade steered the car into the parking space behind the bakery and turned off the engine.

"I'm sorry," he said, twisting to face her.

"Me, too. For your family, I mean."

Wade nodded. "Andi, I hate to leave you at a time like this, but Mama…"

"I know. Thanks for bringing me back. I appreciate it. And thanks for earlier. I was kind of a jerk."

"No problem. I've had my share of being a jerk lately."

Andi snickered. "I won't argue with you."

Wade reached over and placed his hand on top of her hands. "Are you going to be okay? I mean, you're heading home now, right?"

Andi stared at his hand covering hers. It felt nice. When was the last time a man had held her hand? When was the last time a man had touched her other than her father's hug? She recalled the one and only kiss she and Jeremy had shared, the only time they had ever touched other than friendly hugs, pats on the back, fist bumps, or high-fives.

She managed to give Wade a weak smile. "I'll be okay. Helena's waiting up for me, I'm sure."

"Okay, then." He removed his hand, and her hands suddenly felt very cold. "I'll wait until you get your car running. Oh!" He unbuckled his seat belt and reached into the pocket of his jacket to retrieve her keys. "You'll need these."

Andi took the keys and smiled at Wade. "Thanks, Wade. Be careful driving home." She opened the door and hurried to her car, feeling completely drained. She had run the full gamut of emotions that day, and she hadn't had time to come to terms with her loss of control. She was spent and longed for the comfort of her bed.

As she started the car and watched Wade pull away, she wondered if there had been a breakthrough for the two of them. Were they beginning to trust each other?

She put the car in reverse and realized she had confided in Wade, to a small extent, but he still hadn't made any move toward opening up to her. She sensed that the walls he had built up around himself went higher than the loss of his family. There was something else that he was keeping inside, something that kept him at arm's length from the world. Andi couldn't help but wonder what it was.

Ten

"My access to the town budget has never been an issue before. Why now?" Wade tried to remain nonconfrontational as he faced Ted Mitchem.

"You've never asked about the town budget before. You haven't inquired about money at all other than making sure the accountant paid the bills. You were just, ah, how should I put it?"

Wade seethed. "Not doing my job properly? Just letting the town continue to decay? Not caring about the wellbeing and future of my constituents?"

Mitchem was calm, too calm for Wade's liking. "Let's be honest, Wade. They're not really your constituents. They didn't elect you. If the people of the town wanted to, they could rescind your position with a simple referendum."

"And why would they do that, Ted?" Wade placed his elbows on the desk and pressed his fingertips together beneath his chin. "Tell me. For looking out for their best interests? For trying to revitalize the town? For looking into ways to bring in tourists and new residents? For seeking investors to help the citizens of the town open their own businesses? Which of these do you think the people would oust me for?"

Ted breathed loudly through his clenched jaw, his calm beginning to unravel. "Now, look here, Wade. I warned you to put an end to this, and you'd better do what I say. I put you in this office. This whole thing was my idea. I told the council to bring you in as mayor, and I convinced everyone to step down. We counted on you to do what's best for this town and its citizens."

"Is that not what I'm doing, Ted? I'm confused. Which of my actions has been detrimental to the town or the people?"

Ted turned red, finally losing all composure. "I think you've forgotten what our deal was, Mr. Montgomery. You were to help the town die a peaceful death, and I was to bring someone in to take care of the decaying infrastructure."

"To what end, Mr. Mitchem? I never questioned this little arrangement before. And frankly, I didn't care. This was all a means to an end. I needed to take care of my mother, sell the theater, and get back to New York. I didn't stop to ask you what you needed, what you were getting out of this. I was selfish and naïve, but you...You were president of the council, spokesperson for the citizens. I trusted that you had their best interests at heart. Now, I'm wondering about that. I'm seeing a way to help this town that I've actually grown to care about. It's become more than the place I couldn't wait to get away from as a youth. It's become my home, and I mean to protect my home. What is your angle?"

Ted Mitchem stood so abruptly, the chair he was sitting in fell backwards. "This conversation is over. Thank you for your brief but ineffective term as mayor."

"I've got news for you, Mr. Mitchem. I am the mayor, and I'm not planning on resigning any time soon."

Ted looked Wade squarely in the eye. "We'll see about that, son. You'd best start packing your bags." He turned, walked around the fallen chair, and left the office with a hearty slamming of the door.

Wade stared at the back of the door, a million thoughts and questions running through his mind. What had he gotten himself into by agreeing to this position? For the first time, he wondered if he unwittingly aided and abetted something illegal?

He raked his fingers through his hair and picked up the phone. "Trudy, I need to talk to Steve Marshall. Immediately." He hoped the town's accountant would have the answers he needed.

***

"I don't understand," Andi said to Rudy. "I got the loan, you said the contract was good. Why did the deal fall through?" She pushed her laptop away and pressed the speaker button on the phone. She laid the phone on the kitchen table and waited for a response.

"I honestly don't know, Andi. I'm as puzzled as you are."

"Does he want more money? A longer settlement period? What is it?"

"He says the building is no longer for sale. None of them are."

Andi stood. "What? None of the buildings are for sale? How many does he own?"

"Everything for sale but the jail, which is owned by the town, the laundromat, and the theater."

"What about the buildings that are still open?"

"Those belong to the owners of the businesses. All of the closed buildings were bought out by a single entity except for the laundromat. The Hills were out of town when the deal was made, so Wade was able to acquire the building rather easily as they were anxious to unload it."

"Wade? I thought the town bought that building."

"Oh, no. Wade offered a contract a few days after your town meeting. He gave well above the asking price, and they handed the keys right over to him, allowing access to the building before the settlement, which hasn't even taken place yet."

"Wade owns the building?" Andi's mind swirled with questions as she sat back down in the chair.

"Well, he will in a couple weeks, but yes, it was Wade who bought it."

"But the other buildings are what? No longer for sale?"

"That appears to be the case. In fact, I received an email just before I called you that they're set to be demolished next week."

"Next week?" She stood again. Unable to stand still, she walked around the table in a circle. "I don't understand. Is this person or entity, or whatever they are, planning on putting something else in place of the buildings?"

"I'm afraid I can't answer that, Andi. I'm sorry I can't tell you more."

"It's okay, Rudy. Thanks for calling." She disconnected the call and wondered if the town's mayor might have any insight as to what was going on. She picked up her phone to call Wade but thought better of it. She closed her computer, grabbed her keys and jacket off the hooks by the door, and tugged her arms into the sleeves as she left the house.

A light drizzle and chill in the air signaled an abrupt change of seasons, and Andi shivered as she got into her car. She drove through the downtown, peering at the empty storefronts, wondering why someone would want to tear them down. Sure, she saw broken windows and steps in need of repair, but the buildings were in pretty good shape, most built in the 1950s and 1960s when the town experienced its first revitalization after the opening of the movie house, the expansion of the paper mill, and the closing of the 'boarding house.'

Andi parked in the town parking lot and made her way toward Wade's office as the drizzle turned into a shower. She pulled the hood of her jacket over her head as she crossed the street and hurried to Wade's. She bounded up the stairs to the second floor office.

"Hey, Trudy, how are you today?" Andi asked, tugging off the hood and shaking out her hair as she entered the office

"Hmph. Don't ask."

"Uh-oh? Is something wrong?"

"Something's not right, that's for sure."

"Meaning?" Andi moved closer to Trudy's desk but shifted her gaze toward Wade's closed door. She could hear his raised voice.

"I'm not sure. Something with the former council president. Wade's on the phone with the town accountant."

"It doesn't sound good."

Trudy shook her head. "No, it doesn't." She looked up at Andi. "You know, Wade never really cared about being mayor until you showed up. For the first time, he's actually showing an interest in the town, the people, and the inner workings of the job." Trudy's mouth turned down.

"You make it sound like that's a bad thing."

"I have a feeling it might just be a bad thing. I think Wade is stirring the pot, and there are some who are not happy about it."

Andi leaned down toward Trudy and lowered her voice. "Do you think something shady is going on?"

Trudy looked around as if doubting they were alone. "I've always had my suspicions. It looks like your whole revitalization plan may have brought some things to light, or it's about to anyway."

Wade's office door opened, and Andi straightened as quickly as a student caught looking at the answers to a test.

"Andi," Wade said in surprise.

"Hey, Wade. Do you have a few minutes, or is this is a bad time?"

"No. It's perfect timing actually. Trudy, I've got to run out for a bit. Can you hold down the fort?"

Trudy rolled her eyes. "What do you think I've been doing for the past eleven years?"

Wade nodded and looked at Andi. "Ready?"

Andi wasn't sure what he meant, but she nodded and followed him down the stairs and out into the rain.

"Sorry," Wade said, looking up at the sky. "I didn't know it was raining."

"No worries. Where are we going?" She pulled up her hood again and followed him across the empty street.

"Just to the theater." He led the way, hastily unlocked the door, and bolted it behind them. He reached for her hand and pulled her toward the stairs.

For a moment, Andi lost focus as his skin brushed hers. Wade led them down a dark hall that was heavy with the odor one often encountered in very old buildings, of mildew and old wood and musty fabric. At the end of the hall, Wade entered a room and switched on the light of what Andi presumed was his mother's office.

"Take a seat," he told her as he let go of her hand and crossed to a beautiful oak desk. Andi looked around and dragged an antique cushioned chair closer to the desk.

"What's going on?"

"You first. You said you needed to talk to me."

Something was definitely wrong. Andi watched as he nervously shuffled papers, glancing every few moments out the window that looked across to his office.

"My contract was rejected."

"To the bakery? I'm sorry." He finally focused on her and frowned. "Is that all you wanted to tell me? Because I've got a lot on my mind, and I'm hoping I might be able to talk it through with you."

Andi wasn't sure what to say. Whatever bothered him was big, and she hated to add fuel to the fire but…"Wade, there's something going on in this town. The bakery, and all the other buildings that are for sale, other than this one, are slated to be demolished next week. Did you know about that?"

The shock in his eyes answered her question. He blinked several times before speaking. "What did you say?"

"They're all going to be demolished."

"By whom? On whose orders?"

"By the owner, whoever that is."

"Can they do that? Do they need permission from the town?"

"I was hoping you could answer that." Andi watched Wade. He hung his head then put his elbow on the arm of the chair and rested his forehead in his hand. Andi remained silent as he sat with his eyes closed, his fingers rubbing his temple back and forth several times. Finally, he looked at her with pain in his eyes.

"Andi, I think I'm in trouble. I'm in way over my head."

"With the revitalization plan?"

"With everything." He closed his eyes and sighed. When he opened them, he leaned toward her. "I think I walked into something bad. The only way I can describe it is, sinister. I know that sounds ridiculous, but I think I'm being set up to take the fall for some serious stuff."

Andi's heart began to pound. What was he talking about? What had he done? She thought about the new tourist center and the knowledge she now had that Wade had bought it, for more than the asking price, without a second thought. Was his family really as wealthy as she had presumed, or was he on the take?

"Wade." She reached out and laid her hand on his arm. "What's going on?"

He looked down at her hand and back up at her face. "I think my whole meteoric rise in politics was a sham. I think I'm being used." He turned the chair away from her and let out an anguished sound. "Oh, man, what have I done?"

"Wade, back up. Tell me what happened."

He swiveled the chair back to her. "I made a deal when I was hired. It was stupid, I know. In hindsight, I should have known it was wrong. I just wasn't thinking."

Her concern deepened. She reached for him again, taking his hand in hers. "Wade, please, tell me what you did."

He tore his gaze from hers and squeezed his eyes together. His hand involuntarily squeezed hers. Taking a deep breath, he spoke. "I was brash and arrogant and selfish and had no desire to look past my own needs. I was an idiot, thinking I could take this job, sit back and do nothing, close my eyes to reality, and then just walk away."

Andi waited for Wade to go on.

"I never questioned why they wanted me, a virtual outsider who only wanted to sell my family's properties and get out of Dodge. I could say I was flattered, but it was more than that. My self-inflated ego made me think they asked me because I was smarter, more educated, more worldly than anyone else. I thought they wanted someone who would oversee the death of the town and help put it out of its misery so that the citizens, my mother included, could move on. What they wanted was a patsy, someone who would tell everyone he was doing all he could to help them but would never bother to find out what was really happening."

Andi swallowed. "What was happening, Wade? What is happening?"

He hid his face in his hands. "I don't know." He faced her. "Honestly, I don't know. Ted Mitchem came to see me today."

"I remember him. Mean SOB. But what's he got to do with anything?

"He's the former president of the disbanded council, the one who recommended me as mayor and then convinced the council to step down."

"Okay. And he came to you, why?"

"He's been calling the shots all along. Checking up on me, telling me to do this or that, hire this person, fire that one. At first, I thought it was because he knew the town and I no longer did, but after a while, it became clear that he just wanted to control everything. He had ulterior plans to putting me in office. I just didn't know what. I still don't."

"Okay. So, this latest visit?"

"Was to caution me against spending the town's money on this revitalization. He said I had no right to go poking my nose into the town accounts without consent."

"Consent from whom?"

He slowly raised and lowered his shoulders. "From him. He just said that I wasn't authorized to spend any money. I'm the mayor. If not me, then who?"

"What else?"

"I asked to see the latest budget report, and he told me I wasn't authorized to see it."

"That makes no sense. As mayor, you'd be in charge of setting the budget."

"You would think so, but after he left, I called Steve Marshall." Before she could ask he answered. "He's the town accountant. He confirmed that the council secretly passed a statute before I took office that precludes me from seeing the books."

Andi sat back and moaned. "Wade, that makes no sense. Why would they do that"

"Exactly? Why? Unless they're trying to cover something up. I have no idea what's going on with the town funds and no way to find out."

"What was his plan for you once you became mayor?"

"To let the town die." He looked at her. "But then you showed up, and I realized that's not what was best, not what people wanted. What they wanted was hope and promises of a better future."

"Wade, you've got to get a look at those books." She had a sudden thought. "Wade, the buildings, the ones set to be demolished. Do you know who owns them?"

Wade looked at her blankly before understanding began to take hold of his features. "No, but I think it's past time I find out. Let me reach out to my friends in the real estate sector. They don't have any ties to Buffalo Springs. Maybe they can do some digging without bringing my name into it." No longer the picture of defeat, Wade started to rally. He stood and pulled his phone from his pocket. "I'll make a few calls to find out who holds the title. How much time do we have until they're leveled?"

"I don't know. Sometime next week." Andi stood, too, anxious to get to work.

"Why don't I work on this and look into whether or not a demolition permit was filed. I haven't seen anything come across my desk. I'll check with Trudy. She knows all the ins and outs of the bureaucracy of the town."

"What should I do?"

Wade raked his fingers through his blonde locks as he thought for a moment. "What else do we need to do?"

"I can try to look into the banking stuff. I have a former colleague who's with the Treasury Department who might be able to find answers."

Wade's hopeful expression faded. "I don't know…it doesn't feel right having a town resident looking into the financials."

"Suit yourself, but you're taking on a heavy load by yourself, and it's not like you have access to them."

Wade nodded. "You're right. Just be discreet."

Andi rolled her eyes. If he only knew. Discretion was her middle name for ten years. "I'm sure I can manage."

"Okay, let me know what you're able to find out."

"Will do. My friends and I are pretty good at finding answers. I'll be in touch."

Wade smiled for the first time since she'd seen him that morning. "Thanks, Andi, for listening and for all that you're doing for me and the town."

Andi started to leave but suddenly recalled part of her conversation with Rudy. She turned back to Wade.

"Wade, the tourist center…"

"What about it?" He shuffled some papers on his desk, not looking up at her.

"Why did you tell me the town bought it?"

Slowly, he raised his eyes to meet her gaze. "I didn't. I said that I was able to find the funding."

Andi furrowed her brow as she examined his expression. "You led me to believe that the town bought the building, but it was you. Why did you do that, and why lead me on?"

"If you believed the town bought it, that's on you. I never said that." His evasion bothered her.

"You're still not answering my questions."

Wade exhaled, dropped the papers onto his desk, and shrugged. "I didn't want you to think I had ulterior motives. I just wanted to help. And I thought about what you and Jackson said about the buildings and businesses being an investment. I thought, why not invest in the town myself?"

"And you don't see that as a conflict of interest?"

"No. Maybe. I don't know. I just wasn't ready to get the town or my office fully invested. I thought if I kept that endeavor as a personal one, I wasn't risking the town's assets."

Andi stared at him, trying to decide if he was telling the truth, but his expression gave nothing away.

"Andi, I mean it. I wasn't trying to lie or do anything unethical or illegal. I really was trying to help."

She nodded, still unconvinced. "If you say so, Wade." Still uneasy about everything she had learned in the past couple hours, she left the room and closed the door behind her. She made her way down the dark hall and narrow staircase with dozens of questions buzzing in her brains like honeybees in a clover field.

As Andi walked out into the daylight, she wondered if she could trust Wade at all. There was only way to find out. She had to get answers.

***

"Yes, I'll hold." Andi bit into an apple slice covered with peanut butter as the canned jazz music drifted from the phone. She tapped the keys of her laptop, looking for back doors and security breaches that might lead her to what she needed to know.

"Andi, is that you?" Ryan's familiar voice took Andi back several months, and she wondered, if she closed her eyes, could she imagine she was still at work, the guys still alive, and their safety still in her hands? She shook off the thought.

"It's me, Ryan. How are things in Washington?"

"Not the same without your calls. It's so good to hear your voice. Word is, you've had a rough time with what happened."

Andi swallowed. "You could say that."

Though employed by Treasury, Ryan was an expert at intelligence gathering. Trained as a forensic CPA, he provided Andi with crucial information on more than one mission, and he was trusted by people across the intelligence sector. She wouldn't be surprised if he was privy to some of the confidential details about the crash.

"Andi, it wasn't your fault, you know?"

"I'm starting to see that, but it's hard not to wonder what if I had done things differently?." She absent-mindedly spread a layer of peanut butter on another apple slice.

"From what I know, there was nothing you could have done. It happened, and it was out of your control."

"Thanks, Ryan. I'm working on believing that."

After a moment, Ryan spoke. "We all miss you, Andi. I hope you're finding some peace and happiness."

"Trying to," she said with more cheer than she felt. "Anyway, I'm calling because I need some help."

She explained the situation, leaving out Wade's involvement as best she could.

"So, what do you think? I've been trying to find a back door with no luck. As you heard, I don't have a lot of information."

"Let me see what I can do. What's the name of the bank?"

Andi told him and then listened to the sound of Ryan typing. She could hear chatter in the background, and easily envisioned the scene in the busy office at the Treasury Department. She worked closely with the group on many missions and had made friends there, but it wasn't part of the Defense Department, so there was no conflict of interest in her calling. It was good to know she could still count on Ryan to help her out.

"Andi, still there?"

"I'm here."

"I can't find an account for your town or anything that looks like it's a similar name to your town name or any corporation as such in any records at your local bank."

"Hmm. Do you think they kept the money in a bank other than the one in town?"

"Could be. Not very convenient, but maybe a way to ward off questions from the bank staff."

"Can we look at other nearby banks?"

"Do you know what they are?"

Andi ran a Google search and rattled of the names of other banks. "There aren't that many. Do you have time to look?"

"Sure. It's much easier now that most small-town banks have consolidated with bigger, nationally recognized banks. Fewer places to look."

"Great. Do you want to call back or put me on hold?"

"It won't take but a few minutes if you don't mind holding."

After nearly five minutes, Ryan was back on the line. "No luck. Let's try something different. What's the name of the accounting firm the town uses?"

Andi relayed the information Wade had given her.

"Okay, hold tight."

"Are you hacking into the firm?"

"I prefer to look at it as helpful digging."

Andi smiled. It helped to have friends in high places.

"I'm in, but you're not going to like what I have to say."

"Hit me, Ryan."

"I found the ledger for the town's accounts, or what's left of them."

"What's left? What does that mean?"

"They're all empty. Totally drained."

"How can that be? They're still able to pay bills. The town hasn't declared bankruptcy."

"Someone else must be supporting the town."

"But why?"

"Your guess is as good as mine."

"Can you see where the money went? How it was paid out? Anything to tell me what happened to it?"

"Everything is written in code—abbreviations, acronyms, maybe, that sort of thing."

"Can you give me those?"

Ryan read off the list. "Hey, Andi." Ryan lowered his voice. "You better be careful. I don't know what you're walking into, but you're walking in blind and without intel or backup. I don't have to tell you what kind of a mess that can lead to."

Andi felt a lump in her throat. The whole conversation brought back so many memories of the life she left behind, the life she loved, and the people who were a part of it.

"Thanks, Ryan. I appreciate that. I'll watch my back."

"You know better than that. You need someone else to watch your back while you scope out the area or take your shot. You can't go it alone."

She thought of Wade. "Don't worry. I'm not alone."

Ryan paused then asked, "Can you trust him?"

She thought of the tourist center, of Wade's secrecy, of the things in his private life he wouldn't talk about, about the walls he built up around himself, and of his involvement with Ted. How much did he know? What else was hiding?

"I hope so, Ryan. I hope so."

***

New York City Wade, attorney Wade, financial expert Wade was a different man than the one who hunched over the desk in the little office above the movie theater. The old Wade was a mover and shaker, a man to look up to, a man who was ethical in practice but ferocious in getting his clients what they wanted. He was particular about the cases he accepted, requiring meticulous research about the businesses, the shareholders, and the employees. He was an icon in the firm he represented and a much sought after attorney in the world of mergers and acquisitions.

Mayor Wade Montgomery was none of those things, and he couldn't help but wonder when his brain had gone to sleep and how he had gotten into this mess. Everything he'd done since losing Pam was incompatible with the man he was. He had lost himself and his way, and he knew he had to find the path back to the man who always did the right thing even when given another option. As he listened to the voice on the other end of the phone, another piece of the old Wade was resurrected.

"Marcie, can you do some poking around? Find out who's behind the purchases?"

Marcie Hobbs was a paralegal for the New York firm where Wade had spent the better part of his adulthood. She was Wade's go-to person when he needed more information about a merger or acquisition.

Marcie hesitated before answering. "I can, but, Wade, this is easy to find. Titles are public record."

"I know, but I don't want to call the county land records and have it get back to the owners. I'm in kind of a tight spot here. Like I said, I'm trying to keep things quiet. I don't want anyone to know that I'm poking around."

"Wade, you know how much I admire you, so it pains me to ask, but are you in trouble? Are you involved in something that could get me in trouble?"

"Marcie, you know me better than that."

Did she? Did he? Wade barely recognized himself anymore.

There was a pregnant pause on the line, and Wade was sure Marcie was going to tell him no.

"I trust you, Wade. I'll do it. Hold on."

As soon as the soft orchestra music began playing, Wade let out a long, relieved sigh. He waited for Marcie to look up the titles and thought some more about his predicament and how he was going to rectify it.

He turned his chair around and stared out the window as the steady rain fell on the roof of the county municipal building. As far as he knew, nobody else had gone inside, and he'd had no calls or texts from Trudy saying someone was looking for him.

He heard a click on the phone.

"Okay, the buildings were bought by an LLC named, Buffalo Springs Enterprises. Ring a bell?"

"Vaguely. Not sure why except that it's obviously named after the town. Any other holdings?"

"None that I can see. Looks like the LLC is pretty new, established only two years ago."

"Any names?"

"Controlling members are Todd Markham, Samuel Fields, and Douglas MacArthur, all with equal shares."

"I've never heard of any of them, except MacArthur of course. Is that really the name?" he asked as he scribbled down the names

"That's what it says here."

"Strange. Are you sure one is Todd Markham and not Ted Mitchem?"

"Positive."

"Is there an address for the LLC?"

"A P.O. Box. Harrison, Arkansas. Is that nearby?"

"It is. And it's about four times the size of Buffalo Springs."

"Easy to stay anonymous."

"That's what I'm thinking."

174   Amy Schisler

"Anything else?"

"Not right now. Thanks, Marcie. I really appreciate it."

"No problem, Wade. Hey, when are you coming back? It's pretty quiet around here without you."

Wade watched the rivers of raindrops run down the windowpane. "I don't know, Marcie. Things have gotten more complicated here than I bargained for."

"They always do when you go back home, my friend. They always do."

Eleven

Wade stoked the fire in the fireplace before going to the den to return some calls while supper heated in the oven. Andi sat on the footstool by Blanche's chair, painting the woman's fingernails. It was one of the simple pleasures Blanche could still enjoy and appreciate, and Andi liked doing something nice for Wade's sweet mother.

"Did I ever tell you how Jake and I met?" Blanche asked.

"Nope. Why don't you tell me now."

"His sister, Virginia, and I were the best of friends, inseparable from the time we were six years old. We did everything together, including sneaking bottles of wine into the back of the movie theater."

"Blanche, I'm shocked." Andi feigned her shock with an appropriate horrified expression.

"I was young once, you know."

"Of course. So Jack was Virginia's older brother?"

Blanche laughed. "Younger."

"Oh, really?" Andi asked with genuine surprise.

"Yes. He was always pestering us, trying to get us to include him in our games, take him to the movies, buy him ice cream. He was such a nuisance."

"Until he wasn't," Andi said with a smile.

"Until he wasn't," Blanche said wistfully. "Virginia went away to college. I was so envious but proud of her. She wanted to be a teacher."

"Why didn't you go, too?"

"My parents worried about me. You see, one of my legs is longer than the other. Did you know that?"

"I did not," Andi said, glancing at Blanche's legs.

The older woman stretched them both out in front of her. "See? One is a few inches shorter."

"Well, I'll be darned. It sure is."

"I had a hard time as a child. I couldn't run or keep up with the other kids. I had several operations. When I graduated, my parents thought it best that I stay here and take over running the theater. I love the theater, so I didn't really mind. Except it was lonely with Virginia and all of our other friends gone. Her mother invited me over for supper quiet often, and I enjoyed going there. It made me feel like Virginia was still around."

Andi finished the first coat of polish and started on the second coat while Blanche talked.

"Anyway, one night, Jake showed up for supper. We sat there talking, long after the dishes were done, and I realized he wasn't the same little boy who used to follow us around the house. The next time I went for supper, he was there again. Soon, it was Jake asking me to supper and not his mother. Then he started showing up at the theater to escort me home at night. One night, he arrived with a bouquet of red and white roses. I looked at them and just knew he was the one."

"That's so romantic," Andi said, and she meant it. Though she'd never been the sentimental type, she could appreciate a real love story when she heard one.

"Supper is ready," Wade said from the doorway.

"We're ready," Andi said. "Now, don't mess up your nails, Blanche."

"I won't. I want to show them to Jake when he gets home."

Andi and Wade shared a sad look as Blanche shuffled into the kitchen with her cane.

***

After supper, Wade and Andi huddled over their laptops and the notes they'd taken. Papers were strewn across the old farm table in the kitchen. Wade was quiet through most of their meal, and his mood hung over them like a canopy of Spanish moss.

"I can leave if you want, Wade. I'm sure your mind is elsewhere tonight."

Wade looked at her with pleading in his eyes. "No, please, I need this tonight. I need to think about something other than…" He glanced toward the staircase.

"If you're sure."

"I'm sure." He looked at her with admiration. "You're good with Mama. Thank you for that."

"She's a wonderful woman. I enjoy spending time with her."

"She likes you, and the company is good for her." He looked down at the papers before them. "Now, let's get to work. I ordered an injunction to stop the demolition, but once word gets out, things might get messy. We might have a hard time proceeding with our plans."

Our plans.

Andi wondered when that had happened, when the 'Y' had been dropped and the plans went from 'yours' to 'ours.'

Wade read over Andi's notes, and she read over his while Boomer slumbered at their feet beneath the table. "Any idea who these people are?"

Wade shook his head. "No clue. I've never heard of them."

"Todd could definitely be Ted. The names are so similar. What about the other names? Any similarity to other people in town, maybe ones connected to the town council?"

Wade stood and went behind Andi to look over her shoulder. The scent of his soap was now familiar to her, or perhaps it was his deodorant or after shave. Did men still wear after shave? She blinked a few times to bring herself back to the matter at hand, but his closeness was distracting. She tried to refocus, suddenly self-conscious in her sweatpants and faded t-shirt while he stood behind her in his pressed shirt, loosened at the collar, and crisp grey pants.

"What did you say the name of the accountant is?" she asked.

"Steve Marshall."

She looked back at the names. "Samuel Fields. I don't remember anybody by that name living around here."

"Neither do I. What about this third guy? MacArthur?"

"Parents were history buffs perhaps?"

Wade clicked his tongue and stood back, but his intoxicating scent lingered. "Could be. Not from around here though. I'd have remembered the name. Although, the real Douglas MacArthur grew up not too far from here."

"True," Andi said. "You know, you said this Todd guy could be Ted. What about the others? Any other resemblance to names you know?"

He sighed and dropped back into his chair. "Not that I can think of."

"Okay, let's shift gears. Did you look up the company online?"

"I did. Seems legit." He brought up the website. "Just a real estate investment firm. Odd though. It says it's located in Manilla."

"Huh. That is odd. There's a US phone number on the site. Did you call?"

"Yeah. Got a receptionist by the name of Jade. I asked if I could speak with one of the investors, but she says they're all attending a real estate convention, and could I leave my name and number for someone to call back. I said, no thanks."

"How convenient." Andi frowned and shuffled through the papers until she found the one with the list of letters. "Let's move on. How can we find out where all the money went that was in the town bank accounts?"

"We have all these letters—abbreviations or acronyms or something else maybe? What do you think?" She handed the paper to Wade.

Wade scanned the sheet and handed it back to Andi.

"Look how many payouts have the letters BFE next to them. Coincidence?"

Andi looked at the list. "The LLC that owns the buildings."

"The money used to buy them came from the town. Those sons of—"

"We can't speculate. Not yet." Andi pointed to the paper. "There are too many other transactions here, and several have the initials, PS."

"Assuming they're initials," Wade reminded her.

"True. PS could stand for just about anything."

Andi rested her head in her hands, elbows on the table.

"Tired?" Wade asked.

She moved her head from side to side and looked over at him. "Frustrated. Sifting through intel, finding answers, solving riddles, it's what I do. I should be able to look at this stuff and figure it out, but there are too many missing pieces."

"We just have to keep digging." Wade pushed his chair back and stood. "But not tonight. It's been a long day, and you've had a lot of stuff thrown at you. Let's get some sleep and talk again tomorrow."

Andi gave the table a once over before nodding and heaving herself up from the chair. "You're right. My brain is fried. Hopefully things will be clearer in the morning."

"I've got to go to the office first thing. I got nothing done today."

"What exactly do you do? You have no control over the budget. You don't oversee the bills. There aren't council meetings to attend. What does your job entail?"

Wade laughed wryly. "Not a heck of a lot. I've realized that I'm just a figurehead, a man paid to keep quiet and follow orders. At least Trudy keeps me busy."

"Doing what?" She leaned back against the counter.

"Making appointments, like for fire chief or the chief of police. Signing contracts for things like the town gardens, sidewalk repairs, tree trimming. Answering letters and returning calls from people with complaints, like when Ed Arthur's tree grew over the fence and blocked Tessa Muller's driveway." Wade stopped talking when Andi straightened, and her jaw dropped. "What?"

"That's what you do as mayor? Settle disputes over trees hanging across someone's property line."

He shrugged. "That's about as exciting as it gets. Tessa threatened to blow the whole thing away with her shotgun if Ed didn't cut off the offending branch. It caused quite an ordeal."

"You can't be serious." She put her hands on her hips and cocked her head to the side.

"I'm told there was a lot more to do in the past. The mayor used to preside over council meetings, sign or veto town laws and ordinances passed by the council, represent the town in parades and festivals and other town events. Trudy says the office was quite the 'hive of activity' at one time." He emphasized Trudy's words.

"I'm shocked that you haven't died of boredom."

"I'll admit, it's a far cry from the world of high finance in the city that never sleeps."

"I'll say. So, why do you keep the job? Why did you take it in the first place? Why not resign and let the town elect someone else?"

"The truth?"

Andi held his gaze and searched his eyes. She couldn't help but wonder how much truth he was willing to share. This was the most he ever said about himself, and it was all job-related.

"Yes, the truth."

"It was a time filler, something to do while I figured out what to do with Mom. It was supposed to be an easy job with decent pay, and I could take all the time I want to find the right buyer for the theater and a place for Mom to go when the time comes."

Andi thought of something. "Decent pay?"

Wade chuckled. "Well, nothing remotely near what I earned in the Big Apple, but enough to pay Mom's bills without having to dig into my own savings or hers."

"And how are you paid?"

"What do you mean?"

"What account do your checks come out of? If the town accounts are empty."

Wade sat back down in front of his laptop and navigated to his bank account. He let his head drop backwards, hitting the top of chair, and groaned. "I'm an idiot."

"What?" Andi walked around him and looked at the screen. She willed herself to look past the balance in the account. Triple digit income, indeed. Wade was loaded. She focused on the deposits. "Oh my gosh," she breathed.

"I'm being paid by Buffalo Spring Enterprises, not the town."

Disbelief engulfed Andi. "Wade! You said you'd never heard of Buffalo Springs Enterprises. How could you not recognize the name on your own paychecks?"

"I never see the checks," he said defensively. "I look every other week to make sure the direct deposit has gone through. I mean, the name was familiar when Marcie said it, but I didn't put two and two together."

"You didn't know where your money was coming from? That the town wasn't paying your salary?"

He pointed to the screen. "It says, 'Buffalo Springs Enterprises.' Why would I question it?"

"Because an enterprise and an incorporated town aren't the same thing! You of all people know that. How could you be so careless?"

Unless you knew all along…

"Wade, can you look me in the eye and tell me that you're not involved in all of this?" She leaned back, shifted her weight to one foot, and crossed her arms in front of her chest.

Wade closed his eyes and looked away. When he turned back to Andi, his eyes were full of pain and remorse. "You're right. I should have known. Maybe deep down I did. So, how could I let this happen? I'm not a stupid man. I've got multiple degrees, my job in New York required precise attention to detail, I juggled numerous multi-billion-dollar accounts. I worked with contracts every day. Heck, I wrote contracts! I understand fine print and numbers and how finance works. How could I be so careless? So stupid? How could I let these men take advantage of me like this?"

Andi took it all in, let her brain process his words, and compared his actions to scenarios from her experience in the Navy. Did she trust him? Maybe, maybe not, but this wasn't the first time she'd seen this happen.

Andi sat back down and leaned toward him. "Wade, you're not going to like what I have to say but hear me out. I've known a lot of men like you, men who often let their education, knowledge, and intelligence get in the way of making good decisions. In almost all cases, there are two common denominators: ego and lack of common sense. I've seen brilliant men make the most egregious mistakes because they didn't think them through and consider the consequences. It was part of my job to weigh those consequences so that nobody acted out of fear or misplaced honor, or worse, arrogance. Both ego and lack of common sense have been the downfall of many. You, Wade, are a victim of your own intelligence and arrogance, acting as if you knew what was best for everyone, assuming you could let these men call the shots without it coming back to bite you, and closing your eyes to what you had to know was going on and what was right. You leaped in without checking the depth of the waters because you were confident that whatever their endgame was couldn't drown you. You're right that it was stupid, but you weren't and aren't naïve. You knew you were playing a risky game, but you thought you could ride the wave and not get wet."

She expected him to protest, but he hung his head in shame.

When he finally raised his head to meet her eyes, she knew he saw the truth in what she said. "I deserve to be locked up with the rest of them. I've failed this town, and I've failed myself."

"Let's not get ahead of ourselves. You can redeem yourself and put the ship back on the right course, but you're going to have to want to do it, and you're going to have to do it right and make amends."

"Then help me figure out how."

Andi stood and paced for a moment. She took a deep breath and turned back to face him.

"First, I need to know that you aren't lying to me. About any of it. I need to know that you see the big picture now. No more selfish or rash decisions. No more letting chips fall where they may. I need to know that you are honestly going to do the right thing."

He stood and looked into her eyes, their heights matching almost perfectly. "If I wasn't being honest with you, why would I bring you into this? Why would I have you looking into this at all?"

"I don't know. Maybe you're trying to throw shade, to make me think you're innocent, to try to pull one over on your partners. You tell me." She took a step back and crossed her arms over her chest.

"Andi, I'm not involved. I swear to you. I was wrong to not stop them, but I am not a part of whatever their game is."

"But you were brought in to aid in the demise of the town. You went along with the dissolution of the council. You never questioned the budget, or lack thereof." She narrowed her eyes. "Whether you say you are or not, you're looking pretty guilty to me."

The color drained from his face. "Holy mother of… Andi, I do look guilty. Guilty as sin. That's exactly what they wanted. They didn't bring me in just to be a patsy. They brought me in to be the fall guy."

Andi stood still for a moment, gauging his tone, his expression, the tension in his jaw. He certainly looked surprised and, she admitted, scared.

"Look, if you're right, and Ted and the accountant, what's his name, if they know you're starting to look into things, questioning the budget, and trying to restore the town, you may be in danger."

"Then I'm putting you in danger, too."

"I'm a big girl. I can handle it." The phone call nagged at her, but she pushed it away. She wondered again about trusting him. For all she knew, he could have made the call.

Wade grasped her arms with his hands. "I can't let you do this. I can't let you be a part of this." He seemed sincere, or was he trying to get rid of her? That wasn't going to happen. What was the old saying? Keep your friends close and your enemies closer?

"It's too late, Wade. I'm already a part of it."

"But you don't have to be. We can cut our losses. You didn't buy the bakery. Your family doesn't know about any of this. Ted doesn't know what you know. You can still get out. Get your parents to sell the house and leave. Go far away."

"Now you're trying to get rid of me, and I'm not supposed to be suspicious?"

He shook her, not enough to hurt, but enough to really get her to pay attention. Boomer crawled out from under the table and shifted his gaze between the two of them.

"Andi, I'm not involved. I promise you. But I am worried. About me, my mom, and you. I will not let you be in danger. Look what happened at your folks' house. That could have been a warning. Ted's already tried to warn me off more than once. Something is going on here that's bigger than what we see." The worry in his eyes was real.

"Where I come from, we have a saying, 'All in, all the time.' I can't just walk away, Wade. I can't know what I know and leave it alone. I have to get to the bottom of this as much as you do. If that means I'm in danger, I can handle it. And if it means you're involved, I'm going to figure it out."

Wade grit his teeth. "Andi, for the last time, I'm not involved. You have to believe me. Despite all of this mess and how it looks, I'm a good guy. I go to church. I say my prayers. I screwed up, and I know it. I've been to confession. I've asked for forgiveness from God. Now, I'm asking for forgiveness from you."

Andi stared at him, surprised by his frankness. "I don't know what to say."

"You don't have to say anything. Just know that I'm not the enemy. And that I'm giving you an out. You don't have to help me. We don't know what's going on here. We don't know how far these guys will go or what their endgame is."

"No, we don't, but we do know they're up to something, and any SEAL worth his salt will tell you, 'the only easy day was yesterday.' It seems like every day, something has changed, including today. Tomorrow, things could be worse. You can't do this without backup."

"Andi, I'm not going to war."

"Are you sure about that, Wade? Because from where I'm standing, we're both already under fire."

Wade looked down to where his hands held her arms and then moved his gaze back to her eyes. "Are you sure about this?"

In his gaze, Andi saw what she needed to see. Wade was stepping out of his comfort zone. He wasn't used to asking for help, but he needed her. He was frightened and lost. For perhaps the first time since they'd met, he was being totally open and honest with her.

"I'm sure."

Twelve

"I'm finding all of this hard to believe," Jackson told Andi the following morning. "Wade knew nothing about any of this?"

"That's what he says." She downed her coffee and looked at her brother. Her head pounded from mental strain and lack of sleep. Nightmares about the crash bombarded her nights like the blitz over London, coming more frequently than ever.

"Look, I know it sounds sketchy, but I saw the look in his eyes and the shock on his face when he figured out what was going on. I'm sure he's telling the truth. And I'm pretty good at figuring out when someone is lying." *And when he's still holding back.*

"Well, your instincts are better than mine, so we'll go with your gut, but I hope he's not a better liar than you are an intelligence officer."

"Jackson, forget Wade. I need you to look at this puzzle with fresh eyes and help me figure out what we're missing."

Jackson sifted through her notes but shook his head. "You're definitely missing something. Why let the town die? Why demolish the buildings? Unless..."

"Unless what?"

"Unless they're trying to hide something. Has anyone been inside any of the buildings?"

"That's a good question. How would you like to go with me on an intelligence-gathering mission?"

"Me? No way." He held up his hands in front of her. "I'm not breaking into a building and getting hauled off to jail."

"Nobody is going to haul you off to jail. Let's think about this. How can we get inside without being seen?"

"Andi, who are you?" Jackson looked at his sister with wide eyes. "Is that what you learned in the Navy? How to break into buildings and avoid the law?"

Andi gave her brother a shove. "Knock if off. What I learned was how to collect information. The way I see it, nobody is going to be forthcoming with the info we need, so we'll have to find a back door."

"I don't like the use of the word, 'we'."

"Aw, come on, Jackson, you used to love sneaking up on Helena and me and spying on us. Now, you get to do it in real life."

"I don't know about this, Andi. Couldn't we at least wait until it's dark?"

"No. We'd have to use flashlights to look around. That means even more of a chance we'd get caught. We just have to be careful getting in and out."

"And what happens if we do get caught?"

"We say the door happened to be unlocked and we're just checking it out as part of our revitalization plan."

"You've got an answer for everything, don't you."

Andi looked away. "If only that were true, little brother. If only that were true."

***

Jackson and Andi stood behind the abandoned building on a side street behind Rick's Place.

"When you said back door, I didn't know you meant literally." Jackson's voice shook with nerves.

"Quiet down and keep a look out."

The back door was the kind that slid up and down like on a garage or storage unit. Andi had swung by earlier in the day, careful she wasn't being observed, and was relieved to see that gaining access would be easier than she imagined. When she examined the lock, she saw right away that it wasn't a very good one, and she formulated her plan on her short ride to her parents' house.

Andi clamped her father's bolt cutter onto the looped arm of the lock and squeezed as hard as she could. It took three tries, and her hand ached through the latex glove, but the lock fell to the ground. Andi looked around before gently sliding open the door just enough for her and Jackson to crawl through. She quickly reached for the lock and lowered the door, hoping nobody would be dropping by any time soon.

There were no windows in the room, so Jackson pulled out his phone and switched on the flashlight.

"This must be some kind of storage area for the business," Andi said. "Can you see anything?"

"There's a light switch. Should we try it? We should be okay without any windows in here."

"Not yet. Let's make sure there aren't any cameras around."

"How are we going to do that?"

"Look around, high and low, especially in the corners and along the ceiling. Watch for red lights, blinking lights, any type of light actually, or anything that reflects off of your light. Shine the light along the floor to look for tripwires, physical or laser."

"Geez, Andi. Is this the kind of stuff you did?"

"Kind of," she said dismissively.

Andi recalled the many missions she had listened to over communication devices. She tried to imagine what Jeremy would do in this situation. His brain worked like no other. He had a supernatural instinct when it came to danger, like the instinct he had that last day…

She shook away the thought.

"I don't see anything," Jackson whispered.

"Okay, let's try the door."

Andi went to the door and turned the knob. It was unlocked. As she opened it, the light from a nearby window momentarily blinded her, and she had to blink several times to adjust her sight.

"Okay, I'm going in," she whispered.

"What about me?"

"Stay here and listen out. Keep an eye out for any signs of someone coming in the back door or the front door. Listen for any sounds and stay out of sight. If you see or hear anything, let me know. Call me."

Jackson hit the button on his phone, and Andi made sure her new AirPod was secure in her ear. It wasn't the sophisticated comm she was used to, but it was better than her old earbuds with wires hanging around her neck. She'd driven all the way to the nearest Walmart to buy the set so she could easily wear one as she prowled through the house. Luckily, Walmarts were not in short supply in Arkansas.

Andi connected to the call from Jackson, nodded to him, and slipped the phone into the pocket of her dark sweatshirt.

Before going in, Andi swept her eyes around the room. There didn't seem to be any surveillance devices or any alarms. Part of her was shocked, but part of her believed that these people simply thought they were smarter than everyone else. Many people are taken down by nothing more their own conceit. She thought of Wade and what his arrogance had gotten him into. It was a mistake Jeremy never would have made.

She brought her thoughts back to the task at hand. "Building seems empty," she said in a low voice.

The dusty floor revealed footprints leading to a staircase.

"Heading upstairs to check it out. Copy?"

"Copy." Jackson's voice was nearly a whisper, and Andi knew he was discovering that real missions were nothing like hiding under his sister's bed, listening to her secrets.

A large picture window loomed ahead, and Andi moved across the floor like an animal on the hunt; she crouched low and furtively crossed the room toward the stairs. In a flash, Andi took long strides across the eleven or twelve foot room to the side of the window and stood, back flat against the wall. She waited for a moment until she was sure she hadn't been seen by anyone passing by, then she dove for the stairs and shot up them as quickly and quietly as her legs could carry her.

"Three rooms upstairs. Two closed doors. Third door is a bathroom."

"Copy," Jackson replied. "Hurry up."

She ignored his plea and looked around. The building must have been a residence at one time before being turned into the candy store she remembered from her youth. Andi backed herself against the wall by one door and put her ear to the wood. She quietly turned the knob and eased the door open. It was vacant.

Andi moved to the other door like a panther sneaking up on her prey and listened before turning the knob. She peered into the room and gasped. Her heart began to pound, and her base instinct told her to run.

"Holy sh…" Her voice trailed off.

"What? What's wrong?" Jackson's voice rose an octave.

What she saw was certainly not your typical candy, and it rivaled anything she had seen on her missions. Folding tables were covered with weapons, cash, and clear packages. Andi eased into the room and pulled out her phone. She could hear her brother questioning her as she quickly snapped shots of the guns, homemade grenades, piles of money, and plastic packages of crystals, which she assumed was meth. Andi had never been a part of a drug cartel raid or worked border patrol, but she knew that what she saw on that table was no science experiment.

***

Wade scrolled through the photos on Andi's phone, his hands beginning to shake with both fear and rage. He didn't know if he was angrier with Andi or with what she had discovered. When she texted that she needed to see him immediately in his mother's office at the movie house, he had no idea what she had done.

"What the heck do you think you were doing? You could have gotten yourself caught. Or killed!"

"Relax, Wade, I'm fine. I knew what I was doing."

"Knew what you were doing? What do you think this is? Some kind of war game? A military exercise? Whoever this belongs to, they're the real thing, Andi. These kinds of people, they kill over stuff like this."

"How bad is the problem here?" Andi asked without remorse or fear, and Wade didn't know if he was impressed or appalled by her nonchalance.

"What problem?" He put the phone on the desk and looked at her.

"Meth? How bad?"

Wade shook his head and sat on the edge of his mother's desk. "As bad as it is in every small town in America today."

"Did you know there was a local dealer?"

"There's always a local dealer."

"What I mean is, did you know there was an operation taking place right here in town? Do the police know? Are you trying to do anything about it?"

Wade sighed. "The usual. We have DARE in the elementary school, and the police go into the middle-high school and warn the kids about the dangers of drugs. They patrol the streets and alleys at night."

"I've run these streets at all kinds of odd hours, and I've never seen a single police officer anywhere."

"And? What's that supposed to mean?" He felt defensive. Was she blaming him? How was he supposed to know this was happening? What control did he have over where and when the police made their rounds? "We have a total of four officers on the payroll. We're a small town. What did you expect? To see an officer on every corner?"

"Wade, I'm not casting blame. I'm looking for answers."

That was easy for her to say. The truth was, he was to blame. He should have known this was happening. He should have made more of a point to talk to the police, to learn more about the town's drug problem, to help the police with whatever needs they had to get it under control.

Wade stood and paced for a moment before walking around the desk and collapsing into the chair. "I've sure made a mess of things, haven't I? No mayor of the year award for me, I suppose." By the look on her face, Andi didn't appreciate the joke, and Wade couldn't blame her. He ran his fingers through his hair. "I know. I've screwed up everything. From the day I took office, I let others take control without even realizing it. And even if I had realized it, I probably wouldn't have cared." He looked up at her. "What do I do now?"

"Well, the first thing you need to do is contact the police and have them go into that building and all the other buildings."

"On what grounds? What you did was illegal. I can't tell them what you found."

He watched as her expression changed. She took a deep breath through her nose, her lips white as they pressed together.

"I guess you're right, and there's always the chance..." She looked away and sighed.

"What? Just say what you're thinking?"

"How well do you know the police? Any chance they already know about it?"

Wade sat up, opening his eyes wide. "Do you think they're allowing it? Turning a blind eye? Maybe even part of the operation?"

"I don't know, Wade, but there seems to be an awful lot going on in this town right under your nose that you are clueless about. I can't help but wonder how many people are involved in keeping you in the dark."

Wade stood and turned to look out the window, his mind racing. He needed to gain control of this situation. He was smarter than this, more observant. Maybe his focus on his mother and the time spent trying to sell the theater was to account for some of his blindness, but his lack of real interest in the town and his willingness to look the other way were the overriding causes of his fall into the pit. He was tired of taking orders and being blindsided, tired of being in the dark. This was his hometown, and he wasn't going to let it die without a fight.

He spoke without turning around. "Any signs of a lab?"

"Not there. Could be one in another building in town, or the stuff could have been brought in from somewhere else."

As he looked out the window, he imagined an explosion that could wipe out the whole street. No wonder they didn't want anyone opening any businesses on Main Street. The liability was too great.

"They're trying to run everyone out of town." He turned toward Andi. "If they can get everyone out, and Buffalo Springs becomes a ghost town, they can run the whole operation from here without anyone stumbling upon anything."

"But why arrange for the buildings to be demolished? Wouldn't that eliminate their lairs?"

"Good question. Unless they have plans to move the whole operation somewhere else and need to cover their tracks. I'm really flying blind here. This is way out of my purview as an attorney or a businessman. What do you know about drug rings and narcotics?"

"Not much. I was never involved with any of those units. I worked strictly in Eastern Asia and the Middle East. Abuse was a big problem among military personnel back in the eighties, long before I joined. It got better in the nineties but has seen an increase this century. A whole group of SEALs were discharged in 2018 for using meth and cocaine. The nature of the job leads to abuse, but those guys caused a lot of problems and cast a shadow over the rest of us."

"Us? The Navy?"

She didn't blink when she answered matter-of-factly, "The SEALs."

"SEALs? As in *the* SEALs?"

Andi gave one curt nod. "Yes, *the* SEALs. That's all I can say. My job was classified, and I've told as much as I'm able to about it. As far as the meth, the only other thing I know about it is that it's made with certain cold medicines, not sure what other ingredients, and it's hard to eliminate traces of the drug. It hangs in the air and clings to clothes and in the body longer than other drugs."

"So even if the buildings were demolished, traces of it could still exist."

"Probably." She paused for a moment. "Yeah, I think so. Why?"

"If they're going to demolish the buildings in less than seven days, they're going to need to move that stuff out soon."

Andi sat down in the chair across from the desk. "So, what are you thinking?"

"I don't want to alert the local police. You're right. I can't be sure who to trust. I'm thinking I call the state barracks and let them know that I suspect something is going on, see if they want to come to town and keep watch. If nothing else, it might buy us some time. They can't move anything if they're being watched, and they can't demolish with their stash inside. We just have to keep it quiet until the police are in place."

Andi held her bottom lip in her teeth.

"What?"

"It might already be too late to keep it quiet."

"Andi, what did you do?"

"I had to break the lock on the back door. It's not going to take long for them to know that someone was inside."

Wade groaned. "You are going to be the death of me, you know that?"

Andi visibly paled. "Don't say that." The words were almost a whisper, and Wade suddenly recalled what he had said to her at the national park and the night he drove her home. He walked over and knelt by her chair.

"Andi, what is it? Talk to me."

Andi shook her head. "I can't. I…"

Wade took her hands in his. "Andi, that's the third time I've seen you turn as white as a sheet and shut down. Each time had to do with you killing someone. Why won't you level with me? Is it about something you did overseas? Something you were involved in? I know there's a reason you suddenly left your military career and came back here. Why won't you let me in?"

***

Andi searched his emerald green eyes and felt the warmth of his hands. She wanted to trust him. She almost trusted him. At least, she was getting closer. But this, this was not something she was prepared to share with him, not now, maybe not ever.

"Wade, I can't talk about it. Not with you."

"Why? Don't you know that I care about you? I mean, I care what happens to you. You're putting yourself, maybe your life, on the line to help me, and I've been honest with you about everything. Why won't you let me help you?"

"It's not the same." She pulled her hands away and saw a flash of sadness in his eyes. "And I'm not putting myself on the line for you. I'm doing it for my parents, for my neighbors, for my town."

Wade stood and fisted his hands. "For what purpose. Andi? You've been away since you were eighteen. Why come back now and act like you have some kind of stake in this?"

Why was he angry? It wasn't like he confided in her about his own personal life. Everything that she knew about him had to do with his job.

"Maybe I'll level with you when you level with me."

"About what? I've told you everything."

Andi stood and shook her head. "You've told me about the job, about the town, about the council and the accountant. You've never told me anything about yourself. I see little bits and pieces of your life when we're with your mother, but you don't tell me anything."

He rounded on her and stood toe to toe, face to face. "What is it you want to know, Andi? Why do you care about me? My life? Isn't this whole thing just a way for you to forget about whatever it is you're too afraid to talk about and hide out in this Godforsaken town instead of facing real life, of facing whatever it is you did that you don't want to talk about?"

"You have no idea what you're talking about Wade! I have a job to do, a mission to complete. Maybe it's okay for you to sit back and wait for people to die, but I'm not willing to do that again. I can't have more blood on my hands!"

Before Wade could say or do anything, Andi grabbed her phone from the desk and fled from the office. She raced down the stairs and fumbled with the lock, stumbling out onto the sidewalk. She ran toward her car, her hands shaking violently and her stomach convulsing, with only one desire—to flea this town and the man who was causing her to feel things she never wanted to feel again—anger, guilt, fear, and a longing to fall into his arms and let him love all the hurt away.

***

Wade regretted losing his temper, but he was tired of waiting for her to open up, and his nerves were frayed. He sat down and booted up his mother's old computer. He waited impatiently for it to be ready and thought about what to look up. Once he had the search engine open, he typed, *navy seals news.*

He had no way of knowing if Andi had come home right away, or if she had gone somewhere else after she left the Navy. He couldn't remember anything specific in the news lately, but it seemed that there was always something happening with the military. How far back would he have to go? He opened an article about some SEALs testifying against one of their own, but none of it seemed like it would pertain to Andi. There was something about the SEALs going into Afghanistan to recover the body of a fallen soldier. Other than that, there wasn't anything recent. He continued to scroll.

Wade's hand hovered over the mouse as he read the headline from three months prior, *Entire SEAL Team 3 platoon perishes in fiery crash near border of Iran.*

Wade clicked on the link and read the article. He looked at the faces of the men who lost their lives in what was labeled a military exercise.

One of the men was named Jeremy Blake, and something clicked in the back of Wade's mind. Andi had told him that her best friends had all died. One was named Jeremy. He was certain of it. Andi had been on the radio with him when the chopper went down.

Wade leaned back in the chair. The article gave him no more information than Andi had given him. Did she blame herself for the crash? Why? What reason would she have to take that on her shoulders? She wasn't with them.

He thought about the things he knew about her. She mentioned that her job was to sift through intel and solve riddles. Wade hadn't given it much thought at the time. They were too busy looking into the town account and his paychecks, but now…

It was obvious that Andi blamed herself for the death of the platoon. She gathered intelligence and worked with the SEALs. She was on the radio with them at the time of the crash. She must have been one of their command center personnel or whatever you called it.

Suddenly, light dawned in his brain. "Oh, no, Andi. You can't think that. You can't think that you missed something that caused their deaths."

He thought about her insistence that she find answers, the breaking and entering, her vow to save the town and everyone in it. This was Andi's attempt to make up for the deaths of the men she worked with, the men whose deaths she blamed on herself.

What would happen if this revitalization plan failed? Or worse, if they were found out and somebody else ended up getting hurt or killed? Was the rock really a warning for her and Jackson? Was the phone call she received a real threat and not just a mild warning? If somebody ended up hurt, he feared it would be more than she'd be able to stand.

Wade shut down the computer and grabbed his jacket. He hit the light switch as he raced from the room and down the steps. After securing the door, he stood on the sidewalk and looked up and down the street. Where would she go? How could he find her? He ran across the street and up another flight of stairs.

"Trudy," he shouted as he burst into the office. His cousin looked at him with surprise. "I need to find Andi. It's an emergency. I'm starting next door at the library, but if she's not with her sister, I'm going to go to their house to see if she's there. Can you call her brother, her parents, anyone who might know where she is, and let me know?"

"Wade, is everything okay?" Trudy looked worried, but Wade didn't have time to explain. He had no idea what kind of mental state Andi was in, but he knew he had to find her and convince her that everything was going to be all right.

"Just find her, please. It's important."

"Okay, I'll see what I can do." She reached for the phone as Wade turned and ran out the door to and back down the stairs.

As he raced toward his car, the thought struck him that there was more to his feelings for Andi than worrying about her mental state. For the first time since losing Pam, Wade's heart was opening up to someone else. He didn't just trust Andi or want to help her. He thought he might just be falling in love with her.

***

Andi hit the decline button on her phone for at least the tenth time. Why wouldn't he leave her alone? And why was Helena now calling, too?

She walked down the trail toward the river, determined to find some peace and quiet. She hadn't slept in days. Every night she was plagued with images of the falling chopper and the screams of dying men. Her mind wouldn't let her escape the feeling that she could still save them even though they were already gone.

What would her therapist say? That Andi was projecting? That she couldn't save Jeremy and the rest of the guys, but maybe she could save the town and the people in it? That Andi was suffering from a God complex? She shook her head as she rounded a bend. She told Ryan that she was moving past the belief that the crash was her fault. She now accepted that she had survivor's guilt, but sometimes, those feelings roared back like a wild beast that was too overwhelming to fight.

Up ahead, Andi could see a large boulder overlooking the rushing river. She climbed to the top and sat, her chin on her bent knees. She still wore the navy-blue sweatshirt and jogging pants she put on that morning. The rock was cold, and the jogging pants added little insulation. She shivered, but she wasn't sure if it was from the chill in the air or the coldness in her heart.

Why did she have these feelings for Wade? She believed he cared for her, in some kind of way, but she wasn't interested, was she? And if she was, why was she pushing him away? Why did she push everyone away? Was the reason she and Jeremy never got together really because of the platoon or because she never let on about how she felt? Why fall in love when it was doomed to fail?

Nobody ever really understood her. Not her family, not her friends from childhood, not the wives of her team members who always commented on her chosen profession. She was always the outsider, never really part of the group. She was the nerd back in school, the odd student who actually enjoyed writing papers and doing research. At the Academy, she was one of a handful of women in a sea of men. With the SEALs, she was part of the platoon but not part of the actual Team, the ones who went inside and got the job done. Andi was always left behind to do the research, follow up the lead, give the commands, but not holding the gun, covering their backs, or sharing in the excitement of the mission.

And here she was again, digging into the unknown, searching for answers, trying to figure out how to help in a situation where, for all intents and purposes, she just felt like a helpless outsider. Wade was right. She hadn't lived in Buffalo Springs for sixteen years. Why did she feel a need to resurrect the town, to put herself in danger?

And what about Wade? What if, by breaking into the building, she had put him in even more danger? Or her family? What if the phone call and the rock really were warnings?

"Hey."

Andi jumped and nearly skidded off the rock, but she braced herself before looking down at Wade, standing next to the river. She looked around. Was she losing her instincts, too? How did he keep getting the jump on her?

"I've been looking everywhere for you. When you weren't anywhere in town, I thought, maybe, you might be out here."

She scoffed. "Why bother?"

"Andi, I know what happened."

She stared out at the river, not even trying to listen or comprehend what he was saying.

"Andi, look at me."

She refused to look, hoping he would go away.

As if reading her thoughts, he said, "Andi, I'm not leaving until we talk."

She kept her eyes on the river. "Haven't you said all there is to say? You're right. I'm only here because I have no place else to go. I care more about planning and executing a new mission than actually helping the people of the town. I had no business getting involved in any of it, and I won't stick my nose in it anymore. You can do whatever you want concerning the building. I'm out. I'm not putting anyone else in danger."

"Andi, did you hear me? I know what happened."

She slowly turned toward him. "What are you talking about?"

"Got room up there for me?"

Andi reluctantly scooted over, and Wade climbed onto the boulder and sat beside her. He reached for one of her hands and held it between his two palms. Andi felt the urge to pull away, but deep inside, she longed to feel his touch.

"I know what happened," he repeated. "I'm sorry it took me so long to put it together."

"I don't know what you're talking about." But she did. Despite his frequent ease at sneaking upon her, the instincts she had so carefully crafted rarely failed her. Rarely.

"I did a little intel work myself." She could feel him looking at her, but she refused to turn toward him. "You told me about your friends. You called them your 'Team.' Then today, you mentioned the SEALs and how you worked with them. I did a little research. The helicopter accident near Iran a few months back. Were those your friends?"

Andi inhaled through her nose and let it out through her mouth. She looked down at her hand still encased in his. She kept her eyes down as she spoke.

"Jeremy, Evan, Troy, Alan, Ramon, and Ray. They were the senior members of our platoon and my closest friends in the world. We lived a life we could discuss with nobody, not even their wives. We were our own little community, dependent upon each other for everything, even our lives." She raised her eyes to his. "They depended on me, and even though my mind is telling me that everyone is right, and it wasn't my fault, my heart can't help feeling like I failed them."

"What happened?"

She shrugged and looked away. "I can't tell you. There was an accident. I didn't see it coming, but I should have."

"Could you have? I mean, really? Could you have known that this 'accident' was about to take place?"

She sniffed at the thought. "My commanding officers said no. The review board said no. I heard it over and over, 'No INW'—indications or warnings, and I know they're right There was nothing to put me, any of us on alert, but still…" She stared off into the trees on the other side of the water, unable to look him in the eye.

"If you know that, then why do you continue to blame yourself?"

"I don't know." It was the first time she said it out loud, and the realization startled her. She turned to face him. "I don't know. I was the one who was supposed to let them know if, if there was something they should be aware of. I was the one who was supposed to have their backs."

"Andi, if nobody else thinks it's your fault, if your superiors and whoever this board is, if they didn't find you at fault, then why do you continue to shoulder the blame?"

A movement in the sky caught her eye, and Andi looked up to see a bald eagle in flight, soaring over the trees. She raised her hand to cover her eyes and watched it fly until it hid itself among the treetops. Was it a sign? The symbol of their country appearing overhead at this moment? She shook her head.

"I can't explain it. I just can't help asking myself what I missed. What could I have done differently? How could I have stopped it? Logically, I know I did everything right, but the questions still keep coming."

Wade took a deep breath, squeezed her hand, and spoke quietly. "I was supposed to pick up Jolene that day."

Andi's breath caught in her throat. She turned her gaze toward him, but he watched the sky as he spoke.

"I had just gotten my license, and my mom asked me to pick her up after basketball. Jolene had choir practice at the church and would be done about the same time I would be heading home. I got caught up after practice, talking to the guys about the game that Friday. I didn't realize how late it was until one of the guys mentioned that it was getting dark. I remembered Jolene and got out of there as fast as I could." He paused and looked down at her hand, caressing it with his thumb.

"By the time I got to the church, the police and the ambulance were on the scene. We think Jolene got tired of waiting and decided to walk home. She was wearing jeans and a dark coat, and we don't know why she crossed the street in front of that truck, but she did. Maybe she wasn't paying attention, or maybe she thought she could get across in time. Maybe she thought he'd stop and let her go. Whatever the reason, the streetlight was blown out, and with the jeans and dark jacket, well…" He didn't finish the sentence. He didn't have to. The scene he painted hung in the air in front of them.

"Wade," she whispered. "I'm so sorry."

"So was I for a long time. I'm still sorry she's gone and still hate that I didn't get there in time, but I couldn't go on blaming myself. My parents didn't blame me, and heaven knows they could have. It was an accident. I didn't will it to happen, and even though I might have been able to prevent it, that still doesn't make it my fault. It took me a long time to realize that."

"Do you…" She couldn't help but wonder, "Do you ever dream about her? About the scene?"

"Not so much now, but I did a lot back then. Now, it only happens when I'm stressed."

"So, lately, then?" She offered a feeble smile of understanding.

"Yeah, a couple nights ago."

"How did you do it? Get past the guilt?"

"It wasn't easy. I saw someone for a while, a therapist."

Andi nodded. "Same."

"They can only help so much."

"Agreed."

"It has to come from within, Andi. You have to find the ability to forgive yourself. Because that's the key. Nobody else blames you, so nobody else can forgive you. You have to get past your doubts and forgive yourself."

"And how do I do that?"

Wade looked back up at the sky. "I found it up there." He lifted their hands, his fingers entwined with hers, and gestured toward the sky. "My parents had such a strong faith, and I watched them lean on God, and I saw how he got them through that and other hard times—my grandparents' deaths, my father's illness, stuff like that. Leaving town helped me some, but it was talking to our team chaplain at Notre Dame that really did it for me. He helped me understand that I was forgiven by everyone but me. He helped me work through it."

That wasn't something Andi had ever considered—talking to someone other than a therapist. She wasn't sure how much it would help, but the awareness hit her that this helped. Just talking about it to Wade, to someone who understood, helped a lot.

"Thanks, Wade. I needed to hear that, to hear someone say they'd been there and made it through to the other side."

"It's not an easy thing for me to talk about. I've only told all of this to one other person, besides the chaplain."

"Who?"

"Her name was Pam. We worked together in New York. And we were engaged."

Andi gasped and Wade tightened his hold on her hand.

"What happened?"

"She died," he said quietly.

"Oh, Wade, I'm so sorry."

"She had cancer. It was quick, but not painless. I wanted to marry her, but she refused. She said our life wasn't a Nicholas Sparks novel and she didn't need me to marry her to prove I loved her. I wanted to anyway, but it turned out, we didn't have the time. She was gone in a matter of weeks."

Andi took a deep breath before speaking. "I loved Jeremy. It never went farther than a single kiss two days before he died. We left for the mission, and he told me he was worried. He had a feeling it wasn't going to go as planned."

"I thought it was a training exercise."

Andi was silent for a moment, kicking herself for saying too much but trusting it would go no farther than the boulder they sat on. "Anyway, he was gone before I could tell him how I felt."

"Would you have been allowed to be together?"

"And keep working together? Heck no. It's why we kept our feelings bottled up for so long. I know it's not the same at all, and don't take this wrong, but at least you two knew where you stood, how you felt. There were no regrets there."

"You're wrong. It's exactly the same. No matter what words were or were not expressed, you and I both lost someone we loved to tragic circumstances beyond our control. I was pretty depressed for a long time. It got worse after Daddy died. And then one day, shortly after we lost him, I was at Mass with Mama. It was the feast of the Presentation of the Lord, you know?"

She shook her head. "Sorry, I'm a little rusty on some of that." *Most of that.*

"It's when Christ was presented in the temple. Anyway, Father Michael's homily said the real meaning of the feast day is to remind us that Christ is the light of the world. He said that, even in our darkest days—through pain, suffering, doubt, whatever darkness we are going through, Christ is the light. It was kind of an epiphany for me."

Andi thought about that. All this time, she'd been pushing God away, maybe blaming him as much as she blamed herself. Was her mother right? Should she have been going toward him, asking him to help, instead of running the other way? She felt like all she'd been doing lately was running away from someone or something.

"Wade, did you move back home because you were running away from the memories of the person you loved?"

"Are you asking me or yourself?"

They looked at each other with clear understanding and compassion, and neither felt the need to answer the question.

After a while, Wade pushed himself off the boulder and gestured for Andi to come down. She accepted the help her offered and eased herself to the ground. Wade took her hand and held it as they walked back toward the parking lot. The setting sun crowned the trees with a golden halo which made Andi think about what Wade said about Christ being the light. Maybe it was time she let God back into her life. Maybe it was time she welcomed love back into her life, both from God and man.

Thirteen

"It's clean," Officer Hutchens told Wade.
"Forensics will be able to determine what was there and
how many rooms it was in, but there's no trace of
anything now."

The operation had taken place early in the morning
with the hopes of not drawing too much attention, but
Main Street began to fill with curious onlookers.

"Thank you, Sir. I appreciate your people acting so
quickly. I just wish we'd gotten here sooner."

"You're welcome. I wish we had found something.
No telling where it's gone by now."

"Everything okay?" Ted Mitchem asked, coming
between the state trooper and Wade.

"Everything is just fine, Ted. This is Officer
Hutchens with the state police Criminal Investigation

Bureau. He's just following up on a tip that turned out to be bogus."

"What kind of tip?"

"Nothing you need to concern yourself with, Mr. Mitchem. Wade, I'll be in touch."

They watched the officer walk over to another trooper and engage in conversation, pointing to the building and gesturing toward other buildings on the street.

"What's going on, Wade?"

"As the man said, nothing that concerns you, Ted."

"Now, look here, young man. I was president of the town council. If the state police are investigating something—"

"Like you said, Ted, you *were* president. You gave that up. This is my town now, and I don't need your help to run it."

Ted's face reddened as he shoved a fat finger in Wade's face. "I don't know what you think you're doing, boy, but don't you think for one minute you have any real authority in this town. You know who holds the real power."

"I think I do, Ted. I know exactly who holds the power now. In fact, you're looking at him, and he's a very busy man. Now, I've got a meeting at the bank when it opens in…" Wade looked at his watch. "In about three minutes. You have a good day."

Wade started to walk away, but Ted grabbed him by the arm. "What business have you got at the bank?"

Wade met Ted with a cold gaze. "Why, Mr. Mitchem, I don't believe that's any of your business either."

Through clenched teeth, Ted spoke in a low, calculating voice. "You look here, Montgomery. You're getting in way over your head. You need to go back to being the lame duck mayor you were hired to be. Don't do something you're going to regret."

"Too late, Ted. I've done a lot I regret, but that's all about to change."

Wade walked away with a smile on his face and the hope that Ted couldn't hear the pounding of Wade's heart. There were two things of which Wade was certain, that Ted Mitchem was knee-deep in the sewage that was seeping through the town and that he was a dangerous man.

***

Andi's phone buzzed non-stop all morning as she fielded calls from other would-be business owners. The Russos had been notified that their contract had been rejected as had all the other townspeople trying to open new businesses. They were reluctant to share the information with their investors without knowing what was going on—Andi told them to hold tight. Betty Jean called to ask if Andi knew what was happening downtown—she pretended to be unaware of the raids. And Jackson called in a panic that the police would find their fingerprints in the house—she reminded him that they wore gloves, but he was in a state of panic nonetheless.

When the phone buzzed again, Andi was ready to toss it out the window.

"Hello?" she answered tersely.

"I warned you, girl. Back off before it's too late."

The call disconnected, and Andi's hand trembled as she stared at the screen. She nearly dropped the phone when it buzzed again. This time, a Texas area code preceded the number. She answered with a quaking hand and a quivering voice.

"Andi? It's Joe. Joe Blake."

"Oh, hi, Joe." She let out a shaky breath. "I'm sorry. I'm having a bit of a crazy day here. What's up?"

"Andi, I just received a call from your friend, Rudy."

"Look, Joe, I don't know what's going on. I got the same message about the store I'm trying to buy. I'm looking into it."

"I'm not sure I understand."

"Did Rudy tell you that the contract fell through?"

"No, just the opposite. The contract was accepted, and they're willing to sign everything over immediately. That's why I'm calling. Can you give me the name of a good contractor?"

Andi was stunned. "Your contract was accepted?"

"You sound surprised."

"Wow. No, um, that's great. And you need a contractor?"

"Yes, to convert the building into a clinic. Andi, am I calling at a bad time? You sound distracted."

"No, no, not at all. Let me just look up that number for you." She relayed Stan's information to Joe.

"Thanks, Andi. I hope to be up and running soon. I'm guessing three to four months. I hope that works into your plans for the town."

"Perfectly," she said while thinking, *I hope we still have a town by then.*

"Great. I'll be in touch. And Andi? Thanks for letting me be a part of all of this."

When the line went dead, Andi sat and stared at her phone. What was going on? Why turn down everyone else's contracts but accept the good doctor's?

Startled once again by its sudden vibration, Andi let the phone slip from her hand. She bent down and hesitantly picked up the phone. Wade's name flashed on the screen.

"Wade, you're not going to believe what I have to tell you."

"Oh, I bet I can one up you."

Her interest was more than piqued. "Where and when?"

"I'll pick you up in five."

Andi hurried to clear the table and ran to the bedroom to grab her shoes. She paused in front of the mirror, taking in her tee and sweatpants. She hurried to the closet and tugged a light blue sweater from a shelf. Stepping hastily out of the sweats, she pulled on a pair of tight jeans. She ran a brush through her dark hair and decided to leave it down instead of pulling it back into a ponytail. She even dabbed a bit of lip gloss on her lips.

She had almost forgotten what it felt like to dress like a girl, and she smiled at her reflection in the mirror. But thoughts about the calls came to mind. She hated having to tell Wade that she'd gotten another one. At least she'd had one good call that morning.

Wade pulled up to the curb as Andi opened the door. She locked the front door and hurried to his car.

"Where are we going?"

"To the national park, if that's okay. I don't want to talk here in town."

As if her curiosity wasn't already high on the Richter scale, his desire to talk away from the town took it to a meteoric ten-point-oh.

"Do we have to wait until we get there to talk?"

"You know what happened to the cat, right?"

"The cat?"

"Yeah, the curious one."

"Not funny, Wade."

"I'm not trying to be funny, Andi."

***

"You look nice, by the way," Wade said as they walked down the path toward the river, hand-in-hand.

"Thanks." Andi blushed and Wade liked the way the color filled her cheeks.

"Are you going to be warm enough? It's starting to turn colder."

Andi looked down at her jeans and sweater. "I'll be fine, but thanks."

They stopped at the boulder, and Wade climbed up before reaching down to give Andi a hand. He knew she hardly needed help and was probably in much better shape than he was, but she accepted his offer, which made his stomach flutter just a bit more than he wanted to admit.

"So, you said you have something to tell me." Wade looked at her with anticipation.

"Jeremy's brother, the doctor? He called me this morning to tell me his contract was accepted and that he could take ownership immediately. He's buying the Anderson house instead of one of the empty buildings. Anyway, that call came amid the flood of calls from others telling me their investors' contracts were declined. What do you think that's about?"

"Interesting." Wade mulled it over for a moment. "Restaurants, tourist shops, and boutiques get turned down, but a clinic is welcomed with opened arms."

"What do you think it means?"

"Well, if it's connected in any way to what you and Jackson found, I'd say it's about the medicine."

"You mean, like opioids?" Andi asked

"That would be my guess."

"But Joe doesn't have any ties to Buffalo Springs or its meth operation. He's from Texas and had never been here before that day he showed up to talk to me."

Her remark gave Wade even more reason to question Joe's motives. "Not having ties raises suspicion right there, don't you think?"

"Yes, and no."

"Really?" He couldn't believe she was willing to give this total stranger the benefit of the doubt when she just barely trusted him.

"Look, I don't know Joe, but I did know Jeremy, and he and Joe were thick as thieves. Jeremy talked about his brother the doctor and how good and compassionate he is."

"Maybe so, but I've heard of many doctors who've been lured into the opioid business through blackmail, extortion, the promise of money. He may not be involved now, but whoever these guys are, they may have let his contract go through with the hopes they can get him to join their operation at some point."

"Hmm...I hadn't thought of that. I don't know anything about his personal or financial situation. You could be onto something."

Wade was glad to see that she was considering the possibility that Joe might not be the altruistic doctor she thought he was.

"Know anybody who can look into him?"

Andi pressed her lips together for a moment. "I might. Let me see what I can find out."

"Okay," Wade said. "Anything else?"

She pressed her lips together, and Wade scrutinized her expression.

"Andi, what aren't you telling me?"

"I got another call."

"Another call?" His confusion turned to anger as her words sunk in. "Another threat, you mean?"

"All he said was to back off. That's it."

"That's still a threat. Look, Andi, maybe we need to rethink—"

"Forget it, Wade. I told you, I'm not backing down. My only personal concern is that my family is safe. I'm thinking about installing cameras at Mama and Daddy's house and at Helena's."

"Might not be a bad idea."

"Agreed." Andi pointed to a doe as it slowly made its way down to the flowing water. They sat in silence until the deer made her way back up into the trees.

"Wade?" Andi said, looking over at him. "It's getting pretty cold up here, and I can't feel my butt or my legs. Can we walk for a bit?"

"Of course."

***

Wade climbed off the boulder, and Andi followed. Again, he turned to help her down, and she took his hand. She was surprised to feel a wave of disappointment when he let go and started walking ahead of her along the banks of the river.

"You should have brought Boomer."

"I almost stopped by the house, but I didn't want to get waylaid."

They walked silently along the river for a few minutes before Andi looked over at Wade. "So, what's your news? You still haven't told me about what the police found."

"Well, to start, they found nothing."

"Nothing? What the heck?"

"Everything had been cleared out. My guess is, they discovered the broken lock and hauled it all out of there as fast as they could."

"Great. Now what?"

"The police are still investigating. They're looking at all of the buildings and sending in a forensics team to figure out exactly what the stuff was, where it was located, etcetera."

"I guess that's good."

"It's a start."

"What else?"

When he came to where the river widened, Wade stopped and picked up a smooth rock. He rubbed it for a moment before skipping it across the water. He watched it skip and then sink beneath the ripples, and Andi waited for him to talk.

"Ted Mitchem was there. When the police made the raid."

"He was in the building?" Andi asked, surprised by the information.

"No, outside, watching what was going on."

"Oh." She felt a stab of dismay.

"He's in on it, Andi. I know it. What I'd like to know is how many others in the former council are also in on it."

"I agree. He's definitely in on everything."

"And you're not the only one being warned. Mitchem threatened me."

Andi gasped and turned toward Wade. "He what? In front of the police?"

"After the officer walked away. And he was careful. He didn't come out and make an obvious threat, but it was there."

"Wade, maybe you should be the one to back off. You have your mother to think about."

Wade turned and looked at Andi, his face a blend of emotions. "Look who's talking. Andi, if you're in, I'm in. There's no other way."

"Wade, I took an oath to support and defend this country, and that includes this town."

"You're no longer obligated to keep that oath."

"I will always be obligated to keep that oath."

She watched the muscle in his jaw twitch and expected him to argue with her, but after a moment, he nodded.

"Well, I made an oath, too. I didn't take it seriously at the time, but you've changed that. You've changed me. And I need to see this through."

A host of feelings bubbled up inside Andi as he spoke. All her life, she wanted to make a difference in the world, to protect those she loved, to give herself to a higher calling, and to stand up for her country and all it stands for. But that life forced her to make sacrifices. She rarely saw her family. She was never one of the lucky ones able to maintain a long-lasting, stable relationship. She was thirty-four and had never come close to thinking about having children. She never felt like she had permission to cry, to be comforted, or to just rest and relax.

Just as Wade had changed, Andi realized that she had changed. She was slowly becoming a new version of herself, and she thought she might even like the person she was becoming. She admitted that the change began some time ago, when she knew she was falling in love with Jeremy, but it took leaving the military for her to truly allow herself to embrace the change. Part of her would always follow that oath, that urge to protect, that need to find answers, give commands, and stand her ground, but she now realized that it was okay to be both a sailor and a human with feelings.

"Andi? You okay?"

Andi smiled. "Better than okay. Thanks, Wade. I'm not sure I had anything to do with you changing. As you said, change comes from within, but you've helped me realize some things about myself that I didn't know or didn't think possible before, so I guess we've helped each other."

"I guess the bottom line is, we're good for each other."

"I guess we are." She bent down and picked up a smooth stone, caressing it the same way Wade had, and then skipped it across the water.

"Nice one," Wade said.

"Thanks." Andi realized she was smiling a real, genuine smile for the first time in a long, long time. Then she remembered why they were there. "So, we're both in. No more arguing about that. Was there something else you wanted to tell me?"

"Yes, and it's big. I talked to Devon McCoy, president of the bank. I told him everything I know about the accounts, including my suspicion that I'm being set up."

"That was brave. Are you sure you can trust him?"

"I know I can. He was my first basketball coach and my father's best friend and best man. We closed the empty accounts and set up all new ones, which he assured me nobody else would have access to. When this is all over, I'll institute a new council with a real election, and they can decide who has access to it, but for now, it's just going to be me." Wade picked up another rock and hurled it across the water. "There are things I never thought of before. Like, my salary, Trudy's, Marshall's, even the police department's, they all come out of the town budget. We were all being paid through a bogus account. Now that the funds are gone, I've got to come up with a way to pay these people, except Marshall, of course. Devon is going to personally go to the State Comptroller and ask that Buffalo Springs Enterprises and the accounting office of Steve Marshall be investigated."

Andi mulled over the news. "Hmm…can I make a donation to the town? I'm not rich, but I didn't spend much over the past sixteen years. The least I can do is pay for the surveillance."

"We've got some money that the bank is willing to chip in, and I've put a bit in the pot myself, but I'm not going to tell you no if you want to help."

"I do. I'll call Devon McCoy in the morning."

"Thanks, Andi. I appreciate it. I'm going to have Trudy put an ad in the local papers right away. It's just one more thing on my ever-growing list of things that need to be straightened out."

"The you-know-what is going to hit the fan when Marshall and Mitchem find out what's going on."

"It already has, but what else could I do?"

"What happens if they've set things up so that it all leads back to you?"

"Devon and I realize that's a possibility, but all I can do at this point is maintain my innocence. I guess I'll have to face the consequences when and if something happens."

Andi shivered, but she wasn't sure if it was because of the setting sun or the thought of Wade being arrested for a white-collar crime he didn't commit.

"You cold?" Wade took off his jacket and wrapped it around Andi's shoulders amid her protests.

"Don't argue. I've still got my sports coat on, and you're only wearing a light sweater."

"Thanks," she said. "I guess we should get back."

"Hold on." Wade reached into his pocket for his phone and tapped the answer button. "Hello. Wade Montgomery here."

Andi listened to the one-sided conversation.

"Hey Trudy…That's good…Absolutely, I'll be available tomorrow. Go ahead and set it up…Really? What do we do now?. . .Great, thanks, Trudy…Yeah, just lock up…Okay, goodbye."

Andi raised her brow in question.

"I have a phone call tomorrow with the State Comptroller himself. His assistant called my office. In addition, the state police have found overwhelming evidence that you were right. It was meth, and it was in multiple rooms in three of the empty buildings in town. They've officially been designated crime scenes and are off limits to everyone."

"That's good, I guess. But what about the people who are inquiring about them for businesses?"

"I don't know. Hopefully, by the time the police release the sites, we'll have some leverage over Buffalo Springs Enterprises and can get back to the investors with good news." Wade took her hand in his, and she felt another shiver go through her, a pleasant one. "Let's go. Dusk is setting in, and it's just going to get colder. Plus, I've got to get home to my mom."

"How's she doing?" Andi asked as they walked through the darkening wood, his hand still firmly holding onto hers.

"Good days and bad."

"What are you going to do when this whole thing is over? Will you take her back to New York with you?"

Wade took a few moments before answering. "I'm honestly not sure. I'm beginning to think there might be some good reasons for me to stick around here."

Andi let his words hang in the air as they walked. She didn't know if she was one of the reasons, and she wasn't sure she wanted to know just yet. She was still figuring things out for herself. One thing she did know was that it felt awfully nice to walk through the woods with her hand in his.

Fourteen

The next several days were a swirl of activity. Contrary to Andi's prediction, Wade heard nothing from Ted Mitchem or Steve Marshall. The accountant's office had a Closed sign on the door that hadn't been taken down all week, and Mitchem seemed to be MIA. The State Comptroller formally took over the investigation of the bank accounts and was working with the state police to identify any links to the missing meth, weapons, and bundles of cash in the photos Wade had turned over to both agencies. Andi's inquiries had turned up nothing fishy about Joe Blake. He had a clean record and an impeccable reputation. Andi's theory was that his move from Texas to Arkansas wasn't that different from her return home or Wade's flight from New York—the ghost of Joe's dead brother was impossible to avoid even in the great state of Texas.

Trudy alerted Wade that he had a call, and Wade answered, not sure what to expect. "Wade Montgomery, here."

"Wade, this is Earl. I think it's time you and I had a sit-down. Can you come down to the station?"

"To be honest, Chief, I'd prefer that you come here. I'm not comfortable talking outside of my office." Thanks to the police forensics team, he knew his office was safe for meetings.

"What the—"

"Earl, before you get defensive, let me remind you that everything that is going on took place under your watch as well as mine. I'm not going to talk about it in your office. If you want to meet, I'll meet, but it's not going to be in any place I, or we, can't be sure is safe for this conversation."

There was a long pause before Earl spoke again. "And you're sure your place is safe?"

"I am."

"Then I reckon I'll meet you there. In a half hour?"

Wade agreed to the meeting but found himself ill at ease. He still didn't know if anyone with local law enforcement was involved with the phony corporation or with the drug trade. Other than Andi, Trudy, and Devon, he didn't know who could be trusted.

When Earl Manning walked into the office, his height filled the doorway. The man was almost seven feet tall, an imposing figure to say the least. Wade stood and took Manning's outstretched hand.

"Mr. Mayor, thank you for meeting with me."

"You're welcome, Chief."

Trudy followed Earl into the room with two mugs of coffee. Once the men were settled, Trudy left and shut the door.

"I'm going to just come out and say it. I'm insulted you didn't call me before you brought in the state police and contacted the bank. I've known you since you were knee high to a grasshopper. You didn't think you could trust me?"

Wade exhaled and cracked a couple knuckles on his entwined fingers. "Look, Earl, I'm going to be completely honest in the hopes that you will hear me out and understand where I'm coming from. I took this job without fully understanding the role. Over the past couple months, I've come to realize that I wasn't doing my due diligence for the people of this town. I started digging into the town's finances, the investment potential of the empty buildings, and such. What I found are appalling inconsistencies with bank records that led me to further investigate possible embezzlement and money laundering. That forced me to take action which includes looking into the ownership of certain properties in town. Now, like you said, I've known you my whole life, but I've been gone for a long time, and I'm not sure who's to be trusted. I have to operate from a position of caution. I need you to recognize that the only way I could be sure everything was handled on the up and up was to bring in outside help."

"You call Devon McCoy outside help? We went to school together."

"And he's like family to me. If there's anyone in this town I'm going to trust, it's him. The jury is out on everyone else."

"And the Nelson girl you've been seen around town with?"

Wade sat back in the chair, his heart clenching in his chest. "I never said anything about Ms. Nelson."

"You didn't have to. The whole town knows she and her brother came up with this *plan* as they call it, and the two of you have been seen all over town together, including coming out of the empty movie house. People are beginning to talk."

Wade felt his face grow hot with indignation as he leaned toward the chief. Through clenched teeth he asked, "And what exactly are they saying?"

The chief leaned back in his chair and crossed his arms in front of him. "The things people will say about a single man and a single woman prowling around in empty buildings together. There are some questions as to how this supposed stash of drugs was discovered in a locked, abandoned building. Would you and Ms. Nelson happen to know anything about the broken lock that was reported a few days back?"

Wade answered, wearing the same poker face he wore in the boardroom. "Chief, I'm not going to give that ridiculous question any credence, and I'm beginning to wonder if this meeting was such a good idea." Wade started to stand to show the man out, but the chief put up his hands.

"Wade, wait. I'm not done. I'm sorry. I got us off on the wrong foot."

Wade hesitated. What little trust he had in the chief was diminishing with each word that came from the man's mouth.

"Please, sit down. We have a real problem here, and you and I are going to need to work together to solve it."

"I'm not sure that's a good idea, Earl."

"Wade, I've got some information you need to know." The chief looked around and lowered his voice as if someone might walk in at any moment. "Please, I'm already putting myself in danger by coming over here to see you. Now, sit down so we can get this over with."

An uncomfortable feeling washed over Wade, and he found himself looking at the closed door before he took his seat. "So, you do know more than you let on."

"They approached me. A while ago."

"Who?"

Earl shook his head. "I think you know. They wanted me to look the other way on certain nights and to make sure my men were out of the way."

"And did you?"

Earl looked around as he fidgeted with the stirrer in his mug. "I did." He quickly put up his hand. "But I didn't know why. I didn't want to know. I didn't ask any questions and didn't try to find out what was going on."

"Why do it, Earl? Why forsake your promise to defend and protect?" He thought of Andi and how she would never turn her back on those she was sworn to take care of.

"They told me…" He put his elbow on the table and rubbed his fingers across his forehead before looking back up. "They said they'd tell Martha I was having an affair."

Wade felt sick to his stomach. "And you were."

Earl winced. "It was a one-time thing. It was over before it started. I'd never do anything to hurt Martha. Even after thirty-seven years of marriage, I still love her more than life itself."

"You realize, your meeting with me today may cause you to have to prove that to her."

He flinched before swinging his gaze toward the door. "I hope it doesn't come to that, but I couldn't keep this in. The guilt was killing me. I had to tell you what I know."

Wade felt no pity for the man. "I would guess the guilt about being complicit in a crime is only a small fraction of the guilt you're dealing with."

Earl tried to walk it backwards. "I didn't know there was a crime."

"Good luck trying to convince a jury of that, Earl. Now, hand me your badge and your weapon, and let's make this as painless as possible."

Earl's eyes bulged and the blood drained from his face. "You can't be serious. What will I tell Martha?"

"I suggest you tell her the truth before someone else does." Wade held out his hand. "Please, Earl. Don't make this any harder than it has to be."

Reluctantly, the former chief handed over his badge and his sidearm.

"I'm sorry to have to do this, but I'm sure you will agree, it's for the best. I think we're done here."

Wade began going through files on his desk, sending a clear message that they were finished. When Manning stood and left, Wade expelled the deep breath he'd been holding.

Now he had one more thing to add to his ever-growing calendar. He needed a new chief of police, and one that he could trust.

***

Jackson and Andi stared at the tires on his truck.

"I just spent three-hundred dollars on those." His voice was filled with disgust.

"Jackson, I'm so sorry. I hate that this happened. I understand if you want to make some kind of public declaration that you're not helping me anymore."

"Are you kidding?" He looked at her with disbelief. "The heck with that. I'm more determined than ever to make sure this town stands a chance of getting out from whatever is going on here. I'm in, Andi, all the way."

"Thanks, Jackson. I'm glad to hear that." Not that it didn't worry her. "I wish we could trust the local police enough to report it."

"We've got the pictures, and I'll keep all the receipts. We'll hold onto everything until we figure out what to do."

They turned at the sound of the tow truck. After Jackson settled things with the driver, he and Andi headed to her car.

"Thanks for coming to get me."

"No thanks necessary. The way I see it, I owe you for all you've done and for being willing to stick it out."

"And for four new tires."

"That, too, little brother. That, too."

***

"Holy mother of pearl." Trudy shook her head when Wade ventured out of his office an hour later. "You fired Earl?"

"Wade Montgomery!" The familiar voice filled the room as Imogene Baker's petite form appeared in the doorway. "What's this I hear about Earl Manning turning in his badge?"

"Hmph. Word travels fast." Wade held his arm out to welcome the former mayor. "Care to step into our office, Madame Mayor?"

"You bet I would. What is going on in this town? The things I've been hearing over the past week have me wondering if I've woken up in an alternate universe."

"You and me both, Mrs. Baker." He ushered her into his office and closed the door after rolling his eyes at Trudy.

"What's this business I hear about Earl Manning?"

"Mrs. Baker, Earl Manning came to me with a personal problem, and we both thought it best that he step down as chief."

The elderly woman watched him with interest, but Wade had no intention of telling her any details about Manning and his 'one-time thing.'

"And what about this talk about a drug raid?"

"I'm afraid I can't divulge any details about that either. It's an ongoing police investigation."

"Seems like a mighty big coincidence that the chief of police is fired or resigns or whatever right after the state police come in here and take over the town like they did."

"Now, Mrs. Baker. I hardly think the police took over the town. They've declared a few buildings off-limits, that's all."

She eyed him with a renewed interest. "You know, Wade, I was mayor for a very long time. I've seen a lot of things happen in this town, some good and some very bad. I wasn't sure about you, as you know. In fact, I didn't really like you very much." She looked him up and down. "But you're growing on me."

Wade smiled. "Why, Mrs. Baker, I think that's the kindest thing you've ever said to me."

She leaned on her cane as she pushed herself up from her chair. "Now, don't you let it go to your head. You just make sure you and that Nelson girl keep doing what you're doing."

After his conversation with the chief, Wade felt rather protective of Andi and her reputation. "What we're *doing*?" he asked casually.

"Getting this town back in shape, bringing back people's pride in the town and themselves, draining the swamp, as they say."

"Oh, yes, well we will keep working on doing all of that."

A sly smile took shape on her face, and she winked at Wade. "And whatever else you're doing, keep that up, too. It's good for both of you."

Though he should have acted shocked by her assumption and approval, Wade just smiled and shook his head as he watched her leave. It seemed that many people in this town were giving him a lot more credit than he deserved. His face fell as he thought of Andi. Credit for him could lead to shame for her. That was the last thing he wanted.

Wade fully admitted that he had was falling hard for Andi. He didn't know just yet what to do with that knowledge, but it was there just the same, and his feelings grew deeper every day. The urge to protect her was strong even though he knew she was one woman who didn't need protection from anyone. But it wasn't her reputation or her physical well-being that concerned Wade. He found that what he wanted to protect most was her heart.

***

Jackson went upstairs, leaving Andi and her mother alone in the kitchen. Grace did a fairly good job of hiding her concern, but Andi saw the worry lines on her face.

"These are the last of the year's flowers, I'm sure," Grace said as she busied herself with arranging a vase of blue, pink, and purple hydrangea. "Thanksgiving is just a week away. I can't believe you've been home for two months already." She stood back and looked at her arrangement. "What do you think?"

"Your gardens always have been the prettiest ones in town," Andi told her, admiring her mother's green thumb and the way she kept the house looking so nice despite its slow descent into disrepair and the hole in the living room carpet. "And you always do a beautiful job arranging them. I don't know how you keep them all up, but the flowers sure look nice, inside and out."

"I love bringing the flowers inside and adding a touch of the fresh, clean outdoors to the indoors. And I've always believed that one's yard is just as important as the rooms in their house. It's the entryway to the property, after all."

"I never thought about it like that before, but you're right." Andi watched her mother add some sugar to the vase before placing it in the center of the kitchen table.

Grace sat down at the table across from her daughter. "Okay, enough avoiding the elephant in the room. Are you sure you want to keep going, Andi? First the rock, then Jackson's tires. Is all this worth it?"

"Yes, it's worth it. Somebody has got to stand up to these guys."

"And it has to be you?"

"It has to be somebody. Might as well be me." She took a long drink of iced tea. "I guess Jackson and I sure stirred up some you-know-what."

"Well, that was bound to happen. Anytime someone comes in trying to change things and telling others what to do, some feathers are going to be ruffled." Grace peered at Andi. "But it seems like there's a lot more going on than feather ruffling. I'm worried about you both."

"I get it, Mama. I hate that you and Daddy have gotten pulled into this."

"Your father and I have been through a lot in our years together—money struggles, the loss of a baby between your sister and brother, worrying about you all those years you were gone, worrying about the three of you now. It's all part of the package."

"But you were never in danger before. You could be now."

"Your father installed those cameras you ordered on Amazon. We're being careful. Don't you worry about us. It's you and Jackson I'm concerned about"

"We'll be fine, Mama." Andi hoped that was true.

"Andi, honey, what else is bothering you? You've got something on your mind, and I don't think it's all this stuff with the town."

"The stuff with the town is enough."

"But it's not everything."

Andi's mother never went to college, and she only left the Ozarks once in her life—to attend Andi's graduation, but she was one of the smartest and most intuitive people Andi knew though Andi seldom gave her enough credit.

"Someone asked me recently if I came back to town to escape my old life, or the memories of my old life."

"And that hit too close to home."

Andi looked at her mother with renewed admiration though she should not have doubted her mother for a minute. "You knew?"

"That you were running away from something? Of course, I knew. I'm your mother. I wish you'd tell me what it is you're running from though."

Andi thought about how much to tell her mother and then realized it was the whole reason she was there. She wanted to talk it out and hear her mother's advice.

"Mama, I've been blaming myself for something that happened, something that I've been told over and over wasn't my fault, but it's just not that easy to accept that I couldn't change what happened somehow."

"Andi, I'm sure whatever you did or didn't do, you didn't cause those boys to die."

"Mama, you amaze me. How did you know?"

"Andi, honey." Grace reached across the table and put her hand over Andi's. "I watch the news every morning and every night. There's nothing that happens with the Navy, especially the SEALs that I don't know about. Now, I might not know the whole story about what caused that helicopter to crash with SEAL Team Three on it, but I know this: there's no way you did anything, or didn't do something, that caused it to happen."

Andi swallowed and turned her hand so that it grasped her mother's. "I've been down a pretty dark road, Mama. I even thought about..." She looked away, blinking back a tear. "Anyway, I've been doing a lot of thinking and even some listening, and I think I'm ready to move on."

"Move on? In what way?" Grace's hand squeezed Andi's. "Are you leaving town?"

Andi smiled at her mother. "No, Mama, I'm not leaving. I actually like being home."

"These people you're listening to, is one of them our town's mayor?"

Andi felt her cheeks grow warm. "As a matter of fact, he is, but we're just friends, Mama."

"Your daddy and I were just friends for a long time."

"Mama, you've been together since you were fifteen."

"We were friends before that, and after. That's important, you know. To be friends first, last, and always. The spark and the passion, they wear off over time, or someone gets sick or something happens, like with Wade's daddy getting cancer. In times like that your friendship can be just as important as your love, even more so."

"You know, Mama, you're a lot smarter than I've ever given you credit for."

"Oh, come on, now. I could never be as smart as you three kids with all your fancy schooling. But I do know a thing or two about life and love and the things that matter in this world, like following God's plan and seeing where it leads."

Andi thought about what Wade said about Christ being the light in the darkness. "Do you still go to church every week, Mama?"

"Every Sunday and every weekday that I can."

"I might like to join you sometime if that's okay."

Grace's face lit up, and her hand closed tightly around Andi's. "I thought you'd never ask."

***

Andi's phone buzzed as she walked to her car. She looked at the screen and felt a happy, little twinge in her stomach. She typed a reply, agreeing to meet Wade at his house at five.

She pulled out of her parents' driveway and drove toward the library. As she drove, her sixth sense kicked in, a warning she hadn't felt in quite some time. Something was wrong. She lifted her eyes to the rearview mirror and noticed an old pickup truck following her at a distance. She recalled seeing the truck parked across the street when she left her mother's house. Coincidence? She didn't think so.

A million memories flooded her brain, the many communications from Jeremy as he and the platoon moved stealthily through towns, across deserts, and into Taliban caves. So often, she felt what he felt, experienced what he experienced, even as he evaded enemy combatants and she sat in a secure location wearing earphones while sending and receiving intel. She knew when to trust her gut and when to brush something off, and her gut was telling her to tread carefully.

She turned a corner and slowed down, watching for the truck to follow. When it turned, she felt a rush of apprehension mingled with confirmation. She reached for her phone and held in the button for the voice assistant.

"Call Wade," she said, continuing to turn corners and retrace her steps rather than come to a stop.

"Which number for Wade Montgomery? Home, Office, or Mobile?"

Frustrated, she snapped, "Mobile."

"Calling Wade Montgomery, Mobile."

"Hurry up," she pleaded, glancing into the mirror with each turn, rolling through the stop signs.

"Andi, hey. I'm about to go into a meeting with Devon. Can I—"

"I'm being followed."

The line went silent for a beat as she rolled through another intersection without making a complete stop.

***

"Are you sure?" Wade was up and around the desk before she answered.

"Yes, I'm sure. I know when someone is being followed."

"Right, of course, you do. Okay. Where are you?" He passed Trudy, a puzzled expression on her face.

Andi paused. "West and Elm."

"Go straight to the police station. I'll meet you there." He ran down the steps, jumping over the last three.

"Are you on the way?"

"Already heading there." His breathing was labored from both the run down the steps and the frantic beating of his heart.

"I'm only a minute or so away," she said

"I'm almost there. Just keep driving."

Wade reached the station just as Andi pulled into the lot. He kept an eye on the road and watched as a green pickup truck accelerated and sped past him. He read the plates and called to Andi as she opened the door.

"607 SBL. Write that down."

Andi picked up her phone and started typing. Wade reached her side and saw her hands trembling as she attempted to put the number in her notes app.

"Here, let me." He took the phone from her and finished entering the plate, noticing his own hands weren't too steady themselves. He handed her back the phone after sending himself a text with the information.

"Thanks, I guess the adrenaline is affecting my nerves. Did you recognize them?" she asked.

"No, but it won't take long to identify the plates." He took her hand and started walking toward the combination police station/jail, and a conveniently placed adjacent bail bond office.

When they walked in, they were met with stone-faced stares from both officers in the room.

"We're busy right now," one of the officers said. "You'll have to come back later."

Wade tried to maintain his calm. "Look, Eric, I get that you're not happy with me, but I don't have time for these games. I need a license plate traced. Now."

A third officer emerged from a back office and waved him over. "Wade, come on back."

The officer was Dale Mackenzie, and he and Wade went way back though they hadn't fully reconnected since Wade's return to town. Once again, Wade regretted not trying harder to rekindle old friendships. Maybe if he had, he'd have a better idea as to whom he could trust.

"Thanks, Dale. How's your daddy?"

"Ornery as ever." He looked at Andi. "He's pretty excited about the interest you showed in his wood carvings. He's been working on some new pieces so he's ready whenever the artisan market opens."

Andi smiled and nodded but remained silent, and Wade wondered if her silence was due to being followed or because she was a good observer. Maybe it was because she was starting to doubt that there would be an artisan market, but he hoped that wasn't the case.

"And...Ruth?"

Dale smiled, but his eyes conveyed the truth. "She's hanging in. Chemo starts next week."

Wade nodded. "She's in my prayers."

Dale thanked him, and they followed him into a conference room and closed the door.

"Sorry about that." Dale gestured toward the outer room. "A lot of people are pretty upset about what went down this morning."

Wade saw Andi shoot him a look, but he squeezed her hand and nodded at Dale. "Understandable."

"So, what do you need?" Dale took a seat on the back side of the table and gestured for them to take a seat. Wade let go of Andi's hand, and they both sat down.

"I need this number traced. It belongs to a green Ford pickup, older model, rusted tailgate."

Dale glanced at the phone Wade held out and shook his head. "No need. By that description, I'd bet it belongs to Shane Callahan. Bud's his father."

"Bud Callahan, former town council member?"

"That's him. Good riddance as far as him being on the council. He never belonged there. Bad lot, the Callahans, every one of them. What's Shane done now?"

"Nothing yet. He was following Andi."

Dale looked from one to the other. "Okay?"

"I know it doesn't sound like a problem, but—"

"He was watching me, or my brother, or the house. Whichever it was, he was outside my mama's house while I was there this afternoon. I'd just taken my brother, Jackson, home after his tires were slashed at work." Wade tensed at the news. "That truck was at the house, and then he followed me through town. No matter where I turned, he stayed a bit behind me. I think he knew I was on to him. I think it was a warning." She looked at Wade, and his stomach lurched.

"Dale, I know you might think she's paranoid—"

"I don't." He looked at Andi. "I know who you are, what you were, what your training is. If you say he was following you, I believe you. I also know there are some mixed feelings about what you and your brother are trying to do for this town. And you, too." He acknowledged Wade.

Dale glanced up at the window behind Wade and Andi. Wade turned and saw two pairs of eyes staring through the glass. Dale stood, walked to the window, and closed the blinds. He went back to his seat.

"Look, Wade, if you canned Earl, you had to have your reasons, and I know you're working with the boys from the state on some drug investigation. I don't know if Earl was involved in that or not, but I can assure you that I am not. I've never broken a law, taken advantage of my badge, or looked the other way. Whatever is going on in this town, I'm not a part of it. I'm on your side. You have my word."

In the state of Arkansas, a man's word is as good as a blood oath, but Wade was still uneasy. He looked at Andi.

"We've got to trust somebody," she said.

Wade nodded and spilled everything they knew, watching Dale carefully for any changes in expression or demeanor. By the time Wade had told him everything except the bit about Earl's affair, Dale's face showed disbelief before turning to anger.

"That son of a motherless goat. He knew, didn't he? He knew what they were doing?"

"He says he didn't know what, just that they were up to something."

"No wonder you let him go."

"I had to."

"Look, Wade, whatever you need, I've got your back." He looked at Andi. "And yours and your brother's." He paused. "My niece, Audrey, went to the Naval Academy after you did. Did you know that?"

Wade saw a flicker of recognition pass across her face.

"I heard that. I didn't know she was your niece."

"You inspired her. She's serving on a ship in the South Pacific and loves it. I admire what you did."

"Thank you."

Wade knew that meant a lot to Andi, and he felt himself swelling with pride though he had no reason to, and he once again felt the need to protect this woman who needed no protection.

"So, what do we do about this?" Wade asked.

"Not much we can do. Andi, be careful. Don't go anywhere alone if you're not in a highly public place. Park in lighted lots, carry your car key with your finger on the alarm, be aware of your surroundings. In the meantime, I'll try to keep tabs on Shane's whereabouts." He turned to Wade. "Let me know how else I can help. I'm on your side, Wade. This is my town, too, and I'm sick and tired of those jerks trying to keep it down. What y'all are doing is a darn good thing. I'll do what I can to help."

Wade stood, and Andi followed his lead. He reached for Dale's hand. "Thank you, Dale. I appreciate it. Maybe you and I could get a drink one night after work."

"I'd like that, Wade. I really would. Andi…" he reached for her hand. "It was a pleasure."

Wade and Andi said goodbye and walked back through the station, dodging dark stares and hardened faces. When they reached the street, Andi turned to him with fire in her eyes.

"We have to stop them. I will not live in fear, I will not have my family live in fear, and I will not let them hold this town hostage."

Despite the daggers in her eyes, the set jaw, the waves of fury that rolled off her body, and the way she stormed off toward her car, Wade never wanted to kiss anyone so much in his life.

Fifteen

Word spread like wildfire, and the library was once again packed with people. Missing were the men who lined the back wall at the last meeting—Ted Mitchem, Bud Callahan, Steve Marshall, and former council member, Brian Cleburn. Andi wasn't surprised by their absence.

Wade took the makeshift stage. "Thank you, all, for coming out tonight. Ms. Nelson and I wanted to fill everyone in on what's going on."

Andi saw the door open and turned to see Doctor Joe Blake slip inside the room. He caught her eye and smiled. Andi nodded before returning her focus to Wade. She and Wade agreed that it was time to let the town in on what was going on, figuring the more people on alert, the better.

"I'd like to introduce Officer Thomas Hutchens of the State Police Criminal Investigation Division. He's going to try to clarify some of the things you've been hearing and answer questions. Officer Hutchens?" Wade stepped aside so that the officer could take center stage.

"On the night of…"

Andi tuned him out as she looked around the room, allowing her mind to go into mission operational mode. She studied faces, examined expressions, and read body language. She watched for signs of disagreement—crossed arms, angry scowls, flexing muscles, and twitching jaws; and she looked for signs of discomfort—fidgeting, sweating brows, and darting eyes. By the time Hutchens finished speaking, Andi had identified two men she thought warranted keeping an eye on. She noted their facial features, clothing, one's baseball cap, and the other's missing tooth.

"Are there any questions?"

Leonardo Russo raised his hand. "Will the buildings go back on sale once the investigation is over?"

Hutchens moved aside to let Wade answer. "That is our hope. We're still working to identify the individual or individuals who hold the titles to the buildings." He didn't want to give too much away, so he motioned for the next question.

"How long will that take?" Allie Michaels asked

"We're working with state and federal authorities to figure it out. I will let everyone know as soon as we have more information."

"What happened to the drugs and stuff you said were in the buildings?" another man asked.

Officer Hutchens responded, "I cannot comment on that at this time."

Andi watched the two suspicious looking men exchange looks. While Wade and Hutchens continued to field questions, she watched as one man and then the other quietly slipped outside. Making sure Wade wasn't paying attention, Andi squeezed through the door.

Keeping her distance, she followed the men to the parking lot. She crouched behind a truck as she watched and listened.

The one with the missing tooth was speaking. "I told you, they ain't got any idea where the stuff is."

"I still don't like trying to move it while those state troopers are poking around," the man with the ball cap answered before taking a long drag of his cigarette.

"Look, we got all those orders, and that SOB Mitchem is breathing down my throat to get 'em filled. I ain't aiming to get myself killed 'cause you're afraid to do your job."

"Well, I ain't aiming to get locked up 'cause Mitchem is impatient. We need to wait until the heat dies down."

"Don't you get it? The heat ain't going to die down. We gotta move the stuff now before it's found." Missing Tooth sounded nervous.

Ball Cap tossed his cigarette butt into the ground and rubbed it out with the heel of his boot.

"Let's get it done, then. I want out of this thing, and the sooner the better."

"I'll see you tomorrow night. You know where."

The men parted ways, each heading to his own truck.

Andi duck-walked to the front of the truck and hid between the vehicle and the brick wall of the building until the lights of both trucks were out of sight.

"You can come out now," Andi said to the shadow nearby.

"I should have known you'd make me. Jeremy always knew when I tried to sneak by him."

"It's what we do," she said before a stab of pain pierced her heart.

Joe let her words slip by without comment. "Mind telling me who those guys were?"

"I'm not sure. I got a good look at them though."

"Who do you think they are? They were talking about the missing drugs, weren't they?"

Andi found it hard to believe, but in the dim light cast from the lone bulb in the lot, Joe looked even more like Jeremy than he had when she first saw him. She forced herself to get a grip. "I think so." She looked around but saw nobody else coming out of the library. "What are you doing out here anyway?"

"Following you. I saw the way you were watching them and then how you slipped outside behind them. I was afraid you might get yourself into trouble."

"You do remember what I did for the past twelve years, right?"

"Chalk it up to my profession. If I think there's going to be trouble, I get ready to jump in and help as soon as the smoke clears."

"And you assumed there would be trouble."

Joe stood back as if assessing her. "Andi, I'm assuming that trouble has a way of finding you."

"Why would you say that?"

"Your whole demeanor, the way you stare at people like you're trying to analyze them, the way you can't sit still or let go. You're like a smoldering ember waiting to burst into flame."

Andi was stunned speechless, remembering Jeremy's words to her, *You're like a fire in the desert. Once lit, there's nothing around that can put it out. It feeds on the brush and the heat surrounding it until there's nothing left to consume.*

"What? Am I wrong?"

"No, I mean…you're not the first person to say something like that to me."

There was silence for several moments before Joe spoke. "Jeremy."

Andi nodded.

"We always did read people the same way. Our parents said it was a rare talent we had, to see people so clearly. I use my talent to treat my patients. Jeremy used his to save the world."

Andi gave that some thought then said, "Oh, speaking of patients and saving the world, I heard you've opened a temporary clinic."

"Yes, in the house I'm renting. It was on its way to foreclosure, so I'm paying the owner rent, who in turn will be able to pay off some of his debt. It's a win-win situation."

"Andi!" Wade rushed around the corner, almost running into Joe.

Joe put his hands out. "Whoa, there. She's right here."

"He has a habit of running people over," Andi said. "It's okay, Wade. Joe and I were just talking."

"I realized you were gone, and I was…" He looked at Joe and then back at Andi. "Are you sure everything is okay?"

"I'm sure. How are things inside?"

"Intense, but good. Are you ready to go back in?"

"Yeah, but Wade, don't let Officer Hutchens get away before I have a chance to talk to him. It's important."

Wade glanced at Joe once again.

"Not about me, but I can back her up if she needs it."

"What are you two talking about?"

Andi went to Wade and slipped her arm through his. "I think we may have gotten a break tonight. I'll fill you and Hutchens in after the meeting. Let's go back inside."

The three of them went inside, and Andi admitted to herself that after years of feeling like she had to have the backs of six people, it was okay to let others have her back. It was a good feeling to have.

***

Ryan Stewart, Andi's Treasury Department contact in her former life, relayed the information over the phone. As Andi sat at the kitchen table and listened, she downed one cup of coffee and got up to pour another.

"This was not an easy nut to crack."

"How many channels did you have to go through?"

"Too many to count. This isn't your average small town, basement level operation. Whomever these guys work for, he knows what he's doing."

"You're sure there's a higher up?"

"There always is," he assured her. "Unfortunately, they're a lot harder to catch than their local yokels."

"So Mitchem owns the website domain for the corporation. Pretty sloppy of him, wasn't it?"

"Believe it or not, it's pretty common. We're able to trace a lot of shell corporations to individuals through a simple Whois lookup. It gives domain ownership, IP addresses, the physical address the website is connected to, contact information, and website creation dates. Most people never think about that info being connected to their site. A lot of these guys make the mistake of putting in their own names, but even without a real name or address, it's easy to pinpoint the owners through their IPs."

"And you're sure it's a shell? Wade called the number on the site, and he got a real person on the other end, a receptionist named…" She thought for a minute. "Jade. That's it."

Ryan laughed. "Ever heard of jade.com?"

"No. What's that?"

"A virtual answering service. They've got a whole room full of Jades. They're paid to act like they're real receptionists in brick and mortar offices."

"And that's legal?"

"Most of the companies they work for are legitimate. Saves big bucks on having a real office and paid staff."

"Huh. What about the other names I gave you? You said you had hits on them, too."

"Yeah. I just followed the money for that. Buffalo Springs Enterprises is channeling money through several banks using wire transfers, payouts to other shells, and internet money transfers. I traced the paths of the payments to several offshore accounts. Some of those were impossible to see through, but others, particularly in Panama and the Virgin Islands, were pretty easy to follow. I then compared that list of banks to the banks Callahan and Marshall had ties to. Oh, and one other guy from the list you gave me, a Brian Cleburn, was also flagged."

"None of the other former council members?"

"No, just the three. Oh, and the accountant had accounts at the same banks as the corporation."

"Did you go through the ICIJ?"

"Yeah, the International Consortium of Investigative Journalists was the first place I contacted. You know what they do—expose cross-border crime, corruption, and accountability of power."

"Yeah, the Navy works with them to track cartels."

"So does the Coast Guard. And we use them to take down tax evaders, and other high-dollar criminal pursuits."

Andi leaned back in the kitchen chair. "This is great information. So, what do I do with it now?"

"You don't have to do anything with it. It's already been sent to the IRS, ATF, DEA, FBI, and Homeland Security. I'd say it's only a matter of time before your little town is overrun with men in black suits."

"How much time?"

"Well, we are talking about my fellow government associates, so I can't speculate on that. Could be a day, could be six months to a year."

"Great. Nothing like the federal bureaucracy. What about their holdings? Will we be able to purchase the buildings and open businesses, or will they become the property of the US Government?"

"Normally, they would become civil forfeitures and eventually go up for auction if proven to be legally owned by the perpetrators."

Andi groaned. "Then it could take years for us to be able to get our hands on them."

"Potentially, yes, but there are loopholes that may apply here."

Andi sat up. "Like what?"

"Like Buffalo Springs Enterprises doesn't actually exist. There's nobody with legal claim to the properties, so they would most likely be turned over to the local bank for resale or auction."

"How long would that take?"

"That's not my call, but I'll see if I can pull a few strings."

"Do you think it's possible?"

"Andi, anything is possible."

***

Wade was tied up with the state police the entire day, identifying the men from the parking lot and refining the plan to follow them to wherever the meth was being stashed. He took the time to hear Andi's news but those few minutes were the only communication they had all day. Andi wanted to be part of the sting, but Wade and the police forbid her participation. She argued with Wade, citing her military training and experience, but he refused to give in. Feeling at loose ends after talking to Ryan, she spent most of the day pacing in the library.

"For goodness sakes, you're driving me insane," Helena told her around three in the afternoon. "Please, go get in a run or something."

"Fine." Andi huffed and stomped her way out of the library.

She drove to the house, changed her clothes, grabbed her phone and AirPods, and hit the road. She cranked up the music as loud as her ears could stand it, pounding her feet on the asphalt, winding her way around the town, and down the road toward Wade's house. Maybe she'd stop by and see if Boomer wanted to go for a run.

Andi thought about everything that was about to go down in the town, from the drug bust to the impending arrival of the Feds. In her mind, she weaved a web, an image of the threads that connected Wade, the council members, the buildings, the accounts, and the contraband. It was quite the web of deceit, lies, and corruption.

Vehicles passed by, some too close for comfort, and Andi hugged the narrow grassy strip between the shoulder and the drainage ditch as she left the town limits. It hadn't rained in weeks, and dust filled her airways as she ran.

When Wade's farm was in sight, Andi looked both ways and, not seeing any vehicles, crossed the road. She was almost to Wade's driveway when she sensed movement beside her. As *Firestone* by Kygo blasted in her ears, she turned her head just in time to recognize the blunt end of a baseball bat. In less time than it took for her to register what was happening, she was flying into the ditch, blood gushing from her temple, her world turning black.

***

"And you haven't heard from her at all?" Helena looked out the window, her phone pressed to her ear.

"Not today. Is she with Wade?" her brother asked.

"No. He's got his hands full with something. She wouldn't say what, just that he was busy, and she was forbidden from being a part of it. She was fit to be tied, I tell you."

"When was the last time you saw her?"

"Around three, I think. She was going to go for a run."

"Didn't the police tell her not to go anywhere by herself?"

"Yes, but I'm afraid that was my doing. I encouraged her to go."

"It's not your fault. You know how she is about taking risks. Have you called Wade?"

"I don't have his number. I can call the office though."

"I've got Wade's cell. Andi gave it to me the night we, uh, one night that we were out together. I'll call as soon as I get to the house." He hung up before Helena had time to think about what he said.

She went to the kitchen and turned on the hot pot to make some tea. She was a nervous wreck, waiting for Andi to walk in the door. She nearly jumped out of her skin when her phone buzzed. She looked at the caller ID. It was her mother.

"Hey, Mama. What's up?" She tried to keep her voice calm so that she didn't alarm her mom.

"Helena, do you know someone named Joe Blake?"

"Joe Blake? He's a friend of Andi's. Why?"

"I just got a call from him. I didn't answer of course. Those pesky telemarketers. You never know when it's one of them. Anyway, he left a message saying to call him about Andi. I wasn't going to call because I don't know who he is, do you? I couldn't really hear what he was saying. There was a lot of noise—"

"Mama, what's his number?" She grabbed a pen and paper out of the kitchen junk drawer and scribbled down the number. "Okay, I have to go. I'll call you back."

Helena called, and Joe picked up on the first ring. "Hi, Joe. This is Andi's sister, Helena. What's going on?"

"I'm at Washington Regional Hospital with Andi. She's been involved in an accident."

"An accident? What kind of accident?"

"I'm not sure to be honest. She's having some x-rays done now. Can you come up?"

"I'll be there in less than an hour."

Helena switched off the pot, grabbed her purse, and raced out of the house into the cold, autumn twilight. She plugged her phone into her car and called Jackson, telling him to meet her outside of their parents' house.

"Don't tell mom. I don't want to worry her. Let's see what's going on first."

"She's not going to be happy," Jackson said.

"Oh, well," Helena told him. "I'd rather have all the facts before I get her and Daddy upset."

By the time Helena pulled up out front, Jackson was climbing out of his car. "What's going on?"

She relayed what little she knew, but there was little conversation. Helena wondered if Jackson knew more than he was saying about whatever was going on, but Helena was too worried about her sister's condition to pull it out of him.

Joe was waiting for them in the hospital lobby. He was wearing jeans and a button-down shirt that had blood on it. Helena looked at the blood and then at Joe's eyes, clothed in worry.

"Where is she?"

"X-ray."

"What happened?" Jackson asked as they followed Joe to an elevator.

"I don't know. I heard the call on the scanner and went to the scene. They were waiting for the medivac. Said some guy's dog found her lying in a ditch."

Andi was back in her room when they got to the doorway.

"Is she okay?" Helena rushed into the room and sat on the side of the bed. Andi's head was bandaged almost like a mummy, except the bandages were mainly on one side. A nurse checked her monitors.

"She seems to be fine," a nurse said. "You are?"

"Her sister." Helena motioned to Jackson. "And brother."

The nurse nodded in acknowledgment. "She needed several stitches. And the swelling and bruising are pretty bad. She's been sedated for the pain."

"Swelling and bruising from what?"

Joe walked to the other side of the bed. "Some kind of blunt force trauma."

"I need to call mama." She reached into her purse, but Joe gently laid a hand on her arm.

"Of course, but I'd tell her to wait until morning to come see her. She's been given an anti-inflammatory for the swelling and the pain, and they gave her a sedative to help her sleep. For now, she needs to rest."

Helena eyed him suspiciously. "How do I know I can trust you? Where's the doctor on call?"

Joe sighed. "I'm sure he'll be back soon."

"I'll tell him you'd like to see him," the nurse said. She smiled at them and left the room.

Helena lowered her voice as she leaned toward Joe. "Do you think someone did this to her?"

Joe nodded. "I've seen my fair share of assaults, and I'd bet my license that she was hit with something, hard and with a lot of force. She went down hard. Her wrist is swollen. Maybe a fracture. Some scratches on her face where she hit the ditch."

"Who would do this to her?"

"Someone who doesn't like the changes going on around town," Jackson said. "Probably the same person who threw the rock through the window and slashed my tires." He looked at Helena. "We have to call Wade."

"Andi said he wouldn't be available tonight."

"She's right," Joe said. "There weren't even any officers at the accident. The firemen and EMTs had it under control. But I was with Wade and Andi last night when they were talking about something going on tonight."

"Last night was the meeting at the library," Helena said, furrowing her brow as she looked at Joe.

"Yeah, it was during the meeting. I'm not sure I'm supposed to say anything else."

"Could whatever is going on with Wade have something to do with Andi being hurt?" Jackson's voice was flush with anger.

"Related maybe, but I don't think directly."

"You're talking in riddles, and I want to know what's going on," Helena said, her voice shrill. Andi stirred.

"Not here." Joe motioned for them to follow him. He led them to a family waiting room down the hall. It was currently empty, and he gestured toward the orange and tan plaid chairs.

Helena took a seat on the couch, and Jackson sat beside her.

"What do you know?" she asked

Joe sat across from them. "Not much. There's going to be some kind of raid tonight. At least, I think that's what's going on. I'm not privy to anything specific. I only know what Andi and I heard in the parking lot last night."

Jackson and Helena exchanged looks. "Parking lot?" she asked.

"It was during the meeting. Andi followed some guys outside, and I followed her. They looked like trouble."

"And?" Jackson leaned back, his arms across his chest.

"It sounded like they were planning on moving something, the drugs we think, sometime tonight. Andi and Wade let that Officer Hutchens in on it after everyone was gone. I offered to stick around to give my account, but they said there was no need."

"Do you think they knew Andi was there?" Helena bit her bottom lip, fear climbing her spine.

"I don't think so. No, I think whoever hit Andi is probably connected to this whole thing, but I don't think those guys know we overheard them. I could be wrong though." He sat back in the chair and clasped his hands together. "That's all I know."

Helena thought about what he said. She wasn't ready to trust Joe, but he seemed to be genuinely concerned about Andi.

"I'm staying here tonight. I want to be here when she wakes up."

"I don't blame you." Joe stood. "Why don't I see if I can find the doctor and bring him here? Maybe he has some answers from her tests by now." He stood but paused, reaching his hand into his pocket and retrieving a phone and AirPods. He reached out to hand them to Helena. "These are Andi's. The EMT gave them to me at the scene. They're all Andi had on her at the time."

"Thank you," Helena said, taking the phone and putting it in her purse.

After he left, Jackson sat back down next to his sister. "What do you think?"

"I think he's right. Maybe it was the same guy who followed her the other day."

"I think so, too. Most likely the same person who's been doing all this crap." Jackson looked back over his shoulder. "You trust him?"

"Not a bit." Helena pursed her lips. "You don't trust him either."

"I don't trust anybody in Buffalo Springs right now, and I think I should text Wade."

Helena gave it some thought but shook her head. "Not tonight. If Joe's right, he's got enough on his mind."

"He'd want to know."

"I know but wait until tomorrow. Hopefully she'll be awake and will remember something."

"He's in love with her, you know?"

"I suspected as much." She smiled. "You're pretty perceptive little brother."

"I'm not blind. Anybody who sees the way he looks at her would know."

"What about her?"

"I think she loves him, too, but I don't think she knows it yet."

"I think you're right there, too. Let's hope she figures it out before he heads back to New York."

"You think he'll still go back?"

"Do you plan on sticking around town once you have your degree?"

Jackson shrugged. "I don't know. I guess that depends upon what happens with the town."

"Let's hope His Honor, the Mayor, realizes our town is exactly what he needs."

"And that he's exactly what Andi needs."

Sixteen

    Andi stood on the diving board, willing herself not to look down. She'd already seen one of the other girls in her class refuse to jump. She'd been escorted right from the pool to her room to collect her things. To be in the Navy, one had to be willing to plunge into the water, and that meant starting with a ten-meter jump into the pool, and it was Andi's turn to prove she belonged there.

    She looked at the rafters that ran the length of the ceiling in front of her eyes. She was darn high. She swallowed, closed her eyes, and took a deep breath. Following instructions, she jumped as high as she could into the air and away from the board. She felt herself slicing through the air before being consumed by the cold water. She thought her lungs would burst as she plummeted down, but it was her head that was exploding. Pain shot through her brain, and she fought to make it to the surface. She flailed her arms, but water continued to fill her head. She could feel it. Her brain was swimming in the liquid. She had to get to the top.

"Andi, Andi, wake up."

Her eyes flew open, and she gasped for air. Her rapid breathing was shallow, and her lungs burned.

"Andi, it's okay. You're okay."

She turned toward his voice, her eyes locking with his. What was he doing here? He wasn't in her class. He should be…where? Her mind was fuzzy.

"Jeremy?" she croaked out between breaths.

He took hold of her shoulders, his eyes never leaving hers. Those eyes. She would never forget those eyes. But…he was…

"Andi, it's Joe. You're in the hospital. Helena and Jackson are getting coffee."

Andi blinked, breaking the hold those eyes had on her. "Joe," she whispered. She slowly moved her gaze around the bright, unfamiliar room. "I did the jump."

"You jumped? You didn't fall?"

She squeezed her eyes shut, trying to make sense of his question. Her head ached. She opened her eyes and tried to focus both her vision and her mind.

"I jumped from the high dive. I…we had to jump."

"You were dreaming."

No, it wasn't a dream. She did jump. But that was sixteen years ago, her plebe summer. And Jeremy wasn't there.

"What happened?" she asked.

"We don't know. Someone's dog found you in a ditch out on the outskirts of town. Helena said you went for a run."

Andi squeezed her eyes shut and willed herself to remember what happened. "I ran through town, then I headed toward Wade's. Boomer. I was going to get Boomer."

"Boomer?"

"Wade's dog. I was going to take Boomer on a run. I was almost there." Suddenly, her eyes opened, and her heart gave a jump. "A car, or a truck, something. I don't remember. It was too close. I turned to look, and something hit me. That's all I remember."

"That makes sense. You were definitely hit by something. You've got a lot of swelling and bruising. You needed seventeen stitches, some inside and some out."

She reached up and touched the bandages. Just the light pressure of her hand made her flinch. Her wrapped wrist throbbed.

"I was afraid you might have a facial fracture, but you don't. You do have a concussion and a sprained wrist. They did x-rays last night and may do a CAT scan this morning."

"My sister. She's probably worried out of her mind. I've got to call her." She looked frantically for her phone, but the movement made her feel dizzy.

"I told you. They're already here."

Andi's heart did another leap. "Are they okay?"

Joe laid his hands on her leg to still her. "Andi, they're fine. They're getting coffee. They were worried about you. We all were. I got your parents' number from information. I didn't know who else to call since Wade was tied up. Honestly, Andi, I didn't want to involve anyone else."

"Does Wade know?"

"Not yet. I didn't want to bother him with everything else that's going on."

A sudden cold chill ran down her spine. "Wade! Is he okay? Did everything go all right last night?" She started to sit up, but dizziness overcame her.

"Wade's fine as far as I know. I've been here with you all night."

A pit formed in her stomach, and a feeling of dread washed over her. She wanted to see Wade, needed to know that he was okay. Between the dizziness, the news from Joe, her worry about Wade, and the medication, Andi's head began to spin.

"I need…"

"What do you need, Andi?"

Joe took her hand and squeezed it, but she felt herself fading. She sank into the pillow.

"I'm so tired."

"That's normal. I'll tell the nurse you're awake."

She closed her eyes and saw Wade's face floating in front of her.

"Wade," she whispered as she drifted off to sleep.

***

It was almost ten in the morning by the time Wade checked on his mother and fell into bed. Exhaustion invaded every cell of his body yet sleep eluded him. The chilly night gave way to a blustery day, and Wade was glad to be inside the warm house.

The sting had gone as planned. Half a ton of meth was seized in the raid on a local barn, along with more than three dozen weapons of various kinds, and too much money to be counted at the scene. It looked to be a record breaker in the state's drug enforcement history. The take confirmed their suspicions that this wasn't just your average neighborhood operation. These men were raking in big money and probably distributing to states near and far. The one thing that was not found was the lab. With that amount of meth being readied for distribution, a lab had to be nearby.

Wade and the police were just as busy fighting off local press as they were making the arrests. How did the press always know when something like this happened?

Two local ne'er-do-wells had been arrested, their trucks fitting the descriptions of the ones Andi and Joe had given the night before. Along with them was Shane Callahan, son of former council member, Bud Callahan, and driver of the green truck that had followed Andi. It was something Shane had said as he was being folded into the squad car that had Wade rattled that morning.

"That lady of yours had a might pretty face for a squid. Shame it couldn't stay that way."

"Squid?"

"Navy officer," the police officer replied as he shut the door on Callahan. "I've heard my brother use the term. He's Army."

Wade watched the man through the window as the car pulled away, his grin imprinting itself in Wade's mind. Was that a threat? If so, was there still someone around to carry out whatever the threat was? Was Shane just trying to get to Wade? If so, it worked. Wade's sense that something was wrong nagged him for close to an hour, and he grudgingly gave up trying to get any rest.

His phone sat on the nightstand next to the bed, but when Wade tapped the screen, nothing happened. He pushed the button on the side of the device only to continue to see nothing but a black screen. He reached for the cord that hung from the outlet and plugged in the phone. After a second or two, a red battery lit the screen. Wade would have to wait for more charge before he could use his cell. He pulled himself from bed and made his way into the hallway where a central line sat on a small table in case of an emergency with his mother. He picked up the phone and realized he didn't know any numbers off hand. He slammed down the receiver, cursing the pitfalls of modern technology. He picked it back up and dialed one of the few numbers he knew by heart.

"Good morning, Mayor Montgomery's Office."

"Trudy, hey. How are things there this morning?"

"Quiet so far. Long night?"

"Was there a night? Seems like one long day that won't end."

"That bad, huh?"

"No, that good." He rubbed his hand over the stubble on his chin. "Listen, have you seen or heard from Andi this morning?"

"Negative. Are you expecting her?"

"No, not officially." Though he assumed she would've been waiting on his doorstep to hear the details about the raid. "Do you know her number? My cell is dead."

"I should have it here."

Wade knew that Trudy had a habit of copying numbers from caller ID and saving them. It wasn't a stretch to believe she had saved Andi's number weeks ago.

"You want me to give it to you or call?"

"Give it to me. I'll call."

Trudy rattled off the number, and Wade repeated it several times to make sure he knew it before thanking her and hanging up.

Andi's phone went straight to voicemail, and Wade's stomach churned. There was no way she'd turn off her phone or let it die. Not today. He knew she would be chomping at the bit to hear what happened. He tried again with the same result before calling Trudy back.

"I hate to bother you again."

"You're the boss. What's up?"

"You have Jackson's number, right?"

"I do. Is everything okay?"

"I'm not sure. I've got this gut feeling that Andi might be in trouble."

"If there's one gal who can take care of herself, it's Andi. I'm sure she's fine. Ready for the number?"

This time, there line, rang but in the end, Wade's call went to voicemail. Cursing again, he tried to calm his nerves with a long, hot shower.

The shower did little to calm him, but at least he felt more human after having washed off the dirt and dust from the night before. With a towel wrapped around his waist, he checked his phone. It was not fully charged, but it had powered on while he was in the shower. There were no messages. He called Andi, but the call still went to voicemail. Again, Jackson's rang several times, but he didn't pick up.

Trying not to panic, Wade looked up the number for the library. He was about to hang up when the call connected, and Helena's voice came on the line.

"Buffalo Springs Library. Thank you for calling. The library is open Monday through Friday, nine a.m. until five p.m. If you're calling during business hours—"

Wade disconnected the call and threw the phone on the bed, pulling the cord from the wall. He let the towel drop to the floor as he rushed to his closet. He hastily pulled on khakis and a button-down, jammed his feet into socks and shoes, and bolted down the stairs. Blanche sat in her favorite chair, reading a book while Melanie worked on her laptop.

"Good morning, Mama." He leaned down and kissed his mother on the cheek. To Melanie, he said, "Thanks for staying over last night. I've got to run. You okay for the day?"

"We're fine. Don't you want something to eat? You missed breakfast, and it's almost time for lunch."

"No, thanks. Gotta run. Hoping to knock off early today. I'll let you know."

"It's all good. Miss Blanche and I will hold down the fort."

Wade wasn't sure where he was heading, but he'd turn the town inside out before he'd rest. Wherever Andi was, she was in trouble. He could feel it in his bones.

***

"No facial fractures, though it's going to hurt for some time." The doctor repeated to Andi what Joe had already told her. "Your wrist is sprained and will need to be in a splint for about a week, but nothing is fractured or broken there either. You're going to be in pain for some time, but it could have been worse."

"Pain is weakness leaving the body," Andi said despite the throbbing in her face and wrist.

Helena rolled her eyes and spoke to the doctor. "Ignore her. Can she go home?"

"I can release her, but I do want her to take it easy." He addressed Andi. "I won't subject you to a CAT scan, but you do have all the signs of a mild concussion. No running for at least a week, maybe two. Limit any kind of screen time for a few days. Just try to relax."

Helena scoffed. "Do you know who you're talking to?"

Andi blew out an annoyed breath. "I can take it easy, Doc. Don't worry about me."

"I'll make sure she takes it easy. I'm closing the library for a couple days to take care of her."

"Oh, no you're not," Andi protested. "I don't need a babysitter."

"It's either me, or I'm taking you to Mama and Daddy's."

"Please," she implored the doctor. "Admit me."

"Oh, hush now," Helena admonished her, but Joe interceded.

"I don't think she needs to be watched like a hawk, but Andi, he's serious about taking it easy."

"I am," the doctor reiterated.

"Excuse me." Joe pulled his phone from his pocket and looked at the screen. His brows netted in confusion. "I don't recognize this number. Mind if I take it?"

"No, go ahead," Andi told him.

Joe exited through the curtain as a nurse entered with the splint and an Ace bandage to properly wrap Andi's wrist. Joe hurried back in on her heels.

"Andi, it's for you." He reached around the nurse with the phone.

"Me?" She took the phone and held it to her ear with her good hand. "Hello?"

"Andi, thank God. Where are you?"

"Wade? How did you—"

"Your mother. She said the last she heard, you were with Joe. She had his number on her caller ID."

"Is everything okay? How did it go last night?"

"It went fine. I'll tell you later. Where are you?"

Andi hesitated as she watched the nurse expertly wrap her wrist. "Um, well, I'm at Washington Regional Hospital."

"Hospital? Why? What happened? Is someone hurt?"

"I kind of had a bit of an accident."

"Accident? Are you all right?" The panic in his voice was so heart-warming, it made her feel guilty.

"I'm okay. We'll be on the way home soon. Helena is here, too."

"Is she okay?"

"She's fine. She thinks I need a babysitter." Helena stuck her tongue out at her sister, and Andi grinned. "I'm trying to tell her that I'm a big girl and can take care of myself."

"Yeah, I hear that a lot about you. I hope you don't take it the wrong way if I say, I'd like to see for myself. Will you let me know when you get back?"

Andi thought about the bandage on her face that covered the stitches and the giant bruise that stretched from above her eye to below her cheekbone.

"Sure, but Wade, I just want you to know ahead of time that it's not as bad as it looks." She was met with silence. "Wade?"

"Andi, what aren't you telling me?"

"Wade, we think someone hit me. With something like a baseball bat."

"What did you say?" Wade's voice exploded, and Andi had to pull the phone away from her ear. He was still talking when she moved the device closer.

"Wade, stop. I don't know anything else. We can fill you in when I get home. Just…" She hesitated, but her worry propelled her to say what was on her mind. "Be careful, okay? Please, watch your back."

After another minute and many more reassurances, Andi persuaded Wade to hang up. She pressed the button to end the call and looked guiltily at Helena. "He's going to lose it when he sees me."

"That should tell you something," Helena said, gently prodding Andi's shoulder.

While it made Andi's heart swell to think that Wade had feelings for her, she dreaded his reaction to her injuries. She'd witnessed Wade's temper, and though he was good at keeping it under control, she almost felt sorry for the SOB who did this to her if he was within Wade's reach.

***

Wade watched Helena's car pull up to the curb. Though Andi promised to let him know when she was home, he found himself driving down her street and parking his car in front of the house long before she could possibly get there from the hospital. He allowed himself to doze off while he waited, startling with each passing vehicle.

Before Helena was even in park, Wade was standing by the door. He breathed a sigh of relief as he reached for the latch. He could see the sling around Andi's neck, and his fears of worse possibilities drained. Until she turned to get out of the car. Wade's gut wrenched at the sight of her face. He waited patiently for her to stand, then gently pulled her to him, willing himself not to crush her.

"Andi," he heard the anguish in his own voice. "What happened to you?"

"Let's get her inside," Joe said, coming around from his car, parked behind Helena's. "She can fill you in once she's settled." The wind howled, sweeping dust all around them as Joe closed the passenger side door.

Unwilling to let her go, Wade draped his arm around her and walked her up the steps and into the house.

Helena rushed to the couch and plumped a few pillows, motioning for Andi to sit. Wade let go long enough for Andi to get comfortable and then dragged a chair closer to the couch and reached for her hand. Her hand was cold, and he resisted the urge to blow on it and rub some warmth into it. He was afraid of overwhelming her with his concern.

"Can I get you some tea, Andi?" Helena asked.

"Sure, that sounds good." She offered Wade a feeble smile. "I look that bad, huh?"

Joe cleared his throat. "I'll let you all have some privacy. Andi, call me if you need anything. I'll be back at the clinic, setting up shop."

"Thanks, Joe," Andi called. "For everything."

"I'm glad I was here," Joe said before saying goodbye and leaving the three of them alone.

"Where's Jackson?" Wade asked.

"We dropped him off at work on the way into town," Helena said. "I'm going to go see Mama and Daddy shortly if that's okay."

"Of course," Andi said. "Mama is probably a nervous wreck."

"She sounded relieved when I talked to her earlier, but I'm going to make sure she doesn't work herself up into a state. I'm sure she'll be over here before long."

After Andi had her cup of tea, Helena excused herself to run to their parents' house and then to the library for a few hours. Wade promised he'd stay with Andi. When they were alone, he turned to her.

"Are you going to tell me what happened?"

Andi relayed what she remembered. She still wasn't sure what hit her, but she had a vague recollection of a speeding vehicle coming out of nowhere and of seeing a baseball bat coming at her face. She had no idea who hit her, but Wade was pretty sure he knew. His blood boiled, and he was grateful that he had promised to stay with Andi because if he'd been free, he would've driven all the way to the jail in Little Rock and wrapped his hands around Shane Callahan's throat.

By the time Andi finished recalling what she could, her eyes were slowly blinking, and Wade knew she needed to rest.

"Dale's going to come by later, and you'll have to tell all of this over again, okay?"

She nodded sleepily.

Wade reached across her to take down the blanket that was stretched across the back of the couch and gently covered her as her eyes began to close.

"Wade," she whispered.

He took her hand. "I'm here, Andi."

"Don't leave me."

It was only the second time he'd seen her admit her vulnerability, and he was flooded with memories of the night he held her while she cried. It occurred to him that it was that night when he began to fall in love with her.

***

Andi awoke in the late afternoon as the sun created long shadows in the room, and she heard the wind continue to howl. She stretched but winced as pain shot through her wrist and her cheek at the same time. She was stiff and sore and aching to move around. When she pushed herself up to a sitting position, she noticed the figure sprawled in the recliner across the room.

Wade was sound asleep, and Andi realized he hadn't told her anything about the raid. She didn't have the heart to wake him, but curiosity was killing her. She spotted her phone on the end table, and despite the doctor's orders, she reached for it, and plugged it into the charger Helena kept by the couch. It seemed to take eons before it was powered enough for her to turn it on and navigate to the search engine. She scrolled through news headlines until she found what she was looking for.

State and Local Police conduct one of the most successful drug raids in Arkansas history.

The story went on to detail the amount of meth, weapons, and cash found in an old barn on an abandoned property about five miles from town. The owners were an older couple, one dead and one in a nursing home with no local relatives. The raid was conducted, according to the article, by the head of the state police drug task force and the newly sworn in chief of police of Buffalo Springs, Dale Mackenzie.

Wade wasn't mentioned, and Andi wondered if he had purposely stayed away from the reporters. She thought about Dale and his sweet wife, Ruth, now a couple weeks into chemo, and she felt a wave of sadness that she didn't have time to dwell on.

"Didn't Helena say you aren't supposed to be on your phone?"

Andi looked over the phone to see Wade reaching his arms to the ceiling in a long, joint-cracking stretch.

"I needed to find out what happened last night. You don't seem in any hurry to fill me in."

"Hmph. I think we had more important matters to deal with."

He stood and excused himself to use the bathroom, and Andi realized she needed to do the same. She waited for him to come back before taking her turn. When she returned, she saw Wade standing in front of the window, and she went to him. As if it was the most natural thing in the world, Wade wrapped his arms around her and pulled her to him. She rested her head on his shoulder, and the thought occurred to her that she could stay there forever, wrapped in the cocoon of his arm. She breathed a sigh of contentment, but the moment was shattered by a knock at the door.

"I'll get it," Wade said. He escorted her back to the couch and went to the door.

Police Chief Mackenzie inquired about her health, and Andi assured him she was up to answering questions. Just as he wrapped up his questioning, Andi heard a unison of vibrating buzzing.

Wade and Dale simultaneously reached for their phones.

"Mackenzie."

"Montgomery."

Andi was watching Wade and saw his body stiffen. His face was awash with fear.

She blocked out whatever Dale was saying and concentrated on Wade's one-sided conversation.

"Is my mother all right?"

Andi's heart constricted.

"Yes, I'll be right there." He disconnected and shoved the phone in his pocket.

"Follow me," Dale said as he put his phone back in his pocket.

Wade stood and turned to Andi. "Somebody torched the trees along the driveway. It spread to some of the stubble in the field as well. Thank God Melanie saw the flames and called it in before it reached the house."

Andi's hand went to her mouth. "Oh, Wade. Blanche is okay?"

He nodded. "Pretty shaken up. Melanie said she was already having a bad afternoon. I have to go. Eric will be outside if you need anything."

"Okay." She wanted to go with him, but she knew it would lead to an argument, so she didn't ask.

Dale headed for the door, but Wade hesitated for a moment before leaning down and pressing a firm but short kiss to Andi's lips. Without a word, he turned, grabbed his jacket, and followed Dale out the front door.

As Andi watched the men leave, she absent-mindedly lifted her fingers to her lips where she could still feel the tingling sensation of Wade's kiss.

For a brief moment, she thought of the kiss she shared with Jeremy and the power of that moment. It was what she had longed for and prayed for, unlike Wade's unbidden kiss that she hadn't even known was what her heart was hoping for all along.

They were very different men, and the circumstances of her meeting them both could not have been more different. Even the first kiss she experienced with both men were worlds apart. Jeremy's kiss was passionate, full of desperation and heat, but somehow, Wade's short, tender kiss evoked a deeper and more profound wave of emotions within her. Though she had sensed her feelings for him growing and changing over the past couple weeks, she hadn't realized until that simple, chaste kiss just how far she had fallen.

She loved Jeremy and always would. A piece of her died in the desert with him, and he would always hold a special place in her heart. But she now recognized that the rest of her heart belonged to Wade.

Seventeen

Wade screeched the car to a halt at the end of the driveway behind Dale's cruiser. There were fire trucks and an ambulance blocking the entrance to the farm. A sick feeling rose up in him at the site of ambulance. It took him a moment to come to his senses as he watched plumes of smoke roll toward the sky. Shaking himself out of his trance, he jumped from the car and ran to the ambulance, relieved to find it empty.

"Wade!"

He searched for Dale and saw the chief waving to him several yards down the driveway.

"Do you know what the heck happened?" he asked, barely able to catch his breath as his heart drummed in his chest. The beautiful cherry and plum trees that had lined the driveway for three generations of Montgomerys were no more than blackened poles sticking out of the charred ground. Some still burned, and firemen battled the flames. Wade felt the urge to cry as memories of picking fruit with Jolene flooded his mind.

"According to the Chief Rollins, they were torched."

"How does he know?" Wade fought to catch his breath as the stench of burnt wood and grass filled his senses.

The fire chief pointed to the trees. "There's a pattern. Every other tree was intentionally burned. The ones in between ignited from the wind. It's a prime day for a fire to spread - dry and windy."

With this news in mind, Wade surveyed the sight again and saw the pattern. Every other tree was completely gone. The ones in between were in various stages of burning to the ground themselves. There wasn't much the firemen could do other than contain the flames so that they didn't spread any farther across the stubble or get caught and carried by the wind.

"Where's my mother?"

Dale jerked a thumb toward the house. "Inside. Go ahead. I'm going to monitor the scene and assess damage. With this wind, it could have been a lot worse." Dale looked toward the house, and nausea seized Wade as he thought of his mother facing her worse fear.

Wade sprinted the length of the driveway, pushing himself like he'd done in his days at Notre Dame. In the back of his mind, he remembered Andi teasing him about being out of shape. Maybe he needed to start joining her on her runs. He tried to clear his thoughts as he ran to the house, but his mind was all over the place.

He bounded up the stairs and threw open the door. Boomer greeted him with barks and leaps. He jumped up, enthused with more excitement than usual, and slammed his large paws into Wade's chest.

"Oof," Wade exclaimed. "Down, boy." He gently pushed the dog away. "Mama!" he called, running into the parlor only to find her chair empty.

"I had to put her to bed," Melanie said from the stairway. "I gave her a sedative. Between the fire and Boomer's barking, she was really agitated. She wouldn't stop crying and said she needed to get her daddy from the barn."

Wade fought back the urge to vomit. "Her father was badly burned in a barn fire when she was a child. She's always been afraid of any flames bigger than the ones in the fireplace."

"That explains it." Melanie leaned against the wall, looking as tired as all get out.

"Go on home. If you can't get your car down the drive, ask one of the police to take you."

"Are you sure?"

"I'm sure. I won't be going anywhere tonight."

Wade saw the look of gratitude in her eyes, but true to her nature she said, "Call me if you need to leave. I'll understand."

"Thanks, but you get some rest. I'll deal with things here."

"I'll try. I've got a test this week, so I'll be up studying."

"Good luck with the studying. I'll see you in the morning."

"Thanks." Melanie brushed past him and said good night.

Wade made his way up the steps and looked in on his mother. She slept peacefully, sedated by the medication prescribed for her most agitated states.

Wade went back downstairs and poured himself a large glass of iced tea. He watched from the window as the last flames were doused with water. Dale made his way toward the house, and Wade poured a second glass of tea before meeting him at the door.

"Thank you," Dale said, accepting the glass. "May I come in?"

"Of course." Wade stepped out of the way to let Dale enter. "Let's go to the kitchen."

They sat the table, and Wade apologized. "Not what you needed after that long night."

"Same for you, Wade." Dale told Wade what they knew. "No witnesses. No clues found at the scene. They were in and out before anyone knew what was happening."

"They had the weather on their side."

"They did, and possibly numbers, too."

"What do you mean?"

Dale took a long drink before he continued. "There were multiple tire tracks up and down the driveway, but nothing we could trace. Too much foot traffic, emergency vehicles, dragged hoses, and such. Do you have security cameras?"

Wade shook his head. When had they ever needed cameras out here?

"Didn't think so."

"So, there's nothing we can do?"

"I'll certainly investigate. I've got a couple guys tracking down Mitchem and crew, questioning their whereabouts, taking down their alibis."

"They will have covered their tracks."

"I think so, too. They're bound to be hot under the collar after last night."

"You'd think they'd be in Little Rock baling out their thugs."

"No bail. They got Judge North which is bad news for them. He's going to let them sit and stew for a bit before the arraignment. And their passports have been revoked."

"Good. I hope they're getting a good taste of what the rest of their lives are going to look like."

"Bud Callahan made a scene at the station, yelling about us violating his son's rights and how he's going to hire the best lawyer money can buy. I'm sure he'll try to fight this, but we caught Shane red-handed."

"Speaking of Callahan, what are your thoughts about Andi?" Wade asked. "Any chance of being able to file charges?"

"I spoke briefly to Eric outside. When he gets back to the station, he's going to go to the impound lot and search Shane's car for a bat or similar instrument.

Whatever he finds, he'll send to the state to check for DNA. He may need to get a swab from Andi in order to match anything they find. Hopefully it was Callahan's DNA on it, too."

"You think he kept it? I would've ditched it right after the attack."

Dale frowned. "He kept it. Too cocky not to. Anybody who would drive close enough to somebody to hit them in the face in broad daylight isn't worried about getting caught."

Wade considered that. "Makes sense." He finished his tea and set the glass down. "Dale, they knew I was out all night. For all they knew, I was in bed asleep. What if I had been? What if Melanie hadn't been here? My mother never leaves the house except to go to the doctor. They could have burned the house down with us inside."

"If they had wanted to set the house on fire, they would have. It was a warning."

"A warning of what?"

"Any number of things. To stop pushing forward with the plans for the town. Stop breathing down their necks about the money. Stop looking for drugs or a lab. All of it combined. You've made some enemies, Wade. Look at all they've done to Andi and her family. I think they're trying to tell you that they're not done yet. Maybe even trying to get you to step down."

"That's not going to happen." Wade was more determined than ever to see all of this through.

"Then I'm going to put a man on your house twenty-four seven. I can assign someone to you as well."

Wade thought about it. "The house, yes. Me, no. I'll be careful. But Andi, can someone watch out for her?"

Dale grinned. "How do you think she'll take that?"

"Not well."

Dale leaned across the table. "Honestly, they may have taken her by surprise and gotten the best of her yesterday, but my guess is, that won't happen again. And woe be the man who tries to get one over on her a second time."

Wade knew Dale was right, but he wasn't willing to take any chances. Andi was a fighter, but she wasn't fighting at the top of her game for the time being.

"How about you put someone on her temporarily, just until she's back on her feet? And we keep it between us."

"I'll do it, but it's on you if she finds out."

Wade agreed, and he couldn't blame Dale. He'd rather face Ted Mitchem and his gang of outlaws than be on Andi's fighting side any day of the week.

"We have the manpower and budget for this?" Wade asked.

"We'll make it work. I'm not sure how, but if I can get the mayor to approve some overtime, we might be okay." Dale grinned.

"Good luck with that. The town's broke, as you well know."

"I know, but we'll figure out a way." Dale stood and Wade pushed himself up to show him to the door.

"Don't worry," Wade assured him. "I'll see to it that everyone in this town gets what he or she deserves."

"I know you will, Wade. Don't worry about Andi or your mom. We've got it under control."

"I don't know what to say, Dale, except thanks. Thank you for everything. I wasn't sure I could trust anybody, and your loyalty to this town means a lot to me."

Dale stopped in the doorway. "To the town and to you, Wade. We've known each other a long time. I've got your back."

"Those are beautiful words to my ears, my friend."

"The whole department is behind you. We're ready to win this town back, and we've got confidence that you can make it happen."

The men shook hands, and Wade watched Dale walk down the porch before closing the door. He prayed that their confidence wasn't misplaced.

***

Helena was in the shower, and Andi stood at the window, arms crossed, head cocked to the side, and toe tapping the hardwood floor. Exasperated, she went back to the couch and picked up her phone, pecking at the screen with her finger. When Wade picked up, she first asked about his mother.

"Better. She ate some supper and is watching television. How are you feeling?"

"Not good, Wade, not good." Before he could reply, she asked, "What's with the surveillance?"

"I should have known you'd spot them."

"That's not an answer."

"Then how's this for an answer." She noted the irritation in his voice as it raised an octave. "You got lucky. Bruises, scratches, a sprained wrist, some stitches, and a mild concussion. My mother got lucky. She didn't burn to death inside her own house. You may think you're invincible, but you aren't. And neither is your family."

She gulped, knowing he was right.

"You know I'm right. You live with your sister. Maybe they thought I was at home today. Maybe they wouldn't have dreamed of targeting my mother. Do I know that for sure? No. Do you know that they won't target Helena's house while you're in it? No. So, if you don't want someone keeping an eye out for your sake, how about for hers?"

"You're right. I hate it, but you're right."

"And here's the other thing."

Andi braced herself for whatever he was about to say.

"All I want is to be there with you, holding you, making sure you're safe, but I can't. I have other responsibilities and worrying about you interferes with those responsibilities. So, how 'bout you do me a favor, and indulge me this one little thing? Let me put someone on your house, just like I've got someone on mine. Give me the gift of not having to worry about that much. I let this town get to this point. I allowed these thugs to run things while I sat with my legs propped on my desk. I laughed at you and your brother and your pie in the sky dreams, but you made me a better man, and because of that, I've got more problems than I know how to deal with. So, get off your high horse, and let me be assured that somebody has your back. And don't tell me you can take care of yourself. Would you have let any of your platoon fly blind without backup? Because that's what you're asking of me. We don't know what these guys will do next. All we can do is sit back and wait for them to make their next move. Well, I won't do it, Andi. I won't let them win. Am I making myself clear?"

Andi's words caught in her throat. She managed a few feeble breaths before answering.

"I'm sorry. You're right. We have a saying, 'don't run to your death.' I wasn't thinking rationally. I wasn't thinking about Helena or about you or anyone else, and it could have gotten me or someone I care about hurt or worse. I won't fight you on this."

"Thank you." She heard him take a deep breath. "One thing you won't have to worry about is Shane Callahan."

"Why? What's happened?"

"I just got a call from Dale. They found a bat in his truck. There was blood on it. We're sure DNA tests will show that it's your blood. Someone's going to be at your tomorrow to take a swab. The DA has gone back to the judge and added assault to the growing list of charges.

And they've lifted prints off it, so they'll be able to figure out who the passenger was that hit you."

Andi felt a swell of relief. "Thank heaven. But, Wade, if that's the case, then why—"

"He wasn't working alone, Andi. You know that. Maybe it was one of the other thugs that was arrested, but maybe not. Someone torched my trees, so the threat is still out there. We're not taking any chances. Now, I've got to get Mama some supper. Can I call you later?"

"Text me first. Even though I've done nothing but lay down all day, I'm tired. I think everything is catching up with me."

"I know exactly how you feel. Go get some rest."

"You, too, Wade. Give your mama a hug for me."

"I will, and Andi…"

"Yes?"

"I…Be careful."

Though he was gone, Andi held the phone to her ear, wishing he had said something else.

***

"How's your supper, Mama?"

"It's very good. Melanie is quite the cook."

Wade smiled. "I cooked Mama. I can do that, you know. You taught me well."

Blanche looked down at the plate then back up at Wade. "I taught you to make this?"

"Well, not this specifically. I don't remember you making Greek chicken and vegetables. But you taught me how to cook. My range of recipes is pretty wide."

Blanche's confused expression changed into a beaming smile. "I'm glad I taught you something. You have so much of your father in you. Sometimes I'm not sure you inherited anything from me."

"That's not true, Mama. I have your green eyes and your love of the outdoors."

Blanche glanced toward the front yard. "How bad was the fire?"

Wade had to force his dropped jaw to close. He finished chewing and swallowed. "It was bad, Mama, but it could have been worse. All forty trees are gone, but the house is okay. We're okay. Do you know what happened?"

Blanche's brow creased, and she pressed her lips together. "I think the trees were on fire, but I don't know how it happened. It wasn't the barn, right?"

"No, it wasn't the barn. That happened a long time ago."

"When I was a little girl," she said quietly.

"Yes, when you were little."

Blanche looked at Wade. "I know what's happening, Wade. I know that I'm forgetting things and that it's happening quickly."

He felt the lump in his throat and was no longer hungry.

"I want you to know that I will always love you and will never forget you." She laid her hand on her heart. "In here, I will always remember."

Wade couldn't speak. He just nodded and blink away a tear.

"I need you to promise me some things."

"Go on," he managed to say.

"First, when things get really bad, it's okay if I can't stay here. I don't want to burden you."

"Mom." He reached for her hand. "You could never be a burden on me."

"Stop. I can and I will. Never let me or my needs get in the way of living your life. I know you moved back home to take care of me, and I love you for that. But don't stop living your life just because I have to stop living mine."

"Okay, what else?"

"Second, having said that, if you have found a home here, then stay as long as you want. The house is yours. Your father and I put it in your name after his diagnosis."

Wade knew the house was in his name. One of the first things he did when he returned to town, after Blanche's diagnosis, was look into her finances. But hearing his mother say the words touched him in a way he never imagined.

"You can sell it or keep it, but my prayer is that you will raise a family here and will love this house and this land as much the past three generations did."

Wade nodded. He forced himself to speak. "Is that all?"

"And third." She reached across the table for his hand. "Andi Nelson. I like her. She's good for you. And I might miss a lot these days, but I haven't missed the way you look at her. Don't let her go. I like the way she looks sitting at this table. It's like she belongs here. With you. Take care of her."

"You know, Mama, sometimes I worry that you don't know where you are or what you're saying, and then other times, you make perfect sense."

"Remember, Wade…" She returned her hand to her heart. "In here, always."

***

As soon as Melanie arrived the next morning, Wade left for the office. He was barely in the door when Trudy threw herself at him, wrapped her arms around him, and squeezed him so tightly he could barely breathe.

"Wade, I heard what happened. Are you okay? Is Aunt Blanche? I wanted to call last night, but Mama said she was sure you would let us know if you needed anything and to let you rest. She had already talked to Melanie, and Melanie said the police and fire trucks were there. How is the farm? How badly damaged?"

"Trudy, slow down. I'm fine. Mama is fine. Actually, she was quite lucid last night. More so than she's been in months. The farm looks pretty bad. We lost all the fruit trees. But the house wasn't touched."

"Oh, it makes me madder than a wet hen that they did that. How dare they? I mean, forget the trees, what if Melanie hadn't seen the flames and it had gotten to the house? I could just wring their cotton pickin' necks."

"I know how you feel, Trudy, but—"

"Excuse me, are you Wade Montgomery?"

Wade turned to see an impressive looking man in a dark suit, carrying a briefcase, with a bulge on his hip that could only imply one thing. Wade reached out his hand.

"Yes, sir, I'm Wade. What can I do for you?"

The man slid his hand into his breast pocket and pulled out a badge. He held it up for Wade to see.

"Agent John O'Neil, ATF." He put the badge away and lifted the briefcase. "I've got a pile of papers in here that show quite an operation taking place in this town. Is there a place we can talk?"

"Yes, sir, right in here." Wade showed the agent to his office. "Trudy, please hold all calls."

Agent O'Neil stopped in the doorway. "We should be joined shortly by Ryan Stewart of the Treasury Department and Richard Mason from DEA."

"I will send them right in. Would you gentlemen like some coffee?"

"Ma'am, if that's not asking too much, I'd be obliged."

"It's no trouble at all. I'll get right on it."

"Thank you, Trudy," Wade said before following the agent into the office.

**

Andi jumped when the doorbell rang. She hoped it was a visitor—Joe, Jackson, her mother, anyone. She was going stir crazy waiting to hear something. It had been nearly an hour since Trudy's text, telling her about the arrival of the ATF agent, and Andi was anxious to hear more.

She tied the belt of her robe and went to the door, peeking through the window to see who was there. She recognized the police officer Wade had sent over but hesitated to open the door. Could she trust him?

Andi felt buzzing in the pocket of the robe and retrieved her phone. There was another text from Trudy.

Wade needs you at the office. The rest of the G-men are here and want to talk to you. Eric will bring you in.

She cracked open the door. "Are you Eric?"

"Yes, ma'am. I've been given the order to bring you to Mayor Montgomery's office as soon as possible."

"I need to change first. Is that okay?"

"Yes, Ma'am. I'll wait out here."

Andi hurried to her room and opened her closet. What did one wear to a meeting with a bunch of G-Men, as Trudy put it? She fingered her dress blues and thought about putting them on. Unlike the other branches, honorably discharged Naval officers were permitted to wear their uniforms for non-ceremonial occasions, and

Andi was tempted. She would feel most comfortable facing the Feds in uniform, but would that be too ostentatious?

Her eyes strayed to the outfit she had worn to a friend's wedding. The wedding was casual, no uniform required, but when Andi went shopping, she gravitated toward the familiar and ended up buying a dress and matching jacket the exact shade of her uniform. She removed the dress from the hanger and put it on, followed by the jacket. Clenching her teeth in pain, she attempted to slide on a pair of nude hose but gave up and cradled her wrist for a moment. She managed to pull her dark hair back into a bun, though it wouldn't have passed muster, and surveyed her face in the mirror.

The mummy bandages were gone but a large bandage protected the stitches on the left side of her temple. The whole side of her face was black and blue, and Andi did the best she could with what little makeup she had. She couldn't completely conceal the bruises, but she thought she looked a little less like Frankenstein's monster.

After slipping on her sensible navy pumps, Andi opened a drawer and reached for the firearm. Since the attack, she'd decided she would carry it beneath her clothes, having already followed the honorable discharge requirements in the Arkansas concealed handgun statute and gotten her permit. She hadn't told anyone she was armed, including Wade, but it made her feel better to know she would have her weapon at her side. She stopped before picking up the gun. It probably wasn't a good idea to take it to a meeting with a group of Feds. She closed the drawer and took a quick glance in the mirror. Even without the gun at her side, she had achieved the look she wanted—confident and classy with a hint of her military past.

***

When the door to the office opened, and Andi stepped inside, Wade's jaw dropped. All three government men stood. Mason saluted.

"Lieutenant Richard Mason, Retired Naval Special Ops, at your service, Ma'am. It's an honor to meet you."

Wade saw Andi's suppressed smile as she saluted back. "At ease, Lieutenant."

Wade stood. "Gentleman, may I introduce Ms. Andrea Nelson, Navy, Seal Team Three Intelligence Command, honorably discharged." He hoped he got all of that correct and in the right order.

Ryan held out his hand. "Andi, it's good to see you." He paused his handshake and took in the bandage and bruises. "Combat wounds?"

Andi grinned slightly. "Something like that. It's good to see you, Ryan."

Trudy quickly scooted an additional chair over from the corner, and Andi took a seat.

"Gentlemen, if I may speak," Ryan said. "It was Andi, Lieutenant Nelson, who brought these matters to my attention."

"I want to congratulate you on a job well done," Agent O'Neil said. "We've been looking to shut down this operation for quite some time, and while we've got a ways to go to close the case, you've really helped us along."

"You knew about all this?" Wade asked.

"Not specifics," Mason said. "We didn't know the who or the where, but we knew there was a large meth operation somewhere in the Ozarks. It's been many years since we detected this level of activity in the area. Not since 2002 has there been a known meth production of this magnitude in Arkansas. Most of the product comes in from Mexico, but over the past year or so, we've seen a rise in meth use here and in the surrounding states that was of a different grade. It led us to believe there may be a lab somewhere in Arkansas, Missouri, or Tennessee."

"If I may, sir?" Andi asked. "We haven't located a lab. How do you know it's here?"

"We're following the money trail you alerted us to," Ryan told her. "From everything we've seen, we're fairly certain it's nearby."

"How will we find it?" Wade asked.

"The first order of business is the arrest of Ted Mitchem, Brian Cleburn, Bud Callahan, and Steve Marshall. We're told that you already have Callahan's son being held on related charges."

"Yes, sir, in Little Rock," Wade said. "Along with two other men."

"We're going to need to talk to them," Agent O'Neil said.

"That can be arranged," Wade assured them. "What else?"

"We have warrants for the other men and will be executing them today."

"Do you need me to go with you?" Wade asked.

"No, sir," O'Neil answered. "In fact, it would best if you and Ms. Nelson weren't there."

"Understood."

Wade listened as they went over a few more logistics then bid the men goodbye.

Ryan stopped at the doorway and turned back to Andi. "Hey, I found out we have a mutual friend, Margaret Gallagher Turner. She was at the NSA for a while and then worked for—"

"Vice President Malone."

"Yeah. Crazy case, that one."

"Margaret was the one who turned him. I can't get over what he did to his own daughter. I'm glad he got caught."

Ryan nodded. "Thanks to Margaret, they got him on that charge plus abuse of power, using government resources for personal reasons, and a host of other offenses. Anyway, she's at Treasury now."

"Tell her I said hello," Andi told him. "I've always admired her."

"Will do," Ryan said before a final goodbye.

When they were gone, Wade went to Andi and pulled her from the chair, mindfully aware not to touch her bad arm.

"Seeing you like this gives me an idea of how you looked in your uniform. I never considered myself a sucker for someone in uniform before."

Andi smiled, her eyes sparkling with interest. "Oh, really? And now?"

Wade removed the hat from her head and, without taking his eyes from hers, and placed it on his desk. He gently pulled her to him. "You've won me over."

"Was it just the uniform that won you?"

Wade's entire body tingled with anticipation as he searched her blue eyes for confirmation that she felt the same. "I think it was the whole package," he said before claiming her lips with his.

Andi returned his kiss, and all thoughts of drug raids, money laundering, meth labs, burned trees, and lunatics with baseball bats fell away as Wade tasted what he had wanted since the day Andi showed up at his office and accused him of wanting to destroy the town.

"Ahem." Trudy's tactful throat clearing caused Wade to jump away from Andi. "Just wanted to let you know that Chief Mackenzie will be accompanying your friends on their house calls."

"Thanks, Trudy."

She stood in the doorway, giving her cousin a devilish grin.

"Is that all?"

"That's all, Wade, but you might want to wipe off that lipstick before you meet back up with the Feds." She strode from the room with an air of delight and closed the door behind her.

"I think I'll head home," Andi said, backing away from Wade. "You've got work to do, and I'm suddenly feeling a bit light-headed. I'm sure my personal escort, Eric, is waiting for me downstairs."

He promised to call her later and watched her walk away, knowing his life would never be the same.

***

"Gone?" Wade repeated. Dale stood in the mayor's office with a disgusted look on his face.

"Gone. They got the arrest warrants and apprehended the other men, but Mitchem and Marshall were nowhere to be found."

"Marshall's office has been closed for weeks." Wade collapsed into his chair. "I'm an idiot for not trying to locate him and keep tabs on them all."

"It wasn't your fault, Wade. I have been keeping tabs. Marshall's been locked up in his house ever since you discovered the discrepancy with the accounts. I've been making regular checks on him. He's been seen taking out the trash, paying the pizza guy, and fetching the morning paper."

"Then where the heck is he now?"

"I wish I knew. Their assets have all been frozen, so they have no money. Even if they purchased tickets to the Caymans before all this went down, they can't get far. The Feds have been tracking their every move as far as their credit cards and bank accounts go, and their passports were revoked of course."

"Then they could still be nearby."

"I would assume so. We just don't know where."

Wade rubbed his hand on his chin. "Okay, so now what?"

"There's an APB out for them throughout the South. They won't be able to go anywhere without being recognized. In addition to their passports, they can't use their credit or debit cards, and their license plates have been flagged."

"You know how much cash we seized. Who's to say they don't have that much more stashed somewhere? They could buy a fleet of cars with that money. Heck, they could charter a Leer jet."

"I hear ya. We're doing the best we can for now."

"I know you are. Thanks, Dale. Keep me informed."

Eighteen

"Amen." Everyone made the Sign of the Cross before they all started reaching for food at the family's Thanksgiving dinner.

"So what's this news you've got for us, Andi?" Jackson asked as he reached for the basket of rolls. "It's been two weeks since the raid and your attack. I'm guessing you've heard something?"

"Do we really have to bring that up today?" Grace asked.

"Don't worry, Mama. We won't dwell on it, but I've got great news." Ryan called. All of the buildings titled to Buffalo Springs Enterprises are going to be signed over to the town. It will take a few months, but it's going to happen."

"That's awesome!" Jackson said. "How'd he pull that off. Daddy, can you pass the beans?"

"Don't ask me. He told me he might be able to work a loophole. I guess he came through."

"That's wonderful, news, Sugar. Potatoes, anyone?" Grace asked.

"Yes, please," Wade said.

"It's so nice to have you two join us." Grace smiled at Wade. Andi shot him a shy smile.

"We're pleased as punch to be here. Aren't we, Mama?"

"It's just lovely, Grace. Thank you."

Grace reached for the frail hand of the woman beside her. "You are always welcome here, Blanche."

Andi smiled at the two women, long-time friends. Her mother felt guilty about not making the time to visit Blanche and suggested she and Wade join them for dinner. Thankfully, Blanche was having a good day and seemed to be enjoying her time out of the house.

"Any word on Ted or Steve?" Joshua asked.

"Not yet, Mr. Nelson. I keep hoping we'll hear something." Wade took a bite of his roll and reached under the table to squeeze Andi's thigh. She felt like she was back in tenth grade with her stomach full of butterflies and her heart doing somersaults.

"Like Jackson said, it's been almost two weeks. Strange that they haven't shown up anywhere," Joshua mused.

"It gives me the creeps, knowing they're out there somewhere," Helena said as she laid a slice of turkey of her plate. "I'm glad your friend, Joe, is opening his clinic across the street from the library. He's been making sure I get to my car safely in the evenings."

Wade and Andi exchanged looks. "Is that so?" Andi said. "I thought you didn't trust him."

"I didn't, but I may be reassessing my first impression." Helena acted nonchalant, but Andi noticed the blush on her sister's cheeks.

"You should have asked him to join us," Grace said.

"Oh, no, I'm not subjecting him to that any time soon, if ever. Besides, he's in Texas with his family."

"Hey, we're not so bad. Are we, Wade?" Grace smiled at their guest.

"Not at all, Ma'am. I'm having a wonderful time." Wade beamed at Andi, and her heart melted.

When they finished eating and the dishes were washed, Wade asked Andi if she wanted to go for a ride the following day. "I'm not working, and it's really starting to get cold out there. I thought it might be nice to take Boomer on one last hike before the temperatures start dipping below freezing."

"I'd like that," Andi said.

"Great. It's a date. Do you want me to pick you up or meet at my house?"

"I'll drive to your house. It's on the way."

"Perfect."

Grace walked out of the kitchen. "Now, Wade, don't forget to take this plate home for your mother and you to have tomorrow."

"I won't, Mrs. Nelson. Thank you for making it. I gave Melanie the day off tomorrow."

"Honey, I'm happy to help with that. I always have way more food than we can eat."

"She means it, Wade. You should take her up on it. Mom could even relieve Melanie some evenings. I'm sure your mom would like the company." Andi suggested.

Wade frowned, sneaking a look at his mother, sitting in the family room with a dazed look on her face. "I don't know. Today was a good day, but most days, she may not know who you are."

"Oh, honey, that's okay. I'd like to spend time with Blanche. We've been friends since way back when. I'd love to help her remember some of the good times we shared, and I think today was good for her."

"In that case, I'll take you up on the offer." He glanced at his mother once more. "She did seem to have a good time, didn't she?"

"She did. We all did," Grace said. "Bring her by any time."

"Thank you, Mrs. Nelson."

Andi watched the exchange and felt like her heart would burst. The day could not have gone any better.

***

The following morning was cloudy. A cold front was predicted for later that afternoon, and the weathermen were in agreement that the much-needed rain was on the way. Andi had doubled-checked her weather app. They should have plenty of time for a hike before the rain started.

She opted for jeans, a long-sleeved tee, and a sweatshirt. She concealed her firearm under the sweatshirt and brushed her hair into a ponytail before stepping back to assess herself in the mirror. She was satisfied that the oversized shirt hid the bulk of the gun. With her coat on, it wouldn't be detected at all.

Andi drove to Wade's and found him and Boomer waiting in the desolate-looking driveway. It broke her heart each time she saw what was left of the trees. A landscaping company had been hired to replace the trees, but it would be well beyond her lifetime before they reached the grandeur of the ones that were lost.

Andi got out of the car and bent down to give Boomer the loving he begged for and was thanked with a sloppy lick across her cheek.

"I have to follow that greeting?" he said, pulling her to him.

"He's a tough act to follow."

He laughed before showing her what a real kiss should be.

"Wow," she breathed, her feet barely touching the ground. "Boomer's got nothing on you."

"What a compliment

"How's your Mama?" she asked as she walked over to Wade's car. "Will she be okay while we're gone?"

"Father Michael comes to visit her on Fridays. He brings Communion, and they talk about the old days when they were in school together."

"How nice of him. I'm sure she enjoys the company."

"She does, and it's good for her. Somehow, she always manages to stay in the present when she's with him."

"What time do we need to be back?" Andi asked.

"I told him we'd be gone a couple hours. He said he's happy to stay since the church office is closed today. He likes to cook, so he brought some stuff to make lunch for the two of them."

"I've met a lot of priests who like to cook. It must be a good creative outlet for them."

"Must be. We should get going. I'd like to beat the rain," he said, opening the passenger side door. Once she was in, he shut the door and ushered Boomer into the back seat.

***

As they hiked, the temperature began to drop, and more clouds filtered in. Boomer tugged on the leash, shaking his head every few minutes in an effort to get loose.

"Oh, let him run. There's not another soul around."

"Because nobody else would be this stupid. It's freezing out here. I don't know what I was thinking." Wade stopped and unhooked the leash, and Boomer bounded ahead of them, stopped to see if they were coming, and then turned and took off down the path.

"Don't worry. He won't go far," Andi assured him

"That's easy for you to say."

They hiked to the highest point of the park and looked out at the mountains that stretched to the horizon.

Wade pointed to one of the peaks. "It's raining up there. Can you see it?"

"What a beautiful sight," Andi said. "It's been dry for so long."

"I've always loved watching the rain as it crosses the mountains. I'd forgotten how much. You don't see anything like this in the city."

"Do you miss it?"

"New York? Not at all. I think this is where God wants me to be." He turned to her. "What about you? Do you miss the excitement of being with the SEALs?"

Andi shook her head. "Not really. It was an adjustment for sure, but like you said, I think I'm where I was meant to be."

She turned back toward the mountain. "Fire and rain," she mused.

"What?"

"The day your trees were burned down. The fire consumed everything in its path until the firemen got it under control. Every time I drive down your driveway, I think, if only it hadn't been so dry. If only it had started raining, maybe some of them could have been saved."

"Fire is a hard thing to control," he said.

"It is, and only one thing can match its strength and intensity. Water. Rain." She continued looking at the mountain in the distance.

"I'm not sure I get where you're going with this."

"Twice, I've been told that I'm like a fire that can't be put out, wild and out of control, raging, consuming, a force to be reckoned with until my mission is complete."

Wade chuckled. "Yeah, I've witnessed that myself."

Andi turned her face toward his. "You're like the mountain rain. Steady, comforting, reassuring, a necessary, life-giving source. People look up to you, welcome your presence, understand that you are there to help, to bring the out of control into focus, to wash away pain and fear and uncertainty."

Wade traced a gloved finger down the side of her face where only a faint yellow line remained of the bruising. "Is that what I do for you?" he asked quietly.

Andi nodded. "You are the rain that quenches my fire. You keep me from losing myself to the darkness, from letting myself be consumed with doubt."

He laid his hand gently on her cheek, the warmth of the glove and the tender look in his beautiful green eyes melting away all her insecurities.

"I love you, Andi."

Her heart swelled, and she blinked away a tear. "I love you, Wade."

***

About a mile outside of the park, Wade pulled over to the side of the road and stopped the car.

"What?" Andi asked.

"There are tire tracks leading to the mill." He pointed to the dirt road outside her window."

"That leads to the mill? I thought the entrance was off Highway 10."

"The main entrance is. This is the service entrance." He steered the car onto the road. "I just want to check it out."

"Isn't this way outside of the town limits?"

"Yeah, but something just feels off."

"Maybe you should call Dale or the county sheriff."

"If anything looks suspicious, we'll call." He drove slowly down the dirt road, and a feeling of dread snaked down Andi's spine. She patted her waist, reassuring herself that her gun was there.

Wade stopped the car just inside the driveway, about a hundred yards or so before the mill, and turned off the engine. "I'm going to sneak up and take a look. I won't be gone long."

Andi took hold of his arm. "There's no way you're going up there alone."

Wade opened his mouth to protest, but Andi gave him a stern look, and he nodded. "Fine, but I'll take the lead."

"I don't think so," Andi said, opening her door. She stood and reached into her shirt, taking the gun from her side.

"What the heck?" Wade said when he rounded the car.

"I've been carrying it since the attack. Don't worry. It's legal."

"That's not what worries me."

Andi looked at Wade. "You're not afraid of guns, are you?"

"I've lived in New York City for the past fifteen years. Heck, yes, I'm afraid of guns."

Andi dismissed his squeamishness with a huff and a shake of her head. "Come on, follow me."

She left the road and took a route through the dense trees and undergrowth. As they got closer, she heard voices. She looked back at Wade, and he indicated that he heard them, too.

She silently made her way to a thick, sturdy oak within sight of the mill and plastered herself against it, gun at the ready, and peered out to assess the scene. She motioned to Wade to take cover behind a nearby tree, and he silently followed her lead.

Ted Mitchem and Steve Marshall looked like they'd seen better days. Both had several days' worth of growth on their faces. Their hair was unkempt, and their clothes were filthy. One pickup truck had a bed cover on the back that was closed, but the other truck's cover was up, and the men hefted a black trash bag up with the rest of the ones in the bed, wiping their sweaty brows and taking a moment to catch their breath.

Andi turned to Wade and motioned for him to go back to the car and call for help. Wade shook his head, his eyes wide. "No," he mouthed. He motioned for both of them to go, but Andi dug in. "Go," she silently commanded.

Wade looked back at the men before grudgingly scampering back toward the car.

Andi thought through her options. The mantra came back to her, *don't run to your death*. She promised Wade that she would abide by that, so she needed a plan.

Move, shoot, communicate. The functions memorized by every SEAL that demanded perfect execution. The first two, she had under control. The third? Without comms, she couldn't warn Wade that she was going in, and she had no way of knowing if the men were armed. She wouldn't risk him getting caught in the crossfire.

In all her years of service, Andi had never been in a gun fight. She listened to plenty of them over the air, and she heard stories from those who experienced combat, but she'd never personally been face to face with a real weapon outside of military war games. She was an expert shot, but it had been months since she'd fired a gun. She could hit a target if she had to, but could she kill if necessary? She'd always said she could, was trained for it, but in reality? She wasn't so sure.

Despite the cold air, sweat formed on her brow and ran down her face. Her hands felt clammy. She still didn't have a plan, and she knew that the right thing to do was to wait it out, hang tight until help arrived, and then provide backup if necessary.

The muffled bark broke through the quiet, and she watched as both men froze and looked in her direction. She pulled back behind the tree and flattened herself against the trunk.

"Who's there?" Mitchem yelled.

Andi closed her eyes and held her breath, willing them to stay where they were and not come looking.

After an excruciating pause, Marshall said, "There's nobody there. Keep moving."

"I thought I heard a dog bark."

"It was probably somebody out walking their dog or taking it to the park. Get a move on. These orders are already late, thanks to that mayor you chose."

"I told you, I didn't think he'd be a problem."

"Well, you sure had that wrong, didn't you?" Marshall snarled. "Let's get this done before we've got even more targets on our foreheads. Running from the Feds is one thing. Letting down the boss man is a whole different matter."

Andi breathed a sigh of relief and willed herself to remain calm. The calm was shattered when she heard movement and opened her eyes to see Wade hurrying her way. He was too close to the road, not far enough in the trees to remain concealed.

She glanced back at the men, alarms going off in her brain, and saw Mitchem pointing in their direction.

"There's someone there! I saw something."

Before she knew what was happening, a shot rang out, and she saw bits of a nearby tree explode into the air. She ducked and shouted to Wade, "Go back, dammit! Go back!"

With fear in his eyes, Wade dived into the woods. Steadying herself by the tree, she took a deep breath and pivoted out, taking a shot, before pivoting back behind her wooden shield. Another crack rang out, and more bark splintered nearby.

"The cops are on the way," she yelled. "You might as well give up. You keep shooting, and you'll never get out of here alive."

"It's the girl," she heard Mitchem say. "We're being shot at by a girl!"

"Look here, missy," Marshall yelled. "Only one of us is leaving here in a body bag, and it ain't gonna be either one of us. Put that gun down before you hurt yourself, and come out of there with your hands up."

Andi bit her lip to keep from laughing out loud. Were these men that clueless? She could take them out with her eyes closed.

"Now, look, Andi," Mitchem called. "We don't want you to get hurt…"

Her swift movement sent a shot into the tree just an inch from his head. "Consider that your last warning, men. If I aim to hit one of you, I won't miss."

From the distance, Andi heard sirens. "It's too late, Mitchem," she yelled. "Game's over."

She stayed behind the tree until she heard the vehicles racing into the clearing by the mill. She peeked out but neither Marshall nor Mitchem were in sight. A man in a sheriff's uniform exited one of the vehicles.

"They're armed, Sheriff. I don't know where they've run off to, but at least one of them has a shotgun."

"Who's there?"

Andi stepped out, arms in the air, gun held with one finger inside the trigger guard and shouted, "Lieutenant

Commander, Andrea Nelson, US Navy, Seal Team Three, honorably discharged, Sir."

"Drop your weapon, Nelson."

Andi complied while a group of armored men surrounded the mill. She heard shouts and crackles of radio communications. A single shot rang out, and Andi wondered who fired and if anyone was hit. Andi watched the mill, and before long, she saw Mitchem and Marshall being led out with their hands cuffed behind their backs. It was over in a matter of minutes.

Andi stood with her hands still in the air as the sheriff approached. "At ease," he commanded, and Andi loosened her stance.

"I've heard a lot about you," the sheriff said, reaching for her hand. "Marvin Johnson, Van Buren County Sheriff."

"We saw the tracks in the dirt road. Well, not me, sir. Wade Montgomery, Buffalo Springs Mayor, saw them. We stopped to check it out. When I saw Mitchem and Marshall, I instructed Wade to call for backup."

He looked at the hole in the tree. "I take it there were some shots fired?"

"Yes, sir. Do you need my weapon, sir?"

"Was anyone hit?"

"Not that I know of, sir."

"And you have a permit?"

"Yes, sir."

"Very good, then."

They turned toward the footsteps and saw a frantic Wade running in their direction.

330   Amy Schisler

"Mayor Montgomery?" Johnson asked.

"Yes, sir," Wade said, coming to a stop. He looked at Andi, his eyes full of questions.

"We're going to need to get your statements."

One of the deputies called from the mill, "Sheriff, come take a look at this."

Andi retrieved her gun, and without asking permission, she and Wade followed the sheriff to the mill. Andi glanced at the open trash bags in the back of the truck. Plastic packages of meth filled the bags.

Inside the mill was a lab of mammoth proportions.

"Holy motherlode," Sheriff Johnson said under his breath.

No other words could better describe it.

Nineteen

Andi unlocked the door of the storefront and stood inside the building. She meandered around the boxes and odd pieces of furniture and made her way to the kitchen. Dust-covered stainless-steel counters stood in pristine condition across from and next to a six-burner, commercial, double oven. A large triple-basin sink stood to one side, and a commercial dishwasher took up the back corner.

A smile spread across her face as she imagined the pies and pastries she could create in this kitchen of the gods.

"Andi? You in here?"

Andi followed the sound of Wade's voice back into the front of the bakery. The cold February air had followed him into building, making Andi shiver.

"How's it feel?"

"To be the owner of my own bakery? Pretty darn good."

He opened his arms to her, and she went to him, welcoming his kiss.

"How's everyone else?" she asked.

"I stopped here first. I thought you might like to join me in welcoming the rest of the storeowners to their businesses."

"I'd love to," she said, feeling a rush of pride. "I actually made them all welcome gifts. You can help me deliver them."

A light February snow fell as Wade followed Andi to her car where she extracted several baskets of muffins.

"Just something I'm experimenting with," she said with a smile.

"If they taste half as good as they smell, you'll never be able to keep up with demand. I do have a question though."

Andi stopped and looked at Wade, noting the seriousness in his voice. "Yes?"

"Is this going to be enough for you? Running a bakery? Making pies? It's hardly the caliber of excitement you're used to."

"Wade, I've had enough excitement to last a lifetime."

He regarded her for a moment before smiling, seemingly satisfied. "Okay, then. Let's check out the other shops."

They each carried as many baskets as they could hold and started toward the shops. They passed by the tourist center, up and running with a full-wall touchscreen map of the area. It was empty now, but they hoped that by summer, it would be filled with visitors.

"All that money the Feds seized sure came in handy," Andi noted.

"It was huge for us that your friend, Ryan, was able to help us persuade a judge to agree to use a portion of the money to cover the expenses of the meth cleanup and the necessary repairs around town."

"With enough left over to get the tourist center up and running," Andi added.

"It only made sense that the money be used to help the town. It was Mitchem and his associates who caused the town's downward spiral to begin with. Even with the mill closing, people would've been able to survive if they weren't also dealing with rampant drug abuse and a council that prevented anyone from making good with the resources we have. It didn't help that the mayor was a disgrace." Wade's voice was filled with regret.

"I heard the mayor actually turned out to be pretty instrumental in getting the town back on its feet," Andi reminded him. "And I think it was his legal knowledge that prompted the town to petition the court for the money."

Wade smiled. "Yeah, I guess he turned out all right, but only because he had a very determined woman on his side."

"Speaking of determined women. Can you believe that the person behind all of this was a woman?"

"Virtually unheard of from what I understand, but when her husband was killed by a rival cartel, she took the reins."

"I can hardly wrap my head around it," Andi said.

"At least Mitchem and Marshall tipped off the Feds, and they were able to catch her."

"Do you worry that there will be retaliation?" It was something that had been on Andi's mind in the couple days since she heard about the arrest.

Wade looked pensive. "Honestly, I don't know. The Feds feel confident they've shut the whole operation down, but I guess it's hard to know for sure."

Andi thought about that as they walked down the street. She prayed that this whole dark episode in the town's history was over.

They arrived at the soon-to-be Tuscan restaurant where they made their first delivery. The Russos accepted the basket with tears in their eyes as did everyone else.

All of the new business owners radiated enthusiasm. This day had been long in coming since that first town meeting back in September, but all the red tape had finally cleared, contracts were submitted and accepted, and keys were handed out. New locks had been installed, courtesy of the hardware store, where Joshua Nelson had been re-employed, thanks to the surge in building and construction in town. The Jeremy Blake Medical Center, dedicated in memory of the members of SEAL Team Three, was already up and running, and Joe was quickly becoming a highly regarded member of the community.

After they visited all of the shops, Wade walked Andi back to the bakery.

"Tomorrow is Valentine's Day. Care to celebrate early with a night out tonight? I made reservations at Low Gap in Harrison."

"I'd like that. What time?"

"I'll pick you up around five."

They kissed goodbye, and Andi watched Wade cross the street and head inside town hall. She looked through the bakery window but instead of going inside, she followed the sidewalk to the movie house. A lovely couple from Missouri had put in an offer. They were both drama directors at high schools and had decided to open their own theater. From what she and Wade could tell, Blanche seemed delighted to hear that the theater was going to be returned to its original purpose.

Andi thought about Blanche who now had round-the-clock professional care. Melanie had started nursing school full-time, thanks to the newly established Jake Montgomery Scholarship Fund.

Though Blanche told Wade that she was content to go into a home, he refused to send her. No longer able to get around or speak, Blanche spent her days lying in her bed near the window that overlooked the saplings lining the driveway, fingering her Rosary beads. She had gone downhill quickly, and Andi's heart broke for Wade as he awaited the coming of another loss.

Andi turned as she sensed her sister approaching.

"You okay?" Helena asked, putting her arm around her sister's waist.

Andi hadn't realized until that moment that she was crying. She wiped away the tear. "I'm fine. Shouldn't you be at work?"

"I put the 'out to lunch' sign up. I'm dying for a tour of the new bakery."

"There's not much to see at this point, but come on in."

They linked arms and strolled down the sidewalk as snowflakes melted on their noses and eyelashes.

"It's going to be perfect," Helena said as she took in the large kitchen.

"It is, isn't it? I can almost smell the pies."

"Will you have strawberry-rhubarb?"

Andi looked at her sister with surprise. "You hate rhubarb."

"I know, which is why I'll never bake it myself. But it's Joe's favorite."

"Oh, is that so?"

"Why do you say it like that?" Helena pushed her sister away. "He's been very nice to me since he moved here. The least I can do is buy him a fresh, homemade pie."

"Uh-huh. How nice has he been?"

Helena frowned as she batted her hand at her sister. "Just nice. I don't think he's interested in more than friendship, but it's fun to go out."

Andi leaned over and hugged her sister. "Someday, sis, I promise."

"I'm fine, Andi. It's all good. Now you, you look positively radiant. Do you have plans for Valentine's Day?"

"We're celebrating tonight. Just dinner out. Nothing special."

"Well, I'd better go. Have fun tonight." Helena turned to leave.

"Hey, what about you? Plans for the holiday?"

Helena shrugged. "Nothing special. Just dinner out with a friend."

Andi smiled as she watched her sister leave. They might be just friends now, but Andi could see real potential in that paring.

She let out a contented sigh and thought back over the past several months. Coming home had never been part of her plan, and the day she rolled through town, she couldn't see past the road in front of her. She followed the familiar highway without giving any thought to what lay ahead. But her mother was right. Once she put her trust in God, he led her down a road paved in golden promises. She finally understood the full meaning of the word home, and she had no desire to leave it ever again.

***

Wade was nervous as they pulled into the parking lot. "I'm sorry about this. Trudy was just frantic when she called. She's already at the theater in Branson, and she's certain she left the coffee pot on."

"It's okay. We have plenty of time."

"Come up with me. It's too cold to sit in the car."

"Sure."

"Don't get out yet," Wade said as he opened his door. He rushed around to the passenger side and took her hand to help her out. "I'm pulling out all the stops tonight and trying to impress you with my chivalrous ways."

Andi laughed. "I appreciate your thoughtfulness, sir."

He escorted her to the building and unlocked the door, holding it open for her. "Ladies first."

Andi headed to the stairs, but Wade gave her hand a tug. "We can use the elevator tonight. Those heels you have on look painful to walk in."

"They're actually Helena's, and you're right. I'm not sure I'll make it through the night."

He ushered her into the elevator and whistled as the door closed. "Have I told you tonight that you look stunning?"

"I think you alluded to that when you picked me up."

He smiled as he thought of how she took his breath away when she opened the door in a form-fitting red dress, her dark brown hair down on her shoulders, and those spiked heels... Wow. It took him a moment to come to his senses and pull her into a kiss before telling her she looked beautiful.

The bell dinged, and the doors opened to the hallway. He unlocked the door and checked the coffee pot just to keep up the ruse.

"Let me just make sure I turned the heat down in here." He opened the door to his office. "You first."

Andi walked into the office and immediately noticed the vase in the center of his desk, holding two dozen white and red roses.

"Oh my, these are exquisite. Should I be jealous of a secret admirer?"

"They're for you," he said from behind her. He could feel himself beginning to sweat as he held his pose and waited for her to turn around.

"Oh, Wade, thank—" She nearly choked on her words when she turned and saw him on bended knee, the box held out in front of him.

"Andrea Nelson, despite my vow to never risk my heart again, I've been in love with you since the day you first walked into this room. I can't imagine life without you. My mother told me, months ago, that you and I belong together, and she was right. Please say you'll be mine forever."

"No! Really?"

Wade was frozen in place. Those were not the words he hoped to hear. He swallowed and tried to stay calm. "Andi, did you just say no?"

She laughed and reached for him, pulling him up. "Wade, how could I say no to you? I've loved you since that day in the park when we sat on that boulder freezing our tails off. Yes, I will be yours forever."

He removed the ring from the box, set the box on the desk, and slid the ring onto her finger.

"I love you Lieutenant Commander Andrea Nelson."

"I love you Mayor Wade Montgomery."

Wade took her into his arms and kissed her.

***

Andi kissed Wade with a heart full of endless love. Like Wade, she knew love came with no guarantee of forever. There was always the possibility of loss. But even if all they had was this one moment in time, she knew that their love would never die. They were both all in, all the time.

The End…

for Now.

Curious about Andi and Ryan's friend, Margaret Gallagher Turner? Read *Picture Me* to get the whole story.

Acknowledgements

Whenever I begin a new book, I know that one of the number one things I will strive for is authenticity. I want the characters, the setting, and the story to be as authentic and accurate as possible so that they are more than words on a page. They must be real. The characters must possess human characteristics, emotions, and backstories that will ring true to readers. The setting must be tangible, and the storyline must be more than believable. This takes much effort and introspection on my part as well as invaluable help and advice from others.

When I first had the idea of writing about a female veteran and former officer, I knew that Andi had to be a true representation of her upbringing, her military experience, and her femininity—the combination of which make her who she is and will become. In order to do that, I had to rely on my own personal small-town experiences and those of others as well as personal experiences of female Naval officers.

Instrumental in the creation of Andi was my friend, Danyelle Prince, former Naval intelligence officer (with no affiliation with the SEALs). It was her candidness about what it's like to be a young lady at the Naval Academy, a women in the military, a female superior to both enlisted and commissioned men, a wife, and a mother that really shaped everything that Andi is and was. Without Danyelle's help, advice, and openness, Andi would be nothing more than a flat description on a page. I hope that Danyelle and I made you, the reader, see Andi as a real person, perhaps a friend.

Also instrumental in the creation of the book was my dear friend, Tammi Warren. You may recognize her name as a "resident" of Chincoteague, but the real Tammi lives in the heart of the Ozarks. After three years of telling me that Arkansas should be the setting of a series, I took Tammi up on her invitation and spent a week with her in those beautiful mountains and valleys. Tammi took me to small town after small town, regaling me with stories about each place; but it was the town we drove through with broken windows, cracked sidewalks, and a dry fountain that tugged at my heart and cried out to me for salvation. My week with Tammi was more than a research trip. It was a joyous few days spent with someone I love, and I truly am grateful for her friendship, hospitality, and insistence that Arkansas is the perfect setting for a series. I would be remiss, however, if I didn't give a shout-out to our mutual friend, Chandi Owen, for making sure my expressions and colloquialisms are true Arkansas-speak.

I gained valuable insight into the world of real estate and finance through the expert help of Debbie Nisson, Gabriela Jayne, and Paul Duran. I know nothing about finance, banking, investing, or real estate, but each one of these wonderful friends (and aunt) patiently answered my questions and helped me understand how things work in the worlds of banking and investing. Any mistakes or fabrications are of my doing and not theirs.

To my friends, Anne Novey, Cheryl Baumer, and Marian Grammar, I love you all and thank you for your help and encouragement. Beta readers, proofreaders and constant cheerleaders, they are always there for me. I am enormously lucky to have met Tammi, Chandi, Gaby, Anne, Marian, Dotty, Michelle, Victoria, Susan, Laurie, Ronnie, and Jan on a 2016 trip to the Holy Land, and meeting them changed my life forever. Along with these ladies are my sister-in-law, Lisa, and my closest friend, Debbie. All of you are my friends, my sisters, my tribe. A part of each of you lives in so many of my characters, and a part of each of you lives in my heart.

I could not do what I do without the help and support of my loving family. Always there for me, always rooting for me—always at my side for book signings and long car rides—my parents, husband, and daughters keep me going. They are my cheerleaders and coaches. They are, along with my God and Savior, my inspiration and my foundation. Judy and Richard MacWilliams, Ken, Rebecca, Katie Ann, and Morgan, I love you all.

On a side note, the story that Mrs. Blanche Montgomery told Andi about how she fell in love with Wade's father was inspired by the real-life love story of Helen and George Sprance Sr of Long Island, New York. Helen is the mother of my dear friend, George, and she told me her story a few years ago. I told her how much I love it and promised her I would use her love story in a book someday. Sadly, we lost Mrs. Sprance in the spring, but I know that she is now reunited with George, her true love.

About the Author

Amy began writing as a child and never stopped. She wrote articles for magazines and newspapers before writing children's books and adult fiction. A graduate of the University of Maryland with a Master of Library and Information Science, Amy worked as a librarian for fifteen years and, in 2010, began writing full time.

Amy Schisler writes inspirational women's fiction for people of all ages. She has published two children's books and numerous novels, including the award-winning Picture Me, Whispering Vines, and the Chincoteague Island Trilogy. A former librarian, Amy enjoys a busy life on the Eastern Shore of Maryland.

The recipient of numerous national literary awards, including the Illumination Award, LYRA award, Independent Publisher Book Award, International Digital Award, and the Golden Quill Award as well as honors from the Catholic Press Association and the Eric Hoffer Book Award, Amy's writing has been hailed "a verbal masterpiece of art" (author Alexa Jacobs) and "Everything you want in a book" (Amazon reviewer). Amy's books are available internationally, wherever books are sold, in print and eBook formats.

Follow Amy at:
http://amyschislerauthor.com
http://facebook.com/amyschislerauthor
https://twitter.com/AmySchislerAuth
https://www.goodreads.com/amyschisler

Book Club Discussion Questions

1. Andi blames herself for the deaths of her platoon members. Have you ever experienced a situation, totally out of your control, the results of which you blamed yourself? Were you able to move on? How?

2. Scores of veterans return home, suffering from the effects of their service, and many are diagnosed with PTSD. Andi attended therapy sessions in her last few weeks before leaving the Navy but chose not to continue them once she was home, instead, facing her fears and doubts on her own. She hinted to her mother that she even contemplated suicide as many vets do. How can we as a nation help returning vets successfully deal with things that happened during their service and let them know that they do not need to face things on their own?

3. Like so many American small towns, Buffalo Springs is the victim of progress. Have you seen or visited other towns in this situation? What caused their collapse and perhaps ultimate demise? How successful were they at making a comeback? What can be learned from their experience?

4. Andi is determined to save her town. True to her nature, she puts all of her energy into finding ways to revive the failing community. What is her motivating force? Why is it so vital to her well-being that the town

bounces back? How does the state of the town and its fate mirror her own life? In what ways is she projecting her own situation, feelings, fears, and sense of survival onto the town?

5. Belonging is one of the five essential needs as taught by psychologist Abraham Maslow. According to his Hierarchy of Needs, friendship, intimacy, family, and a sense of connection are some of the central prerequisites for happiness and are necessary components of life which must be obtained before we can reach our full potential as human beings. How is Andi the perfect example of this teaching?

6. Buffalo River National Park is a real park in the Ozarks. For both Andi and Wade, it is a "safe" place where they can spend time away from the town to think or just "be." Do you believe that everyone needs a place where they can just "be"? What is your safe place where you can get away and contemplate life?

7. Wade, an intelligent, well-educated man, becomes mayor under false pretenses, risking everything he has worked for throughout his life. How could this happen? What examples can you give of how the mighty have fallen and why?

8. Andi's attitude toward God changed with the loss of her platoon. She alternated between blaming God and doubting his existence. Wade, on the other hand, grew

closer to God after suffering loss. Both were natural responses. Why do you think this is the case?

9. Buffalo Springs faces the same drug epidemic that so many American small towns are facing. Wade says the town's response is, "The usual" with DARE in the elementary school, police visits to the middle-high school warning about the dangers of drugs, and nightly patrols of the streets and alleys. Is this enough? What do you think towns should be doing to combat this growing problem?

10. Upon returning home from the Navy, Andi decides to open a bakery. The two career choices seem diametrically opposed, leading Wade to ask, "Is this going to be enough for you?" Andi assures him it will be. How has Andi changed and grown since she first came to town to allow her to be so positive that this is what she wants and needs? What will owning the bakery do for her mentally and emotionally? Do you think it will be enough? How and why?

Bonus: There is great potential for Buffalo Springs as a town and for these characters to be featured in a series. What do you see happening next?